D0046023

WITHDRAWN

Riverbound

Also by Melinda Beatty

Heartseeker

Riverbound

⁂

MELINDA BEATTY

putnam

G. P. Putnam's Sons

G. P. Putnam's Sons
an imprint of Penguin Random House LLC, New York

Copyright © 2019 by Melinda Beatty.
Penguin supports copyright. Copyright fuels creativity, encourages diverse voices, promotes free speech, and creates a vibrant culture. Thank you for buying an authorized edition of this book and for complying with copyright laws by not reproducing, scanning, or distributing any part of it in any form without permission. You are supporting writers and allowing Penguin to continue to publish books for every reader.

G. P. Putnam's Sons is a registered trademark of Penguin Random House LLC.

Visit us online at penguinrandomhouse.com

Library of Congress Cataloging-in-Publication Data
Names: Beatty, Melinda, author.
Title: Riverbound / Melinda Beatty.
Description: New York, NY: G. P. Putnam's Sons, [2019]
Summary: "Only Fallow sits beside the king to reveal lies, but now she must use her gift and her courage to fight for the kingdom to treat all people fairly"—Provided by publisher.
Identifiers: LCCN 2018035474 | ISBN 9781524740030 (hardcover) | ISBN 9781524740047 (ebook) Subjects: | CYAC: Courts and courtiers—Fiction. | Kings, queens, rulers, etc.—Fiction. | Ability—Fiction. | Honesty—Fiction. | Fantasy.
Classification: LCC PZ7.1.B4342 Ri 2019 | DDC [Fic]—dc23
LC record available at https://lccn.loc.gov/2018035474

Printed in the United States of America.
ISBN 9781524740030
1   3   5   7   9   10   8   6   4   2

Design by Eileen Savage. Text set in Maxime Std.
This is a work of fiction. Names, characters, places, and incidents either are the product of the author's imagination or are used fictitiously, and any resemblance to actual persons, living or dead, businesses, companies, events, or locales is entirely coincidental.

⊁⊰

To all the fierce girls—you are anything but "only"

Riverbound

1

My dearest Only,

I can't tell you how relieved me and Papa were when Lady Hawliss placed your letter in our hands! She's embarrassed us with the kindness of her patronage—she took 4 bushels of apples, 2 barrels of Scrump, and some candied lavender back to Mollier's Hold, and has promised to stop in again on her way north for Princess Saphritte's wedding so we might write you in return. Please give her our kindest thanks when this paper reaches you.

I've been storing up things to tell you, but now that I've took up my pen, they've up and run off because not having you with us is like a hole in the roof. If the harvest goes smooth next summer, maybe we can think of a journey to the capital, providing the king, in his mercy, might let us spend some hours together.

Your brother would like me to tell you not to get bigheaded, but I know so long as you keep us in your heart, we needn't fear. Your non would like me to tell you that I shouldn't be so nosy, and she'll say her piece in the post script.

Be well, my heart, my sweet child,
Your loving Mama

Post Script—You listen to me, Pip. If there's anyone who gives you bother—real bother, mind—you remember what I taught you from little: fists first, knees second, and questions later. You're my tough green apple, and don't you let no one in that palace forget it. X

—Letter to the Mayquin, Only Fallow, from her home in Presston, from *A History of Orstral*, vol. 2

The winged bull was the first thing that greeted me every morning.

It wasn't a real bull, of course, but one that was stitched into the canopy above my bed. I suppose it's so anyone who slept in it was reminded right away whose house they were waking up in. I couldn't forget, not really, even without its angry, flaring nostrils and silver-flecked wings.

Me and the bed both belonged to the King of Orstral.

Winter had begun its cold creep into the north. The mountains I could see from the window of my chamber, blue and purple in the haze, had caps of white on their heads. The first frosts had long since drawn their crystal fingers across my windowpane, and the smell of pine was everywhere in the palace as it busied itself to prepare for Yule.

Back at the orchard, Mama was stirring the suet for the pudding, every day adding a splash more of the dark rum she bought just for the season. When we were small, me, Ether, and Jon would fuss over who got to stir each morning before breakfast. Each turn of the spoon came with a wish—usually for a foolish thing or trinket that would sometimes appear on Long Night. I couldn't help thinking what Mama and Ether might wish for this year as they stood, spoon in hand, in an unusually quiet kitchen.

I gave the winged bull a hard look from my pillow as I ran my fingers over the smooth willowbark of a figurine with a cheerfully burning acorn in the cage of its belly. I'd been careful to hide the gift Lark'd given me back in Presston when we were first acquainted—in the sturdy nameday box made for me by Papa. But some nights, the only way to quiet my noisy head was to take the Jack from its den beneath my Allcloth and let the glamour lull me to sleep.

A tap at the door let me know my lying-about-and-feeling-sorry-for-myself time had come to an end. The hinges creaked and the familiar figure of my friend Lark slipped in—a dark silhouette in front of the bright window.

"Tides," she gasped. "It's colder'n a toad's belly in here! You forgot to close the drapes last night."

"Didn't forget," I mumbled as she scuttled toward the hearth to make up the fire. "I just wanted to look at the stars."

She clucked her tongue. "Stars'll still be there in summer, y'know. No need to turn your chamber into an icehouse!"

I sat up, hugging my knees under the quilt. "I was trying to pretend I was looking out my own window. It keeps the bad dreams away."

Lark poked at the smoldering logs with the fire iron. "Don't remember the last time I had a good dream."

Shame pricked at my heart. I may have belonged to the king, but at least I enjoyed a measure of comfort. Instead of making merry with the rest of the Ordish clans at the Southmeet in Farrier's Bay, Lark was trapped in Bellskeep—a servant, even less her own master than I was. *My* servant, indentured to the king until her father could raise the coin to buy her and her brother, Rowan, back.

I patted the down mattress. "Come warm up while we're waiting for the fire to do its work."

She looked toward the door warily.

"Don't worry, no one's gonna bust in. If anyone complains that I'm tardy, I'll just tell 'em I was being a slugabed."

Lark didn't need more persuading. She climbed up to join me beneath the quilt, taking care not to crease the fine indigo silk dress she'd been given to accompany me on important occasions like the one that morning. She laid her head on the pillow with a sigh of relief.

"The hearth in the indentures' hall burns all night, but it's still not much warmer than out-of-doors since the season changed." She raised her hands to her lips to blow some feeling back into them.

"Mother's teeth!" I exclaimed. "What happened to your fingers?"

She turned them over to look at them, wincing at her ragged red nail cases. "The fabric bunched funny on one of Lady Monkford's gowns and I got the hem crooked. Her ladyship complained to the seamstress, so I spent last evening in the laundry. The lye Mistress Gibb uses is wicked strong."

I took her hands in mine, all cold and cracked, thinking of how warm they'd been in the summer when she'd first led me aboard her barge, the *Briar*.

"A few nights ago, I *did* dream Papa came to get us," she said softly. "The River was a *real* river, and all the barges sailed under the bridges and right to the palace. It *was* good, but I was so sorry to wake up, I'd rather not have dreamed it."

I'd held my peace long enough. I hadn't spoken of it before— not to Lark or anyone—but I couldn't bear the sorrow in her eyes anymore.

"It's not gonna be a dream much longer, Lark."

"What d'you mean?"

"I made a bargain. I hope it'll have us both home before the snowdrops bloom."

Lark sat up like a shot, looking more alarmed than pleased. "What sort of bargain?"

I shushed her. "One the whole palace don't need to know about, so keep your voice down!"

5

"Only, there ain't a soul here you should be making bargains with!" she whispered furiously. "Not for you, and certainly not for me and Ro! You can't trust no one."

"I got dragged here so the king would *know* who to trust, in case you forgot!"

It was the very reason I wasn't stirring the pudding bowl in Mama's kitchen. All because I could see lies. No one could tell one—not about a plot to topple the kingdom or what they had for lunch—without me knowing. Non once compared a lie to a wall the truth had to find a way round. And while I couldn't exactly see the truth, I could at least see the cracks in the wall where it was leaking out. A vivid wreath of color rounded the liar, intangible as will-o'-the-wisp, but revealing all manner of shame and fear, kindness and ill intentions. The Ordish, who knew more about augury than most folk, called it a *cunning*. I called it a curse.

"Course I didn't forget," insisted Lark, slipping out from under the quilt and heading to my wardrobe. "It's just . . . there's things we don't know yet! Like who the fella from the Southmeet was—the one with the port-wine stain who got Jon's lot to attack your carriage. Or who's burning the grain stores!"

I frowned. Two days before, the news had come of another grain store out by Clifflight Watch going up in flames. Folk were blaming the Ordish, but my brother, whose life was now intertwined with the people of the river, told me there wasn't a man, woman, or child among them who'd do anything so wickedly wasteful.

And even worse, hunger was starting to pinch bellies from north to south. Less grain meant less flour. Less flour meant less bread, and less bread meant folk had to part with more coin to buy it. If it was meant to turn Orstral further against the Ordish, it was working.

"I'm not saying . . . ooh, cold!" I yelped as my bare feet touched the stone floor. I danced on tiptoe over to the rug in front of the hearth. "I'm not saying I trust her in particular, but I'd *know* if she was trying to play me false."

The Ordish girl looked at me suspiciously as she laid my morning clothes on the bed. "*She* who? The princess?"

"Not *her*," I whispered, motioning Lark closer. "Lady Folque."

The dish of gold hairpins she was holding dropped to the floor with a *clang*, sending its contents skittering across the floor like bright minnows in a creek.

"Have you got river mud for brains?" Lark exclaimed, dropping down to retrieve the pins. "That woman's a snake! You should hear the things folk around the palace say about her."

I bit back a rough answer as I joined her on the floor. I thought she'd be dead pleased to hear my news.

"Well, those folk ain't got a cunning like I do, and *I* know she'll keep her word!"

Lark didn't look convinced. "What's she promised you, then?"

According to Master Iordan, when a king or queen loses the throne, it's usually 'cause they end up losing something more important—like a war. Or, if they're real unlucky, their head. Me and Lady Folque had more'n a few things in common—we were both cunning. We both wanted what was best for Orstral. And we both thought what was best for Orstral would be if Alphonse Renart wasn't king anymore. But the king didn't have to fear losing his head—while my cunning just exposed the lies people told, Lamia's was of a useful sort for our aim. Her cunning, in small doses, could change minds. In large doses, it could be deadly.

My fear of the councilwoman had vanished like fog when she told me the story of her elder brother—who she begged to save her dog, lost to a raging spring flood when they were whelps. Hit by the full force of her cunning all at once, the boy waded in and was lost, right along with her pet.

It's the sort of tale I'd've took for made-up, but there was no deceit in it—just a woman, sorrowful and guilty over the loss of her brother. Her idea was simple; for the good of the country, she'd persuade the king to step down, leaving the throne to his daughter, Saphritte. The princess didn't care for keeping up any sort of quarrel with the Ordish, so the river folk's troubles would soon come to a halt and the indentured whelps would be returned. Orstral would be content again. Lark and Rowan could go home. And, though Lamia Folque didn't know it, so could I. The princess had struck me a bargain—when she came to the throne, I'd be allowed to return to the orchard. As for the no-gooders trying to make the Ordish look bad . . . we could get to the bottom of that later.

Lark sat back on her knees, taking in my tale. "She's going to *talk* the king off the throne? And then just . . . go home? That don't sound very like her."

"She's leaving her council seat to her daughter. I guess she'll go back to Folquemotte and do . . . whatever it is people with coin do in their free time."

We got to our feet and Lark helped me out of my nightdress.

"If she cares about Orstral so much, why can't she just do it herself, without telling anyone else?" she grumbled. "What's she want with you?"

"Folk'll *believe* me, that's why!" I answered, wriggling into my shift. "The princess, the king, the council—I mean, I still can't say anything that's untrue, but the truth I do tell's got weight to throw behind her cunning. We've had no chance for a jaw outside council meetings, but someone slipped this under my door last night." I stuck a hand between my mattress and the board beneath. The thick, cream-colored paper was folded tight, the wax seal with the dancing rabbit broken open. I handed it to Lark as I put on my greatcoat.

"'You are cordially invited for tea and conversation with His Majesty and Lady Folque tomorrow at the fourth afternoon bell,'" she read, shaking her head. "Sounds to me like she's just invited you for a cuppa and cake with the king."

"Don't you see? She's ready to start trying and she wants me to help! It makes sense, with the wedding coming up and all."

Yule and the tales of burned grain stores weren't the only things stirring up the city. In two weeks, Saphritte would marry Hauk Eydisson, the second son of King Bram and Queen Arnora of Thorvald. Though the prince and a few minor nobles had been in Bellskeep for months already, the rest of the northern folk would be descending on the city in just a few hours. The fact that

Lark'd even got a new frock for the occasion told me the palace wasn't sparing any expense for their arrival. I'd heard whispers round the castle of Thorvald's fierce warriors and strange customs. Gareth said another steward told him King Bram once wrestled an ice bear and won. Master Iordan sniffed at that rumor, telling me it was "truly quite impossible, as an ice bear weighs nearly a ton, stands over six feet on its hind legs, and has claws the size of kitchen knives." The inquisitor was almost always right, but he sure knew how to ruin a good story.

"Master Iordan's been making sure I know a bit before the northern court arrives. Go ahead," I bade Lark eagerly as she pulled a large leather belt round my waist. "Ask me how to say 'good morning' in Thorvald."

She wasn't ready to let go of my deal with Lamia Folque, but she indulged me. "All right, how do you say 'good morning' in Thorvald?"

"*Goden morhen*," I pronounced carefully. "Now ask me how to say 'good night.'"

She sighed. "How do you say 'good night'?"

"*Goda noght*. Now ask me how to say, 'You've got a face like a cat's rear end.'"

Lark's fingers fumbled on the belt. "Why in Deep's name did Master Iordan teach you *that*?"

"Oh, All, it wasn't the inquisitor! Prince Hauk said it to one of the fellows at the table and all the Thorvald laughed. The princess would only tell me what it meant if I promised not to repeat it in polite company."

I pulled on my warm fleece leggings and boots just as there was a sharp knock on the chamber door. I'd know the sound of those knuckles anywhere.

"*Goden morhen*, Gareth," I called.

The steward's freckled face popped round the door. "Did that mean 'come in'?"

"Close enough," I told him. "We won't be a second."

Lark held up my great golden brooch, shaped like an eye, set with a radiant sapphire. She carefully poked the pin through the lapel of my coat.

"Be careful," she said, quiet-like, so Gareth couldn't hear. "Promise me you won't get so wrapped up in your cunning that you forget how to see round the end of your nose."

I put one hand over hers. "We're getting out of here. I promise you *that*."

THE CASTLE WAS bustling as Gareth escorted us toward the banqueting hall—nothing like the lazy winter mornings of the orchard, where chores would wait till the sun had a chance to warm the air and earth. Instead, we would take our ease and break fast with boiled eggs, slices of smoked meat, and hot bread or good apple tart. The early feast would be enough to put warmth in our bellies for the walk toward halls, a goodly way after sunrise. If I closed my eyes, I could almost see the glitter of the frost on the grass and dry thistle and hear the crunch of the cold ground beneath my feet.

The carved stone trees arched over our heads as we entered the banqueting hall. What I wouldn't have given to feel the warm, rough bark of the orchard under my hands! Everything I touched in the palace was smooth—from the walls and the floors to the silver tableware.

My thoughts were lost in the cold stone forest when a nudge at the side of my cloak brought me down to earth with a bump. I found myself staring into the business end of an enormous, hairy snout.

I fixed her with a stern glare. "Shoo, Mizzen!"

The hound fixed her big brown eyes on Lark.

"It's no good looking at me like that," she told the dog firmly. "She's the one with the pockets!"

"Don't be rude, you great mongrel!"

Everard Dorvan's voice boomed through the hall. He wasn't a man who could sneak up on a body—everything about him was enormous, including his dog. He took hold of Mizzen's scruff gently. "Don't take liberties!" he scolded. "My apologies, ladies, for her wandering stomach!"

We'd taken to stashing a handful of nuts and dried fruit or meat in my coat on mornings when we'd be late to break our fast and'd been soft enough to share the spoils with Mizzen once or twice.

"It's all right, master," I said as I scratched the hound beneath her wiry gray chin. "We don't mind sharing." I reached beneath my cloak and brought out a piece of dried beef, which disappeared into the hairy gullet before it could even be offered.

"I think she's just pleased to find that I'm not the only one who likes an early bite to eat," he confided in a low voice. Opening the pocket of his jerkin, he revealed a pile of dates, one of which he popped into his mouth and chewed with great relish.

"Must you bring that beast with you everywhere?" Arfrid Sandkin appeared beside us, his serious, angular face bunched with disdain.

"Of course!" exclaimed Dorvan, placing a great tattooed hand upon Mizzen's back. "The testaments tell us that we're all part of the Mother's creation."

Sandkin sniffed. "Most of the Mother's creations don't create such . . . odors."

The scent of cider vinegar signaled Lady Mollier's approach. "A goodly morning to you, gentlemen, Only, Miss Fairweather." The silver-haired woman moved stiffly beneath her furs—no doubt Mistress Devi had recommended the pungent soak for her sore joints. "It seems the winter bites just a bit harder on my bones with every passing year. I'm afraid I can't recommend growing old, my dear. It really is a trial."

"I imagine it's better than *not* growing old, ma'am," I answered.

"From the mouths of babes!" The councilwoman chuckled. "Truer words were never spoken, my dear."

"Make way for the king!"

The shout of Adria, the royal page, rang throughout the hall. The three council members and I straightened—even Mizzen, well acquainted with the ways of the palace, sat and dipped her noble head. At the top of the grand staircase, King Alphonse appeared, splendid and terrible. His cloak was a regal shade of blue and trimmed with silver fox fur. The crown on his head glittered with sapphires. His long white hair spread across his shoulders, thick and magnificent.

He was the man who'd stolen me, Lark, Rowan, and all the other indentures from our homes, and I hated every inch of him. Unpleasant words formed in my head. *Yor egaen anglet bacrat kottr!* The princess might have warned me against *saying* it in polite company, but there was nothing that could keep me from *thinking* it.

He descended, Adria following with the cloak's hem raised so it wouldn't be soiled. Dorvan and Sandkin bowed and Lady Mollier, Lark, and I sank into curtsies as he passed us by, leaving behind a whiff of amber and liniment. Close on his heels were Saphritte and Hauk. The princess, clad much like her father, walked rigidly on the arm of her fiancé, whose head was high and eager, the copper beads braided into his long beard clicking together spiritedly.

Three more figures appeared on the stair. They looked every bit as majestic as those who came before them—some in the kingdom might say worryingly so. Lamia Folque, her son, Borin, and her daughter, Adalise, were the fire to the Renart ice, dressed all in crimson and gold. Behind me, Lark sucked in a short breath.

"A good morning to you all," Lamia purred graciously as the three joined the rest of us. Even her voice made you feel like you'd been dipped in something warm.

Some of Dorvan's good humor fell away. "Good morning, my ladies, my lord. The Thorvald await. Shall we away?" With no other nicety, he turned and strode out, Mizzen padding faithfully at his heel. Sandkin followed, though Lady Mollier hung back.

"Come, my dear," she said, holding out a hand to me.

"You go ahead, Constance," Lamia cooed. "I'd have a word with our dear Mayquin."

Lady Mollier inclined her head, though her eyes betrayed her distrust of her fellow council member. Cinching her furs, she turned to leave.

Lamia went to drape a scarlet-clad arm about my shoulders, but found it blocked suddenly as Lark stepped to my side, her face polite but her body saying *beware*.

"Oh!" exclaimed the lady. "I see the master of court has finally seen fit to give you a waiting girl."

"She's my friend," I said quickly. "And I trust her. With *everything*." I hoped she'd catch my meaning.

Lady Folque gazed at Lark shrewdly a moment before nodding. "As it should be with one's closest servant. Why, there's nothing I know that my proctor, Master Beir, does not."

I didn't like her calling Lark a servant—it sounded as bad to my ear as "river rat" ever did. But in the palace, I knew what was what. "I got your message, ma'am," I told her.

"Oh, I'm glad," Lady Folque said, clasping her gold-ringed fingers. "And your answer?"

Lark's hand squeezed mine through my cloak. A small, dangerous thrill went through my heart, like the first time I'd held the Jack with the burning acorn in its belly. I felt *hope*. "I cordially accept."

A slow smile spread over Lamia Folque's smooth lips. "In that case, let us go and welcome our northern neighbors." The lady put the hood of her cloak up as the cold drifted into the hall from the great, open doors. "And then you and I shall speak with the king about the future of Orstral."

When shrewd frost bites green stem
Young buds have but two choices;
To shrivel
Or to weather.

—From *A Sower's Companion*, translated from the Thorvald

They came into the city in a great wave of fur and leather.

From where we assembled atop the barbican to watch the approach of the Thorvald court, I couldn't help but wonder if there were a mink, hare, wolf, or fox left living in the whole of the cold north. From cloaks to boots, the men and women marched under layers of pelts, painted shields slung over their backs. They sang as they marched, but there was no melody in it—just a low, loud baying that raised every hair on the back of my neck. It sounded like war.

Hauk clasped a hand to his heart. "It is enspiriting to see, is it not?"

The princess's brows furrowed. "I believe you mean 'inspiring,' my dear."

"Ah yes. Forgive me, *isabrot*. My Orstral is still . . . dirty."

"Rusty," Saphritte corrected again. "Your *Orstralian* is *rusty*."

"Is *isabrot* the word in your language for 'princess,' then, Highness?" I asked the prince.

He laughed. "No, little one. It is a . . . how do you say, a . . . sweet name?"

"A pet name," Saphritte amended quietly.

Eydisson clapped his hands together. "Ah yes! A pet name. It means 'icebreaker.' My Orstral princess and I, we break the ice between our nations." He took Saphritte's hand between his and planted a whiskery kiss on her cheek. "We will bring the new spring between us."

The future queen of Orstral blushed like a maiden and tried to summon a convincing smile for the future prince consort.

The cry of a horn bounced off the palace walls. It was low and wailing, like the bellow of a buck in rutting season. The king's guard and the bailiffs pushed back the crowds in the streets outside. Everywhere, necks were craning, keen to ogle the Thorvald royalty as they emerged from the underpassages. And when they did, oh, what a sight it was!

Bram and Arnora Eydisson sat atop short, muscular stallions with knobbly knees and brown dappled breasts. Their manes hung wild, long and loose about their crests and forelocks. Crowns of bronzed antlers sat upon the king's and queen's heads, the bases studded with amber and garnet. Arnora's hair was the color of late-summer honey. Her face was broad and her strong neck was hung with an intricate knot made of boar's ivory. Bram's beard, secured into three braids with magnificent amber beads, was almost as dark as the fur that covered him, and wheat-blond hair fell past his shoulders. Orrad, Hauk's elder brother and heir to the throne of Thorvald, rode proud behind his parents, carrying the colors of the Eydissons: a red stag upon a white field. He wore plated leather armor with a wolf pelt on his shoulder and a simple copper circlet over his fair brow.

Dorvan let out a low whistle. "Mother's milk," whispered Sandkin. Lady Mollier paled a little. Only Lamia Folque seemed unmoved by the sight of the fearsome army marching toward us—she was holding a hushed conversation with Adalise while her son, Borin, peered disinterestedly over the parapet.

A little shiver ran through Lark. "Tides, they don't half look fierce," she whispered.

"Maybe Master Iordan was wrong about the ice bear," I thought aloud.

The gates rumbled open beneath our feet and a cheer went up from the crowds watching on both sides of the River.

The royal party and their pelt-covered escort began to flow through the gates and we descended through the barbican to the wide front approach of the castle to greet them.

By the time we reached the ground, Bram and Arnora had dismounted. Hauk had already taken Saphritte's arm and was leading her toward the King and Queen of Thorvald, whose arms were open wide to greet them.

The princess sank into a low curtsy before her future in-laws. "Majesties, I'm honored to meet—"

But before she could say more, she was pulled into a rib-cracking hug by Arnora. "Ah, *naerdotter*! I always prayed to Siv to send me a girl, but Sivgar sent me only boys instead. Now I finally have one, eh? Perhaps the goddess will send you several of each!"

Saphritte cleared her throat. "Oh, I hadn't thought—"

Arnora braced her hands on either side of her *naerdotter's* waist. "You are a good, strong girl, eh? Hips made for birthing—you'll give us many grandchildren!"

I thought I was as close as I'd ever be to watching someone die of mortification. Saphritte gulped like she'd swallowed a frog. It was only the arrival of the king at her side that snapped her out of it.

"*Naermoder,*" she said quickly, "I present you my father, King Alphonse."

The three monarchs bowed their heads to one another. The king clasped Bram's hand in greeting. "I am honored to welcome you to our city and to our family."

Saphritte nudged me forward. "And this is our—"

"Your *vardmadrleita*, no doubt—the heart witch," interrupted Bram, inspecting me closely. "Our son and our ambassador have told us much of her. A blessing for your kingdom! And for the kingdom of my son's children."

While Master Iordan had done a lot of talking about how great the northerners were at fighting, it seemed to me they were awful good at making folk uncomfortable, too. The king smiled mildly, not too taken with talk of his crown being usurped by future half-Thorvald get.

Behind us, Hauk eagerly awaited the grooms to help Orrad off his horse. It reminded me a little of how my brother Ether sometimes nipped at Jon's heels, begging for his attention. Once

Orrad was on the ground, the two wrestled and slapped each other on the back.

"*Velkominn, brodir!*" Hauk laughed. "It has been too long."

"It has been, *ulfrlitt*, it has! How is my little wolf cub?"

Hauk glanced around nervously, hoping no one had heard. "We are men now, eh, too old for such names."

Orrad clasped his arm round his brother's head and tousled his hair, like I'd seen my own brothers do a thousand times. "You may be about to inherit a kingdom, but you will always be my *ulfrlitt*, eh?" The elder Thorvald released the rumpled Hauk and looked out at the castle grounds. "This country suits you. It is . . . softer. More comfortable." He gave his scowling younger brother a harder-than-necessary punch on the arm before pointing to his clothes. "Silk and satin, eh, *ulfrlitt*? And even a haircut! Only a few months here and already you're tamer than you were."

Hauk's face darkened further as he tried to compose himself. "I honor my hosts in their home. I have not forgotten our ways."

Orrad grinned cheekily. "If you say it is so, *brodir*, it must be so. Nothing is too good for the wolf cub of Thorvald!" He pointed to the rest of the party, who'd begun to walk toward the castle proper, servants and grooms scampering in their wake. "But we will follow the others, yes? Much to be done, much to be done, *brodir*, before you become a prince of this little paradise!"

Saphritte, held firmly in Arnora's eager grip, had already disappeared indoors. Lady Folque glided over to the two brothers.

"Excuse me, Highness," she said, laying an elegant hand on Orrad's arm. "I'm afraid I have business elsewhere and my son has already returned to his studies at the lyceum. Would you be so good as to escort my dear Adalise back into the palace?"

A wolfish grin spread over the face of the elder Thorvald prince. "Ah, so the tree of Orstral bears many sweet fruits. Perhaps I will be permitted into its branches to pick one for myself." He offered his big, muscly arm to Adalise.

I half expected her to cuff him for being so forward, but Adalise blushed prettily and looked at Orrad under her long dark lashes. "I hope, Highness, that you are skilled at climbing. The reddest apple always grows near the top of the tree."

And is always bird-pecked, I thought, watching the younger Lady Folque play the coquette, her dainty hand disappearing behind the Thorvald's giant elbow. I resolved then and there never to let a pretty face make *me* so soupy.

Orrad grinned broadly, setting off with Adalise. Hauk, looking a little lost, offered his own arm to Lamia.

"Highness," she said, her voice going young and girlish, "I'm honored."

Hauk was a handsome enough fellow but didn't seem the sort that'd set the cool Lady Folque's heart aflutter.

"My dear," said Lamia, glancing back, "the fourth bell. Do not be late."

"We'll be there, ma'am." I linked my own arm through Lark's. "Both of us."

A look of distaste flashed across the lady's face, but it dissolved into her familiar, catlike smile. "Of course. If she has your trust, your girl is quite welcome."

She didn't have time to notice my scowl before turning

back to Hauk and wrapping her jeweled hand round his arm. "Now, Your Highness," I could hear her twittering as she and the Thorvald moved farther down the path, leaving me and Lark on our own, "you *must* tell me absolutely *everything* about your beautiful country!"

"You ain't *my girl*," I told her, my lip curling at the lady's retreating back. "You're no one's but your own."

She squeezed my arm tightly. "I'll act the servant now so long as it'll make me and Ro our own masters by and by."

THE PALACE SOLAR was high-windowed, perfect for trapping the weak rays of sunshine streaming in. Unlike the rest of the coldly blue palace, the room was done out in warm oranges and yellows from top to bottom—a place to escape the winter.

When we arrived, a table had been set not far from the hearth atop a brilliant rug, woven through with golden butterflies. Lady Folque was already seated and servants in Folque livery with their stiff, high collars were swarming about like silent ants, carrying everything you'd need for a real fancy picnic. The vittles set before her, and us still unnoticed in the doorway, Lamia snagged the sleeve of a departing steward.

"A drop of sherry, if you please."

In a twinkling, an amber bottle was produced and a splash of the contents was tipped into the lady's waiting teacup.

"A little more, please."

Another splash.

"Just a touch more."

The steward gave his mistress a sideways look. Lamia returned it, witheringly.

"Perhaps you can leave the bottle with me."

The steward bowed, set the sherry on the table, and scuttled off, determined not to be part of whatever problem was causing the lady to tie on an afternoon snootful. I cleared my throat, genteel as I could.

"Good afternoon, ma'am."

Lamia gave a guilty start, but she didn't spill a drop of the extra sherry she was tipping into her cup.

"Ah, you're just in time," she said pleasantly, still pouring. Her eyes gave the barest flicker toward Lark. "Your girl can stand over there, in the proctors' corner. My own Master Beir will be along shortly."

Shame pinched on my insides again to hear Lark spoken to so, but I remembered her earlier words as she gave my fingers a squeeze and Lady Folque a curtsy before taking her place by a towering suit of armor at the far end of the room.

I shyly took my seat at the table. Lamia picked up the pot and added just enough tea to her cup to deepen the color before pouring a cup out for me.

"You must pardon me, my dear. I'm not usually one to indulge before my daily meetings with His Majesty, but I feel we could all use some fortification for the tasks ahead." She gestured to the bottle. "Care for a drop?"

"No, thank you, ma'am," I replied, reaching for the delicate pitcher of cream that bloomed into my dark cup like a thundercloud. "But you go ahead. Sometimes, when my brothers were acting bedeviled, Mama'd sneak a slug of something behind the barn."

The lady drained her cup in one long gulp and reached for the bottle once more. "I don't mind telling you that between the arrival of the Thorvald and our . . . undertaking, I may find myself following your mother's example."

I'd spent so many hours hoping, wishing, and imagining that Lady Folque's plans would come to pass, I'd clean forgotten the lady herself might be a bit jittery about the whole affair. It wasn't every day a body tried to persuade a king to give up his crown without the king *knowing* about it. I shot an anxious look at the door.

Lamia poured another shallow puddle of sherry into her teacup, noting my bout of nerves. "Don't fret, child. The king will be another few moments yet. You've heard, no doubt, about the grain store by Clifflight Watch?"

I nodded, not wanting to open my mouth on the subject of the Ordish, especially with Lark standing in the corner earwigging. Not to mention it'd be all too easy to talk myself into a corner where my cunning'd oblige me to reveal things—like how me and Gareth made a whole legion of guardsmen do the sour apple two-step to get Jon and his friends out of the king's dungeon. "Master Iordan told me in my lesson yesterday."

"It's the third royal store the river folk have burned. The effects of the last two burnings are already being felt in marketplaces—this one will make the winter all the more painful. The people are frightened. The sooner the princess and her new prince consort can take the reins of power, the better. I believe the time has come to act."

I shoved a tartlet into my mouth to keep it still. I couldn't reveal I was sure the burnings were the work of some other villain—the very same one with the port-wine stain on his arm, who'd sent Jon and his Ordish friends on the fool's errand against the caravan. But all that could be settled after Saphritte's royal backside was safely seated on the throne.

"I'm happy to do what I can, ma'am, but my cunning doesn't leave much room for keeping secrets."

Her ladyship leaned forward, a beam of sunlight setting ablaze the great blue-green jewel at her throat. "I wouldn't wish you to suffer any more pain on behalf of the kingdom. The only help I require from you is that you use your cunning where and when you can to give greater weight to mine. There will be no need for falsehoods." She grasped a pair of dainty tongs and used them to drop a sugar cube into her tea. "And if all goes well, we shall be crowning a new ruler in a fortnight's time."

A swallowful of tea went down my windpipe and I coughed. "Ma'am, are you saying you mean to have the king give up the throne at the *wedding*?"

"It seems a good opportunity, does it not? A strong, young, shining queen and a consort, ready to rule? The people will be overjoyed to get a second public holiday for the coronation, and the Thorvald's royals will be delighted to see their son installed upon a throne directly."

"And the Ordish indentures'll be freed!" I burst out before I could stop myself. I didn't dare look at Lark, but I could tell she'd heard. I cleared my throat, suddenly nervous. "Won't they?"

"If it will put an end to the burnings, I'm sure the new queen will do so," Lady Folque answered, running a well-tended nail round the rim of her cup. "Though it may be ill-received by some in the city. Old grievances are often hard to let go of."

I pictured the angry face of the rector of the Great Cathedra, Curate Heyman, who was more than happy to throw me, the Ordish, and auguries into the same hateful stewpot he fed his flock from every Matins. And I could see those folk in the pews with empty bellies, all too happy to gorge themselves, licking his ugly words from their fingers.

The sound of feet on the flagstone of the corridor sent both of us quickly to our feet. The door groaned open, admitting Adria's high nose first before the rest of her.

"His Majesty, the king!"

Though I'd sat in more deadly boring council meetings and attended more petitionings than I could count over the last few months, a part of me still quailed whenever Alphonse Renart entered the room. I'd never forget the day I was brought before him, scared and alone, and made to tell lie after lie to prove the way of my cunning. Non says holding grudges is like swallowing poison and expecting your enemy to drop dead. But even if Mother All had suddenly appeared before me in all Her glory and demanded I forgive him in peril of my soul, I don't know if I could've done it.

Lamia bowed her head. "Good afternoon, Majesty."

"Yes, yes," answered the king gruffly, waving away her courtesy and sitting down heavily on the gilded chair that'd been prepared for him. "Let's get on with this. I've got a castle full of Thorvald and a wedding to see to."

It was only then he noticed Lark standing in the corner and scowled. "Your proctor seems to have shrunk. And become a young Ordish woman. Do you really feel it appropriate at the moment, with what those devils are doing to our grain stores?"

"No, Majesty, that is the Mayquin's serving girl," Lamia explained, casting an eye toward the door. "Master Beir will no doubt join us. I expect him back any moment."

The king grunted and looked sidelong at the table covered in dainties—tiny cakes and tarts dusted with sugared violet.

"Gareth!" he shouted.

The steward's freckled face appeared round the casement. I couldn't help but smile to see it.

"Majesty?"

"Bring me something with a bit more substance. A man can hardly survive on finger food."

Gareth disappeared so quick, he almost left a Gareth-shaped hole in the air behind him. The king shifted irritably in his seat. Lamia sensed his ill humor.

"How did you find King Bram and Queen Arnora?"

"On my life, that country breeds thick-tongued brutes! The king and queen speak Orstralian passing well, but the rest of them might as well have mouths full of sheep's wool!" He sat forward, pointing a thick finger at me. "I wish I'd had the Mayquin for company—I tell you, that Bram was spinning a tale about an ice bear that was barely to be believed!"

"But their strength, Majesty!" Lamia pressed. "Is their strength not enviable?"

A faint itch sprung to life inside my ears. Even if Master Iordan hadn't *directly* told me sticking my fingers in my ears at tea would be bad manners, I was pretty sure it would be anyway. Trying not to attract the attention of my betters, I rubbed my tongue as far back my throat as I could manage, but it was no good—it was not to be scratched.

My betters, thankfully, didn't seem to be paying attention, particularly the king. He'd settled back into his seat, some of the ire draining out of him. "Well, enviable, of course. That display this morning was enough to put the fear of All into any man."

Lamia nodded in agreement. "Into the enemies of the kingdom, for a start."

The pesky itch flared again and I made an involuntary *guck* noise. Lady Folque eyed me sharply as I muttered a flustered beg-pardon, but the king seemed to take no notice. And that's when it struck me—I was *feeling* Lamia's cunning, even that moment, as she used it on the king.

She'd told me. She'd *told* me what her cunning could do. But I still sat there, unease crawling all over me like ants to see it in the flesh. Thoughts of pity for the old man stirred in my breast.

"They'll give those waterlogged boat villains a thing or two to think about, eh?"

Those thoughts were squashed as quick as they'd blossomed. *Horrid old grasshopper!* I fumed.

"I know I've said it before, Majesty, but I really must congratulate you on arranging such a match. What better legacy to leave Orstral than a bright future?"

Renart's eyebrows furrowed as if he was just considering the notion for the first time. "Yes . . . the future."

"I can picture them, Majesty, can't you? Your beautiful daughter and her strong Thorvald husband waving to the crowd?"

"Yes," the king muttered dreamily, "I can see them."

"They will be adored by the city."

The itch inside my head became more insistent. It made me want to jam the handle of the sugar spoon in one of my ears in order to scratch it, but I kept still, remembering Lamia's appeal to use my cunning where I could to complement hers.

"By the whole country, Majesty," I chimed in.

Alphonse Renart's eyes had become unfocused. He reached out before him in wonder, as if he could touch the scene Lady Folque was describing. His fingers grasped at nothing.

"It's . . . miraculous!" The old man smiled.

The itching subsided as Lamia and I exchanged glances. "What is, Majesty?" asked the councilwoman.

"The butterflies!" His elbow knocked over a teacup as he vainly clutched at the sparkling dust motes in the sunlight. "All round them! Around my daughter and the Thorvald prince. It must be a blessing from the Mother—a blessing on their union!"

"Majesty," I said, beginning to feel alarmed. "Are you all right?"

"His Majesty must be referring to the butterflies on the

carpet beneath the table," offered Lamia hopefully, her voice shaking a bit. "Aren't you, Majesty?"

The king's eyes suddenly sharpened and he blinked furiously, as if he was surprised to find himself sitting in the solar.

"Of course," he said, his voice sounding very far away. "Of course . . . that is what I meant." He shook his head as if the vision of the wedding and the golden butterflies was still fading before him. "I . . . forgive me, Lady Folque, I don't feel I can spare any more time this afternoon. There's . . . much to do."

He rose to his feet, unsteady. Lamia and I followed suit.

"Of course, Majesty," Lamia answered, concern writ all over her face. "I thank you for your time."

"Adria!" Renart shouted.

The page was through the door and summoning the king's guard before the last part of her name was even out of the old man's mouth. The king gave one last look at the sunbeam, still glinting with dust, before disappearing into the hall. The door shut behind him with a loud *clank*.

I spun round to face Lady Folque. "Ma'am, what *was* that?"

Lamia nervously twisted the rings on her fingers. "Nothing to do with me, I fear. My 'cunning,' as you so quaintly call it, has no such effects."

"He said he saw butterflies!" I exclaimed. "Butterflies that weren't there! Don't you think we should tell the princess, ma'am?"

"The princess is preparing for a wedding of enormous importance. I expect the *last* thing we need to trouble her with is a momentary loss of sense by her father." The lady shook her head decidedly. "No, I think we should keep this between ourselves for the present. Agreed?"

It didn't feel right, keeping such a thing secret from Saphritte. And I could tell from Lark's glower across the room that it didn't feel right to her either. If *my* papa started grinning at thin air and trying to catch invisible bugs, I'd sure as sugar want to know. *But,* said the tiny voice in my head, *the sooner she's married, the sooner you and all the indentures can go home.*

"Agreed."

Satisfied with my reply, Lamia relaxed a touch, but there was a twinge of pain in her face. She stared crossly at the door.

"Where in All's name is Beir?" Her brow creased again as she shifted to her opposite foot. "He should have returned by now."

"Begging your pardon, ma'am, but you seem . . . uncomfortable."

Lamia's mouth set in a crimped line. "I'm . . . well, I don't suppose there's any point hiding it from *you,* but I've developed a rather . . . embarrassing affliction."

"I've seen the herbery here, ma'am—I don't suppose there's anything Mistress Devi can't take care of, even if it's some kind of"—I lowered my voice out of modesty—"lady's complaint."

Lamia tsked. "Oh, nothing like that. And it's no slight to Mistress Devi that I've not sought out her healing—it is simply my own vanity. The women of the herbery are dreadful gossips and I shouldn't like the whole palace to know the bottom of my foot is quite covered in . . ." She shuddered. "Warts."

"Warts are nothing to be ashamed of, ma'am! And your

foot's not the worst place to have them, either. Master Bidford once came to Non's 'cause he—"

"Yes, I'm sure I understand," Lamia interrupted. "Nonetheless, I'm loathe to expose myself to the prattle of palace staff. Unless . . . you might be able to offer me some assistance?" Her eyes flicked to the corner where the suit of armor stood in its unending watch. "Especially in light of my missing proctor."

I frowned. "It's my non that's got a talent with herbs, ma'am."

"No, you misunderstand," she said. "Last week, at the guildsmen's banquet, I overheard Lady Gillis telling one of her friends about a book of remedies in the lyceum library. She had her herbist study it to treat a rather indiscreet rash. It cleared up straight away, so she said."

I thought of Non's friend, old Jora Hustfeld, who'd lend books out of her own collection to folk that wanted to read them. "Why don't you just go and borrow the book, ma'am?"

Lady Folque glanced uncomfortably at Lark, who raised an eyebrow. "Well, you see . . . it's a volume of Ordish herb lore. It wouldn't do for me to be seen obtaining such a book, especially under current circumstances. But you would have no such trouble."

I could almost hear Lark's teeth grinding together. "You mean . . . you want *me* to go to the library?"

It was a question, but the lady took it as an offer, bowing her head graciously. "Oh, *thank* you, my dear—I should be most obliged." She reached out to tug a velvet bell cord. "You should have no difficulty at all persuading your tutor to take you. When it comes to his pupils, Master Iordan's vanity quite matches mine."

"But—"

Folque's servants poured into the solar to whisk away the remains of our tea. "I'll have the details sent to your chamber," Lamia continued, as if I'd not spoken. "Now, if you'll pardon me, there are a great many things that require my attention— including the whereabouts of my proctor. Goodly bye, ladies."

And then she was gone in a swish of crimson, directly past Gareth, who entered balancing a heavy tray of meat, cheese, and beer. He looked round the empty room, bewildered.

"Did I miss something?"

I plucked a slice of cold sausage from the platter. "You don't know the half of it."

The next morning, there was a cow at breakfast.

I almost didn't notice straight off since I was still feeling stung by the words me and Lark had in the hallway on the way to the banqueting room.

I knew she was sore about Lady Folque sending us to look for the book. She'd been tight-lipped the day before, but after a night of stewing, she was more than ready to speak her mind.

"So, she's more'n happy to profit from our cures but doesn't want to be seen doing it. Now *there's* a fine thing," she grumbled.

"I know she didn't ask in the kindest way, but if we *do* this—"

"She didn't suggest that *you* weren't worth spit, did she? That you were someone to be embarrassed of? She even called us enemies when she was talking to the king!" Lark shot back. "I don't trust her, Only, not one bit. You said you *felt* her cunning yesterday in the solar. It didn't trouble you any?"

I could almost feel the maddening itch between my ears

again. "Of course it did! But if there was anything ill in it, I'd've known."

"And what did I tell you just yesterday morning? About being able to see past the end of your—"

And that's when we both stopped dead in the doorway of the hall.

Most of the time, palace folk broke their fast in their own chambers. If I was lucky of a morning, Lark would bring up a tray of cold meats, bread, and cheese. But in honor of the Thorvald's arrival, the whole bleary-eyed court gathered in the banqueting hall just after sunrise only to find a sight I was sure would send Lady Folque straight back to her sherry bottle.

The cow wasn't like any I'd seen before, and not just 'cause it was indoors when it ought've been out. It was brindled like a hound, with dark patches round its eyes, two small, but very pointed horns upon its head, and a wreath of flowers woven from straw circling its thick neck. It didn't seem terrible bothered to be standing in the middle of a fancy dining room—it just chewed its cud and looked at us through its huge brown eyes like *we* were interrupting *its* breakfast.

A few of the minor nobles, visiting for the wedding, had already arrived at the morning meal and were clustered in the corner, as far away from our hoofed guest as they could manage. A stout Thorvald in a red jerkin and rabbit-skin boots patted his charge on the back, whispering comforting words into its twitching ears.

Neither me nor Lark could move an inch. She looked behind us and then back at the cow, as if she was thinking about going out and coming in again to see if we were imagining things. Her mouth opened and closed a few times, but all that came out was "Um."

"You can say that again," I agreed.

"Ah, *goden morhen*, friends!"

Orrad Eydisson strode into the hall as if it was the most regular thing in the world to have livestock join him at table. He clapped his hands in delight and went to plant a kiss on the cow's forelock before addressing the cowering nobles. "Is she not the most handsome *veizlakyr* that has ever lived?"

Lark leaned over to whisper in my ear, "Suddenly, doing a whole castle's worth of laundry don't seem so bad." She patted me on the shoulder. "Let me know how you get on." And before I could say another word, she turned on her heel and hotfooted it down the corridor.

The nobles, meanwhile, were all smiling through terrified teeth at Orrad's entreaties. "Come!" bade the Thorvald, thumping the cow on the flank. "Come and kiss! It is good fortune for the bride and groom!"

The nobles clumped so close together, you couldn't slip a piece of parchment between them. Gathering my grit, I stepped forward, doing a little curtsy.

"*Goden morhen*, Highness. Begging your pardon, but—"

"Ah, little heart witch!" he exclaimed, coming to grab me by the hand. "You will come and kiss the *veizlakyr*, will you not?"

The Thorvald dragged me to stand next to the beast. Hot breath from its great, wide nostrils tickled the loose strands of hair on my forehead. Not wanting to be impolite, I gave the cow a quick peck on its wet snout. Orrad and the fellow in the red jerkin beamed their approval.

I cleared my throat. "I reckon this is the first time the banquet hall's ever had a . . . visla-keer in it."

"All's girdle!"

The doorway to the hall had got much more crowded. Lord Dorvan's huge frame filled the entryway along with Gareth, whose eyes were two full moons in his head. A host of faces craned around them to see what the fuss was over. Mizzen, big as she was, whined and shrunk back at the sight of the razor-sharp horns.

Lady Mollier peeked round her fellow council member, looking more weary than shocked. Non said once when you raise whelps, you come to expect the unexpected. Maybe the lady's nieces had never brought a cow to the breakfast table at Mollier's Hold, but she had the expression of someone who wasn't looking at the oddest thing they'd seen that day.

"My good prince," she began gently, as if talking to a small boy, "there appears to be an animal in the king's formal dining room."

The prince grinned. "But of course! It is the feast cow—and she must eat from the bride's hand at her table."

"Do you mean," exclaimed Lord Sandkin, who'd appeared from the corridor, "you've brought dinner to the table *before* it's cooked?" His mouth twisted in distaste. "Speaking as a farmer," he whispered to Dorvan, "even *I* think that's a bit peculiar."

"What I mean, Highness," Lady Mollier continued, "is that His Majesty is rather particular in matters of . . . cleanliness. And while this is clearly the noblest of creatures, I'm sure you wouldn't wish to offend him by its presence at the morning meal."

The cow turned its giant eyes to the councilwoman, lifted its tail, and demonstrated its nobility all over the floor.

"Ah!" crowed Orrad. "That is good luck also!"

"Oh, All," squeaked Gareth.

"Let me through, please," echoed a voice from the corridor. Lamia and Adalise Folque appeared through a gap in the crowd, her ladyship's annoyance writ clear on her face. "Dorvan," she growled, "the kitchen staff is waiting. Why is no one seat—?"

She broke off, as the beast's presence and odor hit her all at once. "Why," she asked in a low and dangerous voice, "is there a cow in the king's banqueting chambers?"

Orrad's face lit up at the sight of Adalise. "Lovely lady! You will come and kiss the *veizlakyr*, will you not? It is good fortune for unwed maidens! Perhaps you will be next to find a husband, no?" He smirked, raising one eyebrow.

Lady Folque's daughter had a smile frozen upon her face. Though she'd seemed rather taken with the Thorvald the day before, she was clearly less enchanted by livestock. I took advantage of their distraction and slipped to Gareth's side.

"The king's going be mad enough to chew silver and spit out cutlery," the steward squeaked. "He had one of his chamber boys paddled last week for a bit of dust left on the windowsill! What's he going to do when—?"

Adria's familiar cry rang through the chamber. "Make way for Their Majesties!"

I cringed. "I guess we're gonna find out sharpish."

The crowd parted nervously, dropping into bows and curtsies as the royal party swept into the hall, led by the king himself, who stopped so short, Saphritte and Hauk nearly ran straight into the back of him.

Orrad's good humor wouldn't be kept under a bushel. *"Brodir!"* he cried, ignoring Alphonse Renart completely. "Is she not grand? Such a feast we'll have!"

Hauk, though he was Thorvald, had spent some time in Bellskeep, and knew all too well what was going through the mind of his almost father-in-law. He shook his head violently at his brother behind the king's back.

"What—" began the king ominously, but he was cut off by the arrival of King Bram and Queen Arnora.

"Oh, Hjalmar," the queen cooed to the red-jerkined man, "you have outdone yourself!"

"She is one of Sivgar's own herd!" added Bram in admiration.

Beside me, Gareth's knees were knocking together at the prospect of the king's temper. Saphritte was of the same mind.

"Majesty," she said, laying a steadying hand upon his arm, "I'm sure—"

"What . . . ," repeated the king, a little louder, but again, he was cut short by the excited Thorvald.

"Naersystr," chattered Orrad, extending his hand to the princess, "come and give Balvark your blessing!"

"Who's Balvark?" demanded Saphritte.

"I'm pretty sure it's the cow, Highness," I chimed in.

"What—!" roared the king a third time.

The whole hall cowered, braced for a royal explosion. Gareth and I shrunk back further against the wall.

"What *a magnificent creature!*"

The buzz of nervous voices quietened instantly. Gareth, who had both eyes squeezed shut, opened one.

Saphritte looked at the king like he'd just stood on his head with no underclothes on. "Father . . . did you say—?"

Then, to the surprise of all assembled, the stately old man laughed and went to embrace the cow round the neck with outstretched arms.

Orrad pointed to king and cow. "Ah, you see, *naersystr*? His Majesty, your father, has given his blessing. Come! Come give yours!"

"Yes!" agreed Alphonse Renart loudly. "Come, daughter! Come and kiss the cow!"

"Has His Majesty been *drinking*?" whispered Lady Mollier to Lord Sandkin.

"It's not like him to overindulge. Particularly before breaking his fast."

"Perhaps some blow to the head?" suggested Dorvan quietly.

An uncomfortableness that had nothing to do with the fact I was eager to break my fast settled in my belly. First invisible butterflies, now raptures over a cow at breakfast?

Lady Folque frowned. "Whatever the cause of His Majesty's . . . mirth, it seems to be doing no harm to our relations with our northern friends. I suggest we all pay our respects to the beast, get through this meal, and seek answers after."

The other three council members exchanged sour looks, but

all four of them went to join the line of Bolvark the *veizlakyr*'s wary well-wishers.

"Master Farway," said Lamia to Gareth as she passed, "perhaps you could run to the stables quickly." She glanced down at the floor beneath the cow's hind legs. "We are in need of someone with a rather large shovel."

"A . . . cow, you say?"

"Aye, master! A real big one."

"And . . . the king wasn't very angry?"

I popped a slice of orange into my mouth. The inquisitor didn't care for food in his lessons, but breakfast had been a little rushed. "Not even a little! He went up and hugged it like it was his mama."

Iordan sniffed. "Between you and me, the cow was likely more affectionate than the king's mother."

"But ain't it—?"

"*Isn't*," he corrected sternly.

"*Isn't* it peculiar, though? I reckoned His Majesty'd go through the roof, and you could've knocked us all down with a feather when he didn't. What d'you suppose happened, master?"

The inquisitor folded his wiry arms. "As one ages, the mind cannot always be relied upon. I told you in the Wood that the king has become more suggestible over the last few years. Perhaps this mania is simply . . . the next step."

As Iordan reached for the magnificent map of Thorvald, ready to unspool it on the table before us, I went over the words me and Lark decided on so I might avoid my cunning giving me away while trying to do Lady Folque's favor. My head still ached at the memory of all the failed attempts.

"Master, I was wondering if we could do something else today."

Iordan puffed up like a rooster ruffling its feathers. "Something *else*? Do you not suppose the Thorvald continent a satisfactory subject for study?"

"No, no," I said quickly. "I just wondered if maybe . . . we could go to the lyceum library? I'd like to have some books for my chamber—I'd much rather read than do the cross-stitch Lady Mollier brought me." I held up my pointer fingers, the meat of them covered in tiny red spots. "I'm not so handy with a needle."

The inquisitor stopped his clucking and examined me, thoughtful. "In light of this morning's happenings, perhaps it *may* be wise to do some more reading on our guests to avoid any more . . . surprises."

My breakfast churned in my guts. I hadn't told an untruth—I really *did* want something to replace the spiky hours I spent on stitching, but the reason behind my suit was bigger than a just way to avoid turning myself into a pincushion. *Warts*, I thought ruefully, resolving never to let *my* vanity get in the way of comfort. I held my breath for Master Iordan's verdict.

"Very well," he said finally, rolling up the map. "I shall call for a carriage."

A sudden fit of inspiration struck me. "May I bring my fr— waiting girl, Lark?"

"The Ordish indenture? Oh no, I don't think—"

"When I first got here, you told me it wasn't proper for a lady to go out in a fella's company without a shap-rone," I reminded him.

"A *chaperone*. And I . . . I am your tutor!" he spluttered. "Hardly, as you say, a *fella*."

"I mean, it's all right with *me* if you're not interested in being proper, master," I said, crossing my arms. "I ain't never—"

The inquisitor threw his hands in the air. "*Haven't ever!* And yes, all right, you can bring your girl! I suppose I should be grateful that you've hung on to *anything* I've taught you since you arrived."

My outside stayed quite sober, but inside, I grinned ear to ear at my own cleverness. If I was going to search a whole library for one book, two pairs of eyes beat one *any* day.

4

No love hath I for anything than that I owe a good book.
For what other thing can make me,
If even for an hour,
Not myself?

—The Most Honorable Madam Eulard,
founder of the Bellskeep lyceum

Though it took a little longer than I'd hoped, Master Iordan managed to get hold of a carriage. With the royal coaches in constant use ferrying wedding guests, the grumpy inquisitor begrudgingly agreed to hire a public coach with the understanding we'd have a king's guard escort.

"One cannot be too careful in the streets during these times," he sniffed.

Though it wasn't as comfortable as any of the palace carriages, Lark gazed out the windows, positively thunderstruck. I'd been goggled by Bellskeep when I came, but the Ordish girl'd never seen the like.

"I ain't left the castle since they brought us," she said, taking in all the hustle and bustle outside. "These folk live as close to one another as we do! You suppose they're all acquainted?"

The inquisitor let out a small huff. "Bellskeep is a city of tens of thousands. One could hardly be expected to know *all* of one's fellow citizens."

Lark eyed the inquisitor with salt. "There's near ten thousand folk at the Southmeet every year and I know all of *them*, master."

"*Tens* of thousands in this city, child," said Iordan haughtily, "and the citizens of Bellskeep prefer to keep a polite and . . . civil distance from their fellows."

The Ordish girl's eyes narrowed further. "Are you sayin' we ain't civilized?"

There wasn't any answer the inquisitor could give that wouldn't make things worse, so I jumped in quick to change the subject, pointing out the window into the market. "What's that long line in aid of, master?"

Iordan's face became grave. "I'm afraid it's a line to buy bread and meat."

The line stretched a fearful distance; our carriage rolled by soul after soul clutching whelps and purses close, looking forward hopefully. They all had a pinched look about them. Lady Folque wasn't exaggerating when she said the grain-store burnings were making for a lean winter. It grieved my heart that people thought the Ordish responsible for it.

"So it's true, then," I said softly. "Folks really are hungry."

Lark pressed her face up against the window, no doubt thinking of the palace stores, filled to bursting with goods for the wedding. "It ain't right—for some to have so much when so many got nothing."

The inquisitor tried to summon some of his peacock pride, but his heart wasn't in it. "Well . . . of course some of the festivities are being scaled back a bit in light of the situation."

Lark suddenly jerked back from the window as a resounding *crack* filled the carriage. A fracture like a spider's web shot through the glass as Master Iordan and Lark recoiled in surprise. Another *crack* followed hard after, though this time we could see its source—a rock thrown by a lean boy in the market line.

"What's one of them indentures doing in the city?" he shouted angrily.

"The rascal!" exclaimed Iordan indignantly. "Who does he think he is?"

But there were more folk shouting now—and more folk bending down to scoop rocks off the road. Their voices rang through the broken window.

"Wetcollar!"

"This is your doing!"

"River rat!"

More stones pinged off the side of the carriage, despite the angry rebukes of the driver and the guardsman riding pillion. Lark shrunk back even further into the plush cushions of the seat, white as frost, and clutched her cloak round her. I grasped her hand tightly.

"They won't let those folk get near. They won't let 'em hurt you." I looked at Master Iordan, hoping he'd have some comfort to offer, but his face was just as pale, and the shouting was growing louder by the moment. Angry citizens were breaking out of the line to hurl stones and filthy curses, closing in round the carriage.

"A bit more haste, if you please!" shouted the inquisitor, rapping frantically on the roof.

An unexpected ring of steel turned even the hottest heads in the crowd. The city watch, alerted by the racket, appeared from between the many stalls with their swords drawn—ready to quiet the unrest. The young woman nearest the coach, wearing a threadbare cloak and carrying a crying babe on her hip, lowered her arm with the rock clenched tight in her fist.

"We'll drive your kind out of Orstral, rat!" she snarled. "Right back to wherever you came from!"

Her furious face disappeared as the carriage lurched forward once more, the watch clearing the way before the nervous horses. Lark buried her face in my shoulder.

I hadn't seen my friend cry once—not once—since I arrived, though All knew she had plenty of reasons for it. But the cruel words of the angry stranger had cut her to the quick, and I couldn't do a thing but pat her knee lamely as she heaved great sobs into the hood of my cloak.

But then my hand was joined by another.

"The history books tell us," began Master Iordan, "that as long as there has been an Orstral, there have been Ordish. Before the construction of Kester's Weir, the clans joined with the crown to repel invaders, build towns, and harvest shared crops. Orstral belongs just as much to you as it does to that hungry woman and her child." He leaned back in his seat, his hard, thin face beat soft with charity. "I hope you will not forget it, despite your present circumstances."

Lark looked up at the scholar and nodded, eyes red but full of gratitude.

As THE COACH turned up the steep path toward our journey's end, we caught our first glimpse of the lyceum.

Its three stories were made entirely of red brick, with dozens upon dozens of windows under pointed gables. The arch of the main gate, flanked by two narrow towers that rose two more stories above the building, boasted colorful tiles beneath a great statue of a woman wearing the long vestments of a scholar and holding a miniature version of the lyceum in her left hand.

"The Most Honorable Madam Eulard," said the inquisitor, noticing my interest. "The founder of our great institution."

I nudged Lark to have a look, but she was as silent and unmoving as the stone scholar above us. I'd tried to wring a few words from her as we wound through the streets and up the steep road that led to the lyceum, but after the marketplace, she wasn't of a humor to speak. She just stared glumly at the floor of the carriage, lost in her own thoughts.

As we rumbled closer, I could see groups of young folk in gray robes and black caps upon their heads scurrying through the cloisters.

"The second morning classes are about to begin," Iordan exclaimed, his mouth crinkled in disapproval. "There are *far* too many late lay-a-beds for my liking. I realize it's the week before Yule, but there's no excuse for sloth!"

It was nice to know, as the carriage rolled through the gate, I wasn't the *only* one the inquisitor told off for being tardy.

We emerged into the courtyard, where I could finally see the whole of the lyceum. It was a great rectangle, connected by four towers. In the middle was a huge, close-cropped lawn, cut into four smaller ones by paths wide enough for a carriage to pass. A herd of sheep grazing the sparse winter grass didn't even look up as we trundled past.

The coach came to a halt at the rear gate, which looked a lot like the one we'd just come in through. This gate, though, boasted only one tower, which rose high above the rest, set with a gigantic clock that began to chime the hour as Master Iordan opened the door and looked up.

"The astronomy tower," he pointed out. "On Long Night, I shall bring some equipment to the hallsroom so we might have a lesson."

"Couldn't I just look out the window of my chamber?" I groaned, not at all keen to spend a cold winter's night in a drafty old tower.

"Not unless you have a large telescope available to you!" snorted the inquisitor.

"A what?"

"A telescope," he said wearily. "It's a device that lets us observe faraway objects more clearly than we can with our own, limited sight. And we must use it in the tower to escape any light of the city that might disrupt our observations."

"You inquisitors should build one out in the countryside, then. It's dark as a watchman's pocket down in Presston."

Iordan stared over his lofty shoulder as he opened the large door before us. "Ah yes, but that would, of course, require us to relocate. To *Presston*."

It did my heart good to finally hear Lark's voice in my ear as the inquisitor disappeared inside. "Want me to get Rowan to squeeze some bittergreen in his tea next time he comes for a council meeting?"

"Don't bother," I told her. "He's so sour anyway, he'd hardly notice."

IT MIGHT NOT'VE been as grand as the halls I walked every day, but I liked the lyceum straight off.

Dark, shining wood replaced the cold stone of the palace. The walls were white daub and hung with paintings. Not boring portraits of sullen, long-dead folk, neither—but paintings of bloody battles, scenes from tall tales, and portrayals of the testaments. There were no bowed heads and hushed tones—the lively chatter of the collegiates followed the creak of their feet on the wood floors as they moved through the narrow hallways.

Me and Lark trailed in Iordan's wake, the young folk parting before him like water before the bow of a boat. "The palace is fancy and all," I said, "but I like this place better. It feels . . . more alive."

The inquisitor's spine seemed to grow another inch. "That is because the palace is the seat of the nation, where its affairs must be conducted with the solemn attention they deserve. The lyceum is the seat of ideas, which must be freely shared, debated, and improved upon."

We emerged into a great hall, where he pointed to a group of collegiates gathered by a grand wooden stair. "Master Sayer! Straighten your cap! Mistress Wimark, have you not noticed your robe is torn at the hem? And, Master Drew, where are your tassels? Return to your chamber and collect them at once!"

The young folk scattered like mice, all eager to be out of Iordan's sight. "I s'pose they're not allowed to debate the *inquisitor's* ideas," I muttered to Lark as we started up the stair.

We came to a halt before a grand door, where our guide turned, surveying us sternly.

"Usually, it is only students, faculty, and patrons who are permitted to enter the library. However, since you are under my tutelage, exceptions can be made. And unlike the scholars, you will be able to remove books from the collection. If you come upon a title that piques your interest, find a docent to unchain it for you."

"What d'you mean, 'unchain it,' Master?" I asked warily.

"All of the books in the library are chained to prevent their being removed from the premises without the express permission of the docents."

Blast! I'd hoped for a little more privacy, for Lady Folque's sake if nothing else. "My non's got a whole library full of books, too," I protested, "and I've never seen *her* chain one down."

"Your esteemed grandmother does not have to deal with an army of light-fingered collegiates," the inquisitor answered drily.

With a click of the latch, he opened the door into the library. It took a minute for my eyes to adjust to the dim light inside, but once they did, there was such a sight to behold!

The windows, with their diamond panes, were all set with deep amber glass. Covered lanterns guttered among the stacks that stood in straight lines like dark wooden soldiers in the center of the room, each guarded by tall gates. More shelves ran along every wall, the long chains that held the books in place glittering in the lantern light. A huge wooden desk sat in the entryway, a tightly grated fire burning in a sunken hearth behind it. The woman sitting with her nose buried in some ancient volume didn't even look up at our approach. Dressed in deep brown scholar's robes, she almost seemed to be part of the library herself—at least half Acherian, her light umber skin glowed as warmly as the stacks.

"Ah, Mistress Lall, a good morning to you," remarked Iordan, approaching the desk.

"And to you, master," she replied, still not looking up from the large volume she was studying. "How can I be of assistance?"

"I was wondering if you might allow my pupil to choose some appropriate reading material to take back to the palace."

The woman's head snapped up. She picked up a small pair of spectacles and perched them on her nose, peering out at me and Lark with her deep green eyes.

"Oh, so you're the Mayquin, are you?"

"Yes, ma'am," I replied timidly.

She leaned forward in her seat. "And do you know how to treat books, Mistress Mayquin?"

I nodded. "Like a stranger made of glass who arrives on your doorstep, ma'am—with kindness and caution. My non taught me that."

"She taught you well, then." Some of the wariness went out of her as she turned to Master Iordan. "Your pupil is welcome to browse at her leisure."

"I thank you, mistress." The inquisitor turned back to us. "I shall be in the reading room. When you've made your selections, have one of the docents bring you there."

And with that, he turned on his heel and disappeared into the stacks. Mistress Lall had already gone back to her reading, so me and Lark crept into the library, reluctant to disturb the silence with even our footsteps.

I'd never seen so many books in one place before. I took a deep lungful of the dry air—dust, paper, leather, and oil flooding my nose in a pleasant combination.

A tug at my sleeve brought my attention back to Lark. "Only, I just wanted to say . . . what I said this morning . . . about Lady Folque—"

"You haven't got a thing to be sorry for, Lark Fairweather, not a thing!" I whispered urgently, but she shook her head.

"I ain't apologizing. I don't trust her any further than I could kick her, and I think her cunning's dangerous, but after what I saw in the market . . ." She swallowed hard. "If her plan'll get you, me, Ro, and the other whelps out of here, you won't hear me say a word against her from this moment after."

I nodded solemnly. "Non says sometimes you gotta make a deal with a wolf so as not to get et by a snake."

Lark shuddered. "A whole city's worth of snakes." Her eyes traveled up the groaning shelves. "So, how're you going to find the book you're looking for?"

"How're *we* going to find the book I'm looking for, you mean," I answered, peering through one of the stack gates. "That's why you're here, remember? I can't look through 'em all on my lonesome."

"But there're so many!" she complained. "Master Iordan'll come for us long before we find it."

The gold leaf on the book bindings winked at me. "Old Jora Hustfield in Lochery's got a little library of her own. I've been a few times with Non when she got stumped with some ailment. Jora keeps her books by what they're about, just like Non and her herb cupboard, but starting at the beginning of the alphabet. So, books about flowers would be under *F*, books about birds under *B* and the like."

"Look there!" Lark pointed to a large carved letter *H* on the side of a stack. "Maybe this library does it the same. What's the book called again?"

I pulled a folded scrap of paper from the pocket of my coat with the title written in Lady Folque's elegant hand.

"*Healing Waters—Remedies, Herbs, and Lore of the River Folk*," I read. "It's a bit of a mouthful. But what d'you reckon it'd be under? *O* for Ordish? *H* for herbs?"

"Could just as well be *R* for remedies or *L* for lore," Lark suggested.

"Oh, this place is too big!" I groaned. "I wish Lady Folque'd told us where to look!"

Lark put a hand to my arm. "Hold on. At least once a winter, we have to hire a cart at the Bay to go up to Blessing for supplies. There's a fella up there who does pretty much what Auntie Maven can do—says he's a *physik*. When I asked Papa what the word meant, he said it was just a fancy word for healing and medicines." She pointed to all the glinting spines. "This seems like a place they'd use all sorts of fancy words. So . . . maybe it's under *P*?"

I stared down the endless rows of books, feeling daunted. "We've gotta start somewhere, I suppose."

The old floor of the library groaned under our feet as we shuffled along the stacks, following the trail of golden letters until we reached *P*. I pushed open the gate at the end of the stack and began running my fingers over the spines, the chains jingling gently.

"*Sightings of Phenixes . . . Phlegm: The King of Humours . . .* Oh, Lark, this is no good!"

"It's 'cause you're on the wrong end!" Lark whispered, her finger traveling carefully down the row of titles. "*Physik* is spelled *p-h-y* . . . Oh!"

I went to join her at her end of the stack at her quiet squeak. "Here! *Healing Waters—Remedies, Herbs, and Lore of the River Folk!*"

I could barely stop up my excitement as I reached for the book. "Can you believe it, Lark? I didn't expect it to be so eas— *Sweet All!*"

My fingers had hardly touched the spine of the book when an all-too-familiar agony exploded inside my skull. I fell to my knees with a thud, tears squeezing out the corners of my eyes.

Lark was at my side in an instant. "What is it? What's wrong?"

"Oh, to the seven hells with it!" I replied through gritted teeth as the pain turned to a dull ache. "It's my cunning, though I'm not sure why it's got its britches in a bunch about me touching a *book*."

The Ordish girl pulled her knees up to her chest. "What did you tell Master Iordan about why you wanted to come to the library?"

"I told him I wanted to— Oh!" I exclaimed. "I told him I wanted to take out some books to read in my chamber. That's true, mind you, but I guess my cunning knows *that* book ain't one of them. It knows I want it for Lady—"

"Can I be of assistance?"

Both Lark and I jumped as a young man appeared at the ungated end of the stacks by the amber windows. He wore the gray robes of a collegiate, covered by a fawn-colored smock. *A docent!* I thought. But his face was familiar to me—though I'd never been to the lyceum, I'd definitely seen him before at court.

"Are you . . . Lord Folque?" I asked.

The lantern above us caught the pin at my throat. Lady Folque's son put a hand to his breast. "Oh, forgive me, Mayquin! I'd not thought to . . . but where are my manners? We've not even been introduced properly!" He offered me the hand that wasn't full of books. "Borin Folque, at your service!"

Lamia had a chill about her, despite the silky voice and summer trailing behind her wherever she went. But Borin seemed to have more than enough warmth for both of them, shining right through his dark, friendly eyes.

I let him help me off the floor, still feeling shook. "It's a pleasure, your lordship. This is Lark Fairweather."

I could hear Master Iordan's voice chiding me for "introducing an indenture to nobility" or some such nonsense, but Borin grasped Lark's hand in greeting.

"Pleased to make your acquaintance, Miss Fairweather."

Lark was struck speechless. I'd have wagered coin Lord Folque was the first noble to have had any gentle words with her since she was brought to Bellskeep. And on a day when she'd heard others use terrible words against her, it made me like him even more.

"Was there a book you were interested in?"

I glanced quickly along the row of books, all held to the shelf by the same chain. Lady Folque seemed very keen to keep her affliction a secret, and even though Borin was family, he was like not to want to know anything about his mother's foot warts.

"Uh—"

"The Mayquin was looking at some of the books on . . . um . . ." Lark cast a frantic eye over the shelf. "Pheasantry."

A startled look crossed the docent's face. "Pheasantry?"

"Oh, sure! Only's always going on about pheasants! From the minute she opens her eyes in the morning, it's always, 'Oh, how I miss my pheasants back in Presston!' or 'Do you suppose I could find a tame pheasant at the market?' or 'I'd give anything to hear their silly, creaky song once more!'"

The whole stack of books was cast in the blue glare of the lie along with Lord Folque, who was luckily so busy listening to the babble coming out of *Lark's* mouth that he didn't notice *mine* hanging wide-open.

"And when she ain't *talking* about pheasants, she's *thinking* about 'em. Chances are, if I find her staring out the window in her chamber, she'll be dreaming about their long feathers and their speckled breasts and their—"

Lord Folque held up his hand politely. "Clearly, her dedication to the birds is quite . . . noble." He pointed to a narrow volume on the shelf. "This one—*The Art of Pheasantry*—should satisfy your interest."

He took a key, which hung from a rope on his belt, and clicked open the padlock. It was then I saw what Lark had in mind. In order to unchain the book he *believed* I wanted, Borin would also have to unchain the rest of the shelf, leaving *Healing Waters* free for the taking—*Lark's* taking.

She positioned herself to his right, near the books of physik, and gave me a knowing wink. I realized I'd have to catch his attention somehow, making sure he was looking at me and not at Lark. Lord Folque came back and plucked the book on pheasantry off the shelf. The chain behind it slacked and slithered noisily out of the rings, unbinding the entire row of books. Lark's fingers twitched and she flashed me a look. *Well, what are you waiting for?*

I barely had time to think. I couldn't say anything that wasn't true, like *Look over there, Lord Folque—it's a sheep wearing a housecoat!* So I just did the first thing that came to mind.

"*Screek, screek!*"

The docent was so surprised by the noise I made, he nearly dropped the book altogether. Behind him, I just glimpsed Lark's hand shooting out toward the shelf and snapping back under her cloak, leaving her covered in a faint red glow. We'd gotten what we came for.

Borin looked at me like he thought I might suddenly sprout wings and a beak. I could only smile weakly until Lark appeared at my elbow.

"What did I tell you, sir?" she said, patting me on the head. "Pheasants on the brain. A good imitation, though, wasn't it? It's just her way of saying she's excited to read the book."

Lord Folque inclined his head politely. "Yes . . . well, it's been a pleasure, ladies." He held out the book, which Lark quickly snatched up with her free hand. "I must be about my duties. If you find yourself wishing to read on any *other* subject, please don't hesitate to ask."

He gave a little bow and disappeared round the corner of the stack, eager to be away from all talk of wildfowl.

Lark's shoulders slumped with relief, but hunched up once more as I gave her a sharp pinch.

"Ow! What was that for?"

"Pheasants?" I hissed.

"I didn't know what anything else on the shelf *was*!" she protested, rubbing her arm. "Would you rather I'd picked—" She squinted at another volume on the shelf. "Phil-an-thropy?"

"No, but I'll be sure to ask Master Iordan what it is so I'm ready *next* time we have to do some fool thing like this."

"Hopefully the next time her ladyship needs some fool thing like this doing, she'll just send her proctor," declared Lark. "That is, if she can find him."

I'd forgotten entirely about the missing Master Beir. "He didn't come back yesterday?"

"Nope. There's a girl in the kitchen he sometimes makes eyes at. One of the Folque stewards was asking her if she'd seen him and she said she hadn't."

I didn't care for the shrewd, manicured Folque proctor, but his absence sure was curious. "*I* wouldn't want to get on the lady's bad side by not turning up for work."

Lark snorted. "He's probably just holed up in an alehouse somewhere."

"If even half the tales they tell are true, no proctor worth his salt'd cross the Folques. And definitely not for a few pints of ale."

"Well, it ain't none of our business, that's for certain. Let him turn up with a sore head and spend a few days in the dungeon—it don't mean a lick to us." She took my arm. "Come on, let's find the inquisitor before anyone notices there's a book missing."

"I wonder what the punishment for thieving a book from the library is?" I said under my breath as we headed back toward the great desk. "I'd probably end up sharing the dungeon with Master Beir."

"Just think of it this way," whispered Lark. "You'd have plenty of time to read about pheasants."

"*Screek!*"

Our giggles were loud enough to earn a shush from Mistress Lall.

5

The news from Bellsbrake came the next morning, even more unwelcome than livestock at breakfast.

We were all roused from our beds just after the fourth morning bell. Non says only ill news can't wait till sunrise, so when Lark appeared in the dark before dawn, I knew something was afoot.

"They didn't say why?" I asked, my tongue still sticky with sleep.

Lark shook her head as she handed me my heavy dressing gown to pull over my nightclothes. "Usually it's one of Mistress Abbot's girls that wakes us. But it was a soldier this morning—and she weren't gentle about it. Said you were wanted right away, no matter what you were wearing."

The throne room was dark and cold when I arrived—the servants still scrambling to light lanterns. Lord Sandkin stood by the slow-waking flames in a thick green bed jacket and a nightcap covering his ears, tied firmly below his chin. Lady Mollier stood next to him, her long white hair spilling down the back of her fur-lined robe. Dorvan yawned broadly while Mizzen lay before the hearth, her long legs splayed, trying to warm her belly. Only Lamia was entirely dressed—her peach-colored gown pressed, her great fiery jewel about her neck, and not a single hair out of place.

"Ah, the Mayquin's here," Sandkin said as he noticed me. "Good, I'm glad she'll be present for the hearing of this."

"Good morning, my lords, my ladies," I said. "The hearing of what?"

Constance Mollier's face was grim and drawn in the flickering flames. "There's been another burning, my dear."

A sick feeling crept into my belly. I'd been so wrapped up in my part of Lamia's plan, I'd pushed the man with the port-wine stain and the question of who was *actually* setting light to grain stores right to the back of my mind. It wasn't the Ordish—I knew that much—but there was no way to prove it. And with every attack, the hearts of Bellskeep became angrier and their larders became emptier. The face of the woman in the market who'd shouted at Lark the day before was fixed in my head.

"It's far closer this time," Lamia added. "In Bellsbrake."

Bellsbrake was a town about ten miles to the northwest, with a lot of farms that fed the royal city. Their wheat and corn were ground in the nearby mills, their vegetables and fruits sold in the market stalls. If there'd been a burning there, it meant Bellskeep was about to get a whole lot more jumpy.

The door to the left of the dais, reserved for the royal family, flew open with a bang. Saphritte barreled into the chamber before Adria, who was hot on her heels, could even announce her. The princess had taken a moment to change into her field clothes, her sword hanging at her side in readiness.

"This isn't an hour for good tidings."

Sandkin looked round, confused. "Highness, will . . . your royal father be joining us?"

The princess hesitated, just a moment too long for comfort. "I thought I'd spare the king such a rude awakening. I'll share the news with him personally once our meeting is concluded."

It's clear she didn't notice me before the lie slipped out of her mouth. The light of it played over her face, making the circles beneath her eyes all the deeper. The council'd remarked on His Majesty's peculiar behavior the day before—and I'd seen it with my own eyes in the solar. Master Iordan called it *mania*, which Non said was a serviceable word for "all manner of head nonsense." Maybe it'd rattled Saphritte, too—enough to let the king sleep through news of a threat to the kingdom.

When her eyes did find me, they held me a moment, knowing what I saw. But they flicked down and away as she motioned for me to come to my place behind the throne. "Adria, have the man brought in."

"Her Highness summons the witness!" the page bellowed.

The large doors at the end of the throne room cracked open to admit a small, stocky fellow in a fur riding cloak, who approached the throne clutching a thick woolen hat.

"A good morning to you, master," said Saphritte. "And you are?"

His voice trembled. "Master Remond Wilchard, Your Highness. I'm an alderman of the town council of Bellsbrake. I own the tavern, the Goose and Gander."

"And you witnessed the event last night?"

"I did, Highness," he answered bitterly. "I wish I hadn't, but All help me, I did."

Saphritte opened her hands. "Then, by all means, speak."

"Well, I'd only just nodded off, a little before midnight, when my goodlady wife shook me, shouting she could see flames out the window. At first I thought the tavern alight, but I ran to the casement only to see it was Sam Percy's mill."

"A mill, not a storehouse?" asked Lord Sandkin.

"Just so, my lord. And it didn't take long for the canvas on the mill's sails to set the roof of the house burning. Half the town was out at the millpond already, trying to douse it, but it was too late."

Lady Mollier leaned forward, anxious. "Was anyone hurt?"

Wilchard's face went hard. "Sam Percy got all five of his whelps and his wife out of the house, but took too much smoke. He went to the Mother early this morning."

"Is the cause of the fire known?" Lady Folque asked gently. "Is there any chance there was a candle or lantern left burning?"

"Nothing so innocent, lady," he spat. "It was them river devils."

I peered hard at the alderman, willing some light of untruth to appear round him, but none came.

Saphritte inclined her head in my direction, and I nodded, reluctant. "Are you sure, master?"

"They were seen!" insisted Wilchard. "Running from the mill after the deed was done!"

"Begging your pardon, Highness, Master Wilchard," I heard myself saying, "but how do you know the folk were Ordish?"

The man all but bared his teeth at me like a dog. "What do you mean, how do I know, whelp? Everyone knows it's them river rats!"

"I believe the Mayquin is asking what *exactly* the witnesses saw," Saphritte explained. "And though I understand your anger, I would ask that you keep a civil tongue."

Wilchard hung his head. "Apologies, Highness. It was Mistress Percy and her son Nole that saw the devils as they fled— all dressed in red, they were, with kerchiefs covering their faces!" A frightening hard gleam lit the alderman's eye. "We may not be near water, Highness, but the town council couldn't help but remember you got nearly three score of the wretches right here in the palace."

Saphritte was silent a moment. "My father's indentures are kept under close watch, Master Wilchard. They are children and could hardly be responsible for the fire."

"An adder's still an adder, even if it's newly hatched, Highness," the man answered hotly. "All I'm saying is there are some in the town who'd like an answer for what them wetcollars done. To see justice for our Sam."

Cold as the throne room was, the temperature went downright frosty. Everyone felt it, even Wilchard, who shrank back from the chill.

"I hope, master," the princess began, ice forming on every

word, "that you are not suggesting I turn over an innocent to face the . . . justice . . . your town council has in mind?"

"N-no, Highness," he stammered, an explosion of dazzling greens and blues covering him like a cloak. "I—I didn't mean—"

But Saphritte didn't need me telling her what he'd meant. "Because I'm *sure* a wise alderman such as yourself knows that a wrong cannot be undone by another wrong."

The man had bent so low, his nose almost touched his knees. "Of course, Highness. Forgive me, Highness."

The princess stood and walked down the steps of the dais to stand before the cowering Wilchard. "We cannot let our grief make monsters of us. I will send a troop of guard to patrol Bellsbrake until the offenders are caught. Master, please carry our thoughts and beseechments back with you for the family of Sam Percy. Our might shall follow soon after."

Eager to put his embarrassment behind him, the alderman bowed again, muttering thanks, and set off as quick as his legs would carry him.

The princess paced the length of blue carpet that ran from the dais to the doors and back again, her hands flexing restlessly at her sides. She stopped and looked up toward the throne, as if it was the scale she used to weigh her thoughts.

"The city will be in a state of alarm when word gets out," she said finally. "As if it weren't enough to lose the grain, now there's one less mill to turn it into flour!"

"Shall we send for Alderman Wilchard again?" asked Dorvan. "We could ask for his silence a little while longer."

Saphritte shook her head. "It wouldn't make a difference. Ten miles is not far—all of Bellskeep will know by sunup."

"Then we must make sure the knowledge doesn't cause panic," Lord Sandkin declared.

"Agreed," said Lady Mollier. "Seeing the king's guard in the streets would do good for many fearful hearts. Particularly before the Day of Misrule tomorrow."

Saphritte's jaw clenched. "I'm not certain the festival should continue. With the unrest already in the streets, the celebration might just tip into *actual* misrule rather than the usual tomfoolery."

"The people are in sore need of some entertainment, Highness," Lady Folque said. "I fear canceling the festivities may create more problems than it solves. If it will ease your mind, I'll send my fastest messenger to the Motte—I can have another five score men in the city by sunup tomorrow to keep the peace."

Saphritte still didn't have much love for Lady Folque. She'd've had less if she'd gotten a whiff of Lamia's plan, but she knew good sense when she heard it. "My thanks," she answered, climbing the steps of the dais to where Adria stood waiting with the door held open. "My lords, my ladies, Mayquin, I'll take my leave to deliver this heavy account to my father."

WHEN I'D SEEN about nine summers, Mama told me old Vernor Wainwright had been tried for stealing all the lettuces out of Mistress Umble's garden. They found his footprints and the old copper amulet he wore about his neck in the soil near the destroyed vegetable patch. He'd been forced to sit in stocks all day even though he swore blind it wasn't him that did the stealing. Not two days later, another neighbor of Mistress Umble's caught the old woman's daft sheepdog gobbling the lettuces out of *her* garden. Poor Vernor had been telling the truth all along. His only crime had been having a bit of Scrump down at the Bird in'th Hand and stumbling through Mistress Umble's patch on his way home, where his amulet had fallen off. "It don't pay to jump to conclusions, Pip," Non said after. "It'll just lead to a heap of misery."

And it was that misery I was aiming to end. The Ordish *weren't* doing the burning—I knew it as sure as I knew my own name. But what *I* knew wouldn't mean a flea breaking wind to folk now worried about feeding their families through the winter. Alderman Wilchard's visit made me sore afraid for the indentures.

And what would be the king's reaction when Saphritte delivered the news? Would it be the reaction of the Alphonse Renart I first faced when I came to Bellskeep or the one of the man swatting at thin air in the solar? It didn't bode well for anybody either way, as far as I could tell.

The door to my chamber creaked open loudly, but it didn't disturb Lark, who'd fallen asleep on my bed. I lay down beside her and closed my eyes, hoping for sleep to find me again, but it was no good. My brain was brim-full of thoughts that wouldn't be quietened.

Reluctant, I gave my sleeping friend a poke in the ribs. She woke with a snort.

"I was just resting my eyes, honest!"

"It's only me, you goose. Where's the best place in the castle to go if you want to get the keenest gossip?"

"Pffft," she scoffed. "That's simple—the kitchen. Jaws down there are flapping a mile a minute. Ro's always overhearing things he probably ain't supposed to."

I slid off the bed and went to open the doors of my great wardrobe. Shoving aside satin, velvet, and lace, my hands landed on what they were looking for.

Lark sat up. "Only, what're you doing?"

I tossed the stable boy's breeches and tunic onto the quilt.

"I wanna find out what's goin' on outside the palace walls. And I'm not gonna get any answers lookin' like the Mayquin."

THOUGH THE MORNING upstairs hadn't hardly begun, there was chatter rising from the kitchens.

Me and Lark tiptoed down the steps into the giant world under the palace. I'd only been there once before, and I'd been trapped in a crate at the time, so I gave myself a moment to take it all in. Long, arched windows looked down on the enormous rooms, each serving a different purpose. The delicious smell of meat on the spit wafted through from the roasting room. The mellow tang of yeast hung in the air from the bakery. And the earthy scents of onion, carrot, and spices rose from the cutting tables. There was a twinge in my heart to smell preparation of Long Night vittles along with the day-to-day scents—brandy pudding, candied oranges, and rum buns.

It was blessedly warm—like it was a different season from the rest of the palace. But the sweat standing out on the brows of the cooks and indentures made me think summers in the kitchen would be a special kind of awful.

No one paid us any notice as we moved through the bustle. In my traveling clothes, I felt invisible—able to poke my nose anywhere I liked. But Lark handed me a large mixing bowl.

"Best to look like you got somewhere to be. Mistress Abbot don't hold with idleness."

My eyes flicked past all the faces, bent over mortars or chopping blocks, rolling dough, or hurrying through with bags of flour, until they landed on the one I'd been searching for. Rowan, Lark's brother, was sat in the corner with a pail, a pile of potatoes bigger than he was, and a scowl set upon his face.

"He must have cheeked one of the porters again," Lark whispered as we slid by some of the busy cooks. "That old hag Abbot's twigged he hates peeling more'n the pox, so it's an easy penance."

The Ordish boy looked at us twice as we came to stand by him and the enormous pile of spuds.

"What're you doin' down here? If Mistress Abbot catches you, she'll birth kittens on the spot!"

"Forget Mistress Abbot *and* her kittens for a minute," I told him. "You haven't heard or seen anything peculiar this morning, have you?"

"Not with my own ears or eyes. Though Barrow Reed saw a bunch of Thorvald out at the pond in the altogether, shouting and whipping themselves with birch switches."

My mouth dropped open. "Isn't there snow on the ground?"

Rowan shrugged and tossed another potato into the pail. "They broke the ice on the water and went for a dip after, so I heard." He shivered. "Better them than me!"

I shook my head, trying to rid thoughts of bare Thorvald from it. "Anything from the city?"

He squinted at the high windows of the kitchens. "Still early. A lot of the help from outside's not here yet—though I think that steward you're friendly with is busy in the silver store."

Lark picked up a dull paring knife from one of the sideboards. "I'll help Ro with this lot for a bit. You go see what Gareth's got to say."

"No, leave it," Ro said, waving her off. "We'll both get a hiding—me for having help and you for helping me."

"I ain't scared of old lady Abbot," Lark said, pulling up a short stool and giving Ro a friendly pinch on the cheek. "Go on, Only. I'll keep an eye out."

Tall dressers ringed the chamber, piled high with plates that gleamed silver and gold in the dim light. Candlesticks of every shape and size covered tables, along with all manner of cutlery. The room smelt strongly of wax, vinegar, and the soft red grease used to polish the precious metal. The sharp scent wormed its way up my nose, and before I could hold it in, a sneeze exploded out. I clapped my hands over my mouth just as a head popped out from behind one of the large dinnerware dressers.

"Only?" asked Gareth, his hands full with a stack of silver dishes. "What—?"

I shushed him. "I can't stay long. I just wanted to know whether you'd heard the news or not."

Gareth made a pained face. "I saw it with my own two eyes, down by the pond. There's about a dozen Thor—"

"Not *that* news," I said quickly. "I mean about Bellsbrake."

The steward sat himself down at the long, stained table and swiped a rag through the bowl of polishing grease. "My brother Gable told me this morning on his way in. Said word was all over the Shallows, so it won't be long till it hits the reputable parts of the city."

"The Shallows?"

"It's not a place most folk want to be seen. At least not if they care how they're thought of. It's packed full of thieves, smugglers, forgers—all sorts of no-gooders." He polished hard at a stubborn spot on a silver cup. "Gable fits in there just fine."

"Did he tell you what they were saying? In the Shallows, I mean?"

Gareth shook his head. "Just that there'd been another fire and someone'd been killed."

"Did they say anything about the Ordish?"

"I only spoke to him for a second!"

I pulled up a chair next to the steward. "It's just, the fella who came from Bellsbrake with the news was so angry, he wanted . . ." Wilchard's angry face, red and unpleasant, jumped to the front of my memory. "Because some folk in red tunics were seen running away, he wanted to do something awful. To the indentures."

Gareth looked up from the cup. "The king wouldn't allow that. At least . . . I don't think he would."

I scooted closer. "The princess took the news herself. Didn't even want to wake him up."

"I'm not surprised after the last month or so. No one's got any idea what he's going to be like one moment to the next." Satisfied with the polish on the cup, he took up a plate. "And then yesterday, with the cow in the morning and in the afternoon—"

"What'd His Majesty do in the afternoon?"

The steward peered out the door and bent his head toward mine. "So, he was supposed to meet with the curate round fifth bell and *no one* could find him."

"He disappeared?" I asked, wildly curious. "Where'd he turn up?"

"That's the thing," Gareth explained, laying down his cloth. "A few of the maids found him in the main ballroom. There's a big glass vase in there—almost life-size—shaped like a woman. The king was *dancing* with it."

I could hardly imagine the fierce and dour Alphonse Renart doing something as fanciful as that. "Dancing?"

"It took two of his valets to convince him it wasn't the Duchess of East Lodeston. I know the princess asked them to keep it quiet, but nothing stays secret for long round here."

"Hold on—the princess *knows* he's been like this? And it's been happening for a *month*?"

He scratched his nose, leaving a smudge of polish on it. "Of course she knows! Who else would everyone be afeared enough of that the news didn't leave the castle? His fits are usually over pretty quickly, but it's still got everyone walking on eggshells."

If everyone from the princess to the palace maids knew about his "fits," how in the name of All didn't Lamia Folque know? The thought of the councilwoman reminded me of another lingering question.

"You've not heard anything about Master Beir, have you—you know, Lady Folque's proctor?"

"*Everyone's* tongues have been wagging over *that*. It's not every day one of the big houses has a proctor go missing. Some of the kitchen girls think he went off chasing a pretty frock. The porters think it's more likely he got robbed and done in." He wiped the polish smudge off with his sleeve. "Either way, Lady Folque is probably beside herself. No one wants the fellow who knows all their secrets to go missing, do they?"

"Depends on what sort of secrets they're keeping."

I didn't mean the words to come out sounding so direful, but Gareth and I looked at each other with the same wary expression.

"You think something's going on?" he asked quietly.

"Non says if a bird looks like a goose and tries to bite you on the backside like a goose, it's like to be a goose."

Gareth shook his head. "Your non says some awfully peculiar things, but I think I take your meaning."

A shout from the kitchens rang through the silver store.

"*What is* she *doing down here? I thought I told you to peel every last one of those on your* own!"

I jumped up from my seat. "Sounds like I need to get back

abovestairs before someone decides to cook *my* goose. Can you keep your ear out—for anything about the king or Master Beir or what the city folk are saying about the indentures?"

"Keeping an ear out's what I do best," he said with a sly grin. "I'm not *just* good at folding pointy napkins, you know."

6

Dear Mama, Papa, Ether, and Non,

I must've just about cried myself dry after I broke the wax seal on your letter and saw your lovely writing. Seeing it made me feel like you took me in your arms from halfway cross the world.

The Thorvald arrived here a few days ago. I wish you could have seen them—I think Ether's eyes would have popped clean out of his head! They've got some peculiar ways of celebrating a wedding, that's for certain, but they seem to be good folk, nonetheless.

By the time this letter gets to you, it'll be past, but Long Night is coming and I miss you more than ever. It's been three whole months now I been in Bellskeep. It feels like years and yesterday all at the same time. I hope when you light your candle for

the Stranger on Long Night, you think of me. I'll be
doing the same here, thinking of you.

All my love, from the river
to the house and back again,
Your Only

—Letter from the Mayquin, Only Fallow,
to her home in Presston, from *A History of Orstral,* vol. 2

The Day of Misrule had the city in high spirits. But just like Saphritte said, there was something going on just under the sound of vendors selling their wares, the children shrieking with glee, and the cheerful singing of Yule songs that made a body feel like it would only take one dish breaking or one cross word to tip the whole celebration on its head.

I leaned against the velvet-covered wall, eyes closed, trying to block out the noise. I'd barely slept a wink the night before, even though the fire was warm and the bed soft. There was so much going on in my head, I felt for sure it must've been leaking out my ears onto my pillow.

The king's fits. The anger of a hungry city toward the indentures. The fire that took the life of the poor miller and the folk who were *really* responsible. And lastly, Lady Folque's missing proctor. All of the facts tumbled round and round like a waterwheel, leaving me staring hour after hour at the hated bull on my canopy.

"Do sit up straight, dear. You don't want to bend your lovely mask."

I didn't give a fig for my mask, but I sat up all the same. Lamia straightened the satin bow that held it to my face. "There. It does look awfully fetching on you."

The Day of Misrule in Presston was something me, Jon, and Ether would look forward to all year. Mama and Papa'd get up early and good-naturedly do our chores while we lazed in our beds. All the orchardmen and the ladies of the bakery'd exchange clothes for the day, and we'd laugh ourselves silly at Old Teague, with his great woolly beard and Mistress Garvery's frock, pretending to be a blushing maiden. In town, the burgher would sit in the stocks and folk would pay a coin or two to throw snowballs at him. Folk would ride their horses back to front through the square, say good night in the daytime and good day at night. The day would finally end when they brought out Master Litton's ass to crown it Mule of Yule, and with its bray, the upside-down world would be turned right again until the next year.

But I was disappointed to find wearing fancy masks was what passed for mischief in the king's court. The king himself was said to despise the celebration, thinking it vulgar, so the folks in his circles confined their revelry to covering their faces. It was this that led me to sharing a coach with three giant rabbits.

Lamia, Adalise, and Borin all wore finely painted leather masks that looked like the Folque hare—Lamia's in gold, Adalise's in white, and Borin's in brown. I, on the other hand, wore the face of a narrow-eyed hawk with a third eye set in the middle of the dappled feathers that rose from my forehead. I'd seen it in the glass after Lark'd tied it on. I didn't look fetching—I looked cruel. The only decent thing about it was that the feathers shaded my eyes, letting me stare at anything for as long as I liked without seeming discourteous, so I chose to study Lord Folque.

Out of his scholar's robes, Borin seemed smaller and less easy. The rich chocolate-and-gold coat he wore looked well on him, but behind his mask, I'd've bet a copper there was a proper sulk going on. He didn't seem the sort that enjoyed the noisy uproar of the holiday any more than His Majesty.

I was proved right just moments later when Lamia let out a sigh. "I didn't suppose I'd have to tell *you* not to slouch, Borin. You look like an old fishwife, all hunched and irritable."

"I'm a grown man, Mother, I'll slouch if I like." The rabbit's head turned toward the window. "I'd rather be back at the lyceum."

"I don't know how you prefer that dusty old place to court," Adalise said, delicately straightening her mask's whiskers. "I think I'd be bored senseless within an hour."

I didn't much care for his sister's tone. "I spent *two* hours there, your ladyship, and I didn't get bored once."

Even through the holes in his mask, I could see the thanks in Lord Folque's eyes. "And how are you finding the book?" he asked.

Truth was, I'd only just cracked open the cover and was promptly so bored, I'd shut it almost straight away. "It's . . . um . . . very pheasanty."

Ignoring her brother, Adalise turned her head to Lamia. "Mother, you've not heard anything from—?"

"No, I haven't," snapped Lamia. Then, thinking better of her manner, she patted her daughter's hand. "Forgive me my sharpness, dear, but it's been weighing rather heavily on my thoughts."

My ears pricked up. "You've still had no word from Master Beir, ma'am?"

Maybe she didn't want to discuss the matter—or maybe she just didn't want to discuss the matter with *me*—but my question was dismissed with a wave of her hand.

"I've men searching for him. He'll be found soon enough."

But deep in the eyeholes of her mask glinted a hard diamond of worry I wasn't likely to crack.

The carriage rolled to a halt outside the royal box—a stand that towered above the madness of the streets where the court could enjoy the misrule without needing to be in the middle of it. Long silks bearing the king's colors fluttered in the breeze from its balconies, their silver stitching catching the light. The footman opened the carriage door to help Adalise down. Borin disembarked next, holding out a gentlemanly hand for his mother and then for me.

The Cathedra Square was packed to overflowing—hot breath meeting cold air in a fog above the crowd. Folk both high and low crammed the streets, all wearing a dizzying motley of colors under a sea of masks. Some were no more than a piece of cloth with holes cut round the eyes, and others were even more ornate than the one that hid *my* face. Master Iordan told me the masks were so you could get up to no good without anyone knowing who you were. When I complained my mask wouldn't leave anyone doubt as to who *I* was, he gave me a haughty look.

"I believe it's safe to say that *you* will not be participating in any of the low pleasures of the festival."

I didn't know what the inquisitor meant by "low pleasures," but I supposed it was probably anything most ordinary folk would just call "fun."

By the time we'd climbed the stairs to the top of the box, a slippery layer of sweat had formed between me and my clothes, even though the afternoon itself was frosty. I flapped the opening of my cloak, letting in the cold air coming from the open balcony.

Riotous laughter sounded from the front of the covered stand. Orrad and King Alphonse, having spotted something in the crowd that tickled their fancy, were braying like donkeys, the horns and antlers of their masks almost crashing together. At their side, Saphritte looked on through her own, more delicate horned mask, concerned and uneasy at her father's guffawing.

Gareth stood dutifully in the corner, wine pitcher in hand and an equally worried brow. He spotted me through the simple blue-and-silver mask that covered his eyes, but not so fully I couldn't understand what he was trying to tell me.

It's happening again.

Lord Folque pointed to a gilded seat next to the King and Queen of Thorvald. "I believe you're meant to be there."

The fearsome Eydissons were decked in matching stag masks—great golden antlers rising far above their heads. They looked just as dangerous as the day they arrived.

I gulped. "Thank you, sir. Maybe I'll see you the next time I come to the library."

He gave a slight bow. "I shall look forward to it."

I screwed up my courage and made my way down the narrow aisle to the seat next to the Queen of Thorvald.

"*Goden dag, vardmadrleita,*" said the handsome woman as I curtsied. "Today we see your *dogrróta*—your . . . no rules day?"

"*Goden dag*, Majesty. The Day of Misrule, yes, ma'am."

She craned her neck, gazing out over the heaving square. "It does not look so unruly to me. Where is the wrestling of the bears? The blind swordplay?"

Sweet All, I'd hate to be in Thorvald for their Day of Misrule! I thought. "I've never seen any of those things, Majesty, but I think I see a fellow down below wearing lady's bloomers on his head."

"No bears?" Arnora sighed. "Such a shame!"

Bram poked his head out from behind his wife, frowning. "No bears," he grunted. "Just hats made of *undirkrakr.*"

My tongue felt as if it'd been tied in a knot. No one'd ever taught me how to hold a polite conversation with two people who really just wanted to watch a fellow get torn apart by a bear. "My tutor, Master Iordan, said there'd be music, bawdy shows, and clockworks, Majesties."

Arnora inclined her antlered head. "What are these . . . clockworks?"

I'd only ever seen little ones at the fair in Roundmarket. Traveling toymakers delighted folk with little mechanicals— milkmaids that carried tiny pails, blacksmiths that pounded on tiny anvils, and dancers that kicked their miniature legs in the air. Papa explained they worked the same way a clock did, with gears and springs. But Gareth told me the clever guilds of Bellskeep made mechanicals especially for Yule—giant ones, pulled by horses. Bram's and Arnora's mood sweetened a bit as I explained.

"*That* will be worth seeing," mused Bram, bobbing his antlers in time with the pipes and reeds playing below. "Almost as good as bears."

I peered over the heads in front of me, hoping to catch a glimpse of the king. The old man roared his approval at two mummers wearing giant glue-paper heads of Colomba and Trufflo, the dumb-show puppets, beating each other with sticks. I managed to catch Gareth's eye again. He was just as confused as the rest of the courtiers round His Majesty—the old man seemed to be heartily enjoying a festival he professed to despise.

A commotion louder than His Majesty's was making its way through the streets, coming closer to the Cathedra Square. I hoped whatever was coming next might be enough to snap the king out of his fit, but the moment it rounded the corner, I knew it'd do no such thing.

It was one of the guilds' clockworks. I'd been curious to see one, but as it came even closer, all I wanted was for it to disappear. A painted mechanical of Alphonse Renart sat on a great throne. At the end of one of the clockwork's legs was an enormous boot, which slowly extended out to connect with the rear end of another figure, all dressed in red. Its ugly face was caught in a grimace, surrounded by thick braids strung with beads. It was the most horrible thing I ever saw.

King Bram shouted his approval. "The people, they know, eh? They know their king will be strong against their enemies!"

"This is very good," echoed Arnora. "Our *naerdotter* has a mighty sire!"

For the first time that day, I was glad of the mask covering my face. If anyone could see underneath it, they'd've seen my sore desire for the body who designed the clockwork to be brought to the whipping post. The terrible thing was a match in a powder keg, and the king was fanning the spark on the fuse.

The loud hooting and hissing turned to cheers as the clockwork passed before the enclosure. The king, in his humor, waved merrily to the citizens below. It was a humor that might give an angry crowd just what they wanted—and what they wanted was now ringing off the front of the Great Cathedra.

Wetcollar! Wetcollar! Wetcollar!

The princess leaned in toward the king.

"Majesty, do not encourage this. It's dangerous."

But to the king, hers was just one more voice in the crowd he was busy chanting along with. She leaned closer.

"Sir, you must call for calm."

The king and the crowd only got louder. The council were on their feet now, just as alarmed as the princess at the vengeful tide of noise below. Frustrated, Saphritte grasped the shoulders of the king and turned him to face her. "Father, what is the *matter* with you?"

A mighty bellow topped the baying crowd. The king's furious eyes went wide and afraid, and in a voice that sounded more like a frightened child than a man, he whispered, "What was that?"

The princess searched her father's face for answers—the moment of danger had passed, but whatever afflicted the king remained, shaking him as if he was feverish. The ugly chant below was replaced with gasps of delight as the bellow sounded again, louder. King Bram leapt to his feet, the antlers of his mask nearly poking a hole in the canvas roof.

"By the ax of Sivgar! It is magnificent!"

Another clockwork had rounded the corner into the square. Whichever guild designed it was clearly trying to court favor with the visiting Thorvald, for moving slowly down the street was a rearing stag, its legs slowly kicking out before it. Steam fumed from its nostrils and bent-glass lanterns lit its eyes. A bone horn was lodged in its mouth, blown by an unseen guild member. As it neared the enclosure, it sounded once more, rattling my teeth in my head.

At the sight of the apparition, the king gave a shout of horror. He flung his hands before his face as if they could hold back the sight of the clockwork beast. "No! No! I beg you, no!"

"Guard!" Saphritte shouted, trying to shield her raving father. "See to the king! He is not well."

The king's guard appeared from the sides of the stand, surrounding the delirious man. I thought it was at least partly to hide him from the crowd, where masked faces turned upward, craning to see the commotion in the royal enclosure. The king's wails of fear could be heard halfway across the square, but with the old man himself out of sight, it could always be denied later. The tight knot of guardsmen wrestled the frenzied king down the steps, followed by Gareth and Saphritte, who ripped the mask from her face and threw it aside. The horned silver thing clattered to the floor by my feet. I bent to scoop it up, only to notice I'd been joined by Lord Folque, staring anxiously down the stairs after the princess.

"What's gotten into the king?" I asked.

"I don't know," he answered, his own mask forgotten back at his seat. "But it bodes ill, don't you think?"

A fire. A furious city. A wedding. A king struck down with madness. It didn't seem it could get much more ill than that.

But it wouldn't be long before I discovered just how wrong I could be.

WHEN I GOT back to the palace, I could tell someone had been in my chamber.

Every morning, after I was carted off to lessons, one of the chambermaids would come to tidy up any disorder I left behind. It wasn't much, 'cause no matter how many times I was told it wasn't my concern, I couldn't let someone else make my bed or hang my clothes. But I'd got used to the little signs of their presence the maids left behind.

While I'd been at the Misrule procession, I'd been visited by a stranger—one who'd had a good nose-round, by the looks of it. It was little things—the dish of hairpins was on the opposite side of my dressing table to where I'd left it. The door of my wardrobe was slightly ajar. The tight corners I tucked into the bedsheets were loose and the pillows rumpled instead of smooth.

I knew whoever it was had gone, but felt spooked nonetheless. I trailed my fingers over the desk, noticing the paper askew around the letter I'd written home that I hadn't sent yet. I peered under the bed. *You're making something out of nothing,* I told myself. *You just got upset by the procession, that's all.*

I took off my greatcoat, laying it carefully on the bed so's not to wrinkle it, and pulled the chair from my writing desk close to the windowsill. I'd discovered a way up onto the thick wooden beam that crisscrossed my chamber—it was as close to the branches of a tree as I was like to get round the palace—and I found it an agreeable place to perch for thinking. It'd taken a few pairs of torn leggings before I'd learned to do it without leaving evidence of my mischief—no doubt I'd be subject to some lecture on being unladylike by either Master Iordan or the seamstress.

I'd just settled my back against the wall, dangling my feet over either side of the beam, when a knock sounded below. I started, not wanting to be caught on my perch, but relaxed as Lark's face popped in, looking confused at my absence.

"Up here."

The Ordish girl's eyes flicked upward.

"Mistress Tomson's like to give you a hiding if you ruin another pair of leggings."

"Keep your bloomers on," I said, scooting up my shift to show her I'd not done any damage. "I've got it sorted now."

Lark was even quicker up the wall than me. Her steady feet crossed the beam and she dropped down in front of me.

"You weren't in here when I was gone, were you?" I asked.

"No, I've been in the laundry since you left. Why?"

I looked down at the chamber. "I know this sounds peculiar, but I think someone was ferreting around in here."

"You think they took anything?"

"What've I got to take? The dearest thing I have is that stupid brooch, and I wear it all the time."

A second knock at the door gave both of us a start. Quick as a wink, Lark was across the beam and swinging to the floor. Less surefooted, I leapt up, catching the hem of my shift beneath my boot and immediately losing my balance—a nasty business, if not for the canopy above my bed. I tipped sideways, arms flailing like a windmill, and crashed straight through the embroidered linen with a mighty rip. The ornamental cap on one of the enormous bedposts broke with a *crack* and flew across the room, shattering the looking glass on my dressing table.

The chamber door flew open before Lark could answer, and Gareth skidded into the room.

"Sweet All, are you all right?" He glanced at the wreckage of my chamber. "How . . . how did that happen?"

I groaned, looking up at the tatters of the hated bull. "I think Mistress Tomson might give me more than a hiding."

Lark grimaced. "I think you can count yourself lucky your backside's under the king's protection. That was a pretty fancy piece of knitting." She stared in dismay at the shards of glass all over the floor. "Don't know if he can protect you from seven years' bad luck, though."

But I didn't really want to dwell on my ripped canopy, the broken glass, or my luck. "What happened to the king?" I asked Gareth. "Have you been in to see him?"

The steward shook his head. "He sees no one but the healers, princess's orders."

"He's never been that bad before, has he?"

"No, never," said Gareth. "He *hates* the Day of Misrule—everyone knows that."

The horrid chanting of the crowd still rang in my ears. "Well, he sure picked a bad day to start enjoying it!"

"What are you doing up here, anyway?" asked Lark, examining the snapped threads of the canopy.

"I was looking for you, actually. I think you may need to have a word with your brother."

Lark's head snapped up.

"Rowan? Why?"

"One of the porters picked a quarrel with him. Well, I say it was a quarrel—the porter made an uncivil remark about . . ." Gareth reddened to the roots of his hair. "Well, about your parentage, and when your brother came to give him an answer for it, the porter picked up a knife and threatened to 'Kester' him."

"The tale of Kester's Weir," Lark said flatly.

I felt sick. "The prince who killed the Ordish boy with his sword."

The steward nodded. "If the feeling out in the streets is starting to leak into the castle, the indentures aren't going to be safe here. Not for long."

As Lark pressed Gareth for details of Rowan's scrap with the porter, I slid off the side of the bed to check on the wreck of my dressing table. The golden pins lay scattered among the jagged slivers of glass. The silver handle of the boars-hair brush was deeply dented. But worst of all was my nameday chest, which had taken a blow from the broken post cap.

My heart gave a little lurch of despair to see the cracked

lid that Papa's hand so lovingly sanded and oiled. I opened it, to make sure nothing inside was broken, and was immediately struck with a deep dread.

"I think I know what whoever was in my chamber was after."

Gareth and Lark stopped their jawing and looked at me.

"The Jack is gone."

7

Those who seek to fight an unknown adversary must use different weapons from those who spend their rage on the field of battle. To fight what remains unseen, a warrior must put away the sword, the bow, and the ax. Instead, they must take up the head, the heart, and the gut.

—From *The Craft of Warfare* by Asfrid Alrik,
translated from the Thorvald

Despite Gareth and Lark trying to reassure me the theft of the Jack was probably done by an indenture, sad and sick for home, I found the notion harder to stomach. The indentures were canny, especially with all the evil feelings toward them abroad in the streets—getting caught with an Ordish token in such a time didn't bear thinking about. The disappearance was still weighing on me the next day, on the morning of Long Night—when Adria came to take me from Master Iordan's hallsroom to meet with the council.

"I trust you remember our appointment this evening?" the inquisitor asked.

"Pardon, master?"

Iordan harrumphed indignantly. "The appointment in the

hallsroom to observe the heavens? If you remember, I mentioned it to you on the day of our visit to the lyceum."

My troubled spirit sunk lower. "Oh, that's right. To look through your telly-scoop."

"*Telescope*, yes. If we're fortunate, we may even be able to observe the constellation of *Helvia Hyalus*, normally too low in the sky and too faint to be seen from the city."

"The council did say *now*, Master Inquisitor," Adria scolded from the door.

"Yes, yes, all right," he muttered, shooing me away. "Be prepared at seventh bell."

An evening spent in the company of my dry tutor made my heels drag, even as I came into the cheerful warmth of the council chamber, where Lord Sandkin and Lady Folque were engaged in some testy conference.

"It should be postponed," snapped Sandkin, "until the king is well enough to give his blessing!"

Lamia threw her hands in the air. "The king gave his blessing long ago when he agreed to the terms of the marriage—this . . . affliction should not matter in the slightest! Besides, I have still been conducting my daily meetings with His Majesty, and while he is not recovered, I can say there has been some small improvement in his condition. The wedding should go on as planned."

Lady Mollier was uncomfortable to take Lamia's side in any argument, but even more uncomfortable to support Sandkin's on this occasion. "Be reasonable, Arfrid. There are thousands of people already in the city for the celebration—a good many of them bringing badly needed coin. Do you really think putting off the wedding is going to be good for the public order?"

Sandkin frowned, begrudging. "Has anyone consulted Her Highness on the matter?"

"The princess spends all her time by her father's bedside," Lamia replied, "but I'm sure she would wish to do her duty."

"It just doesn't seem right, with His Majesty so . . . affected. And with the tragedy in Bellsbrake—"

"We all share your concerns for His Majesty, my lord," Lamia interrupted. "While it is regrettable, there is nothing we can do to change it. And as for public order, I have another four score men arriving this evening from the Motte with their own supplies so they'll not tax the city's resources. No citizen need fear mischief from their fellow citizens *or* the river folk."

The serious councilman sat back with his flagon of ale. "Yes, quite. Especially when our invited northern guests are mischievous enough!"

"I don't know," Dorvan boomed, helping himself to a large piece of bread and cheese. "I rather enjoy them. It's good to stir things up now and again."

Lady Mollier humphed indignantly. "Well, there *was* the matter of that dreadful wedding play yesterday evening. Has the pig's blood come out of the banqueting hall's drapes?"

"I believe the chambermaids and the mistress of the laundry are still scrubbing." Lady Folque grimaced.

"I've never seen a play with so many murders in it," I said. "We only get boring virtue plays in Presston." I reached for a handful of grapes. "Master Iordan says the Thorvald believe entertainments like that scare away ill spirits that might want to do mischief on the newlyweds."

Lady Mollier threaded her fingers together. "Well, I do hope the bride feast this afternoon is a little more reserved. What is it called again? I have a terrible ear for the Thorvald language."

I couldn't help but puff up a little, eager to show off my learning. "The *fyrstagildi*, ma'am. Is it just a feast, then, or do you think there'll be another play?"

"All preserve us!" exclaimed Lady Mollier.

"I believe the princess has expressed her desire that no further dramas be enacted in the palace," Lamia said drily. "*The Wedding of Ottar and Sigrid* was quite enough for one marriage celebration."

I tried to hide my disappointment. "Oh, so just eating, then?"

Lady Mollier reached for her lace handkerchief to dab at the tip of her nose. "I believe we can safely say that nothing is 'just' anything when it comes to the Thorvald. The ambassador for the northern folk has mentioned dancing, toasts, and a few traditional games."

The thought of games perked me up. "Like Find Your Brother Blind or Catch the Ring?"

"Thorvald games, my dear," answered Dorvan. "And I imagine they have very different rules."

To be honest, it was only after they let the pig loose that I decided to crawl under the table.

For weeks, the palace seamstresses had been working till

their fingers bled to outfit the court for the wedding festivities. In fact, almost every able body who could thread a needle in fifteen miles had been commissioned for work. The clothing for the *fyrstagildi* was the plainest by far, with all the women in roughspun yellow shifts to honor the day and the men in dark blue tunics and leggings for the night. It was strange to see the whole court, no matter how high or low, all wrapped up in the same togs. Saphritte and Hauk were the only two that stood out, in the dullish gray-white of undyed wool. Though I'd seen her in fine gowns and battle-pitted armor, I never thought the princess looked so well as she did that evening, her dark hair loose and a crown of pine on her head.

It all started out quite regular, but Lady Mollier was right; it sure wasn't "just" a feast. After courses of seal, lamb, and the unfortunate Bolvark the *veizlakyr*, the special wedding ale the Thorvald brought was broken out, and that's when the afternoon stopped looking anything like an ordinary dinner. The aftersweets had hardly hit the table when some of the men, including Prince Orrad, stripped off their tunics and began slathering themselves with strips of seal blubber. There were gasps from the ladies of the Bellskeep court who couldn't find a place to look that wasn't taken up with half-bare Thorvald. Bram, Arnora, and Hauk clapped loudly as one of their serving boys brought in a struggling bundle of cloth.

Saphritte pinned her almost father-in-law with a nervous eye. "Majesty, what entertainment is this?"

"Ah, *naerdotter*, it is for the young men to prove their quickness! The victor will be the next to be wed."

From across the room, Orrad aimed a wink at the scandalized Adalise Folque.

"The victor?" asked the princess. The wedding play had made a home in her head, stoking suspicion of further Thorvald "entertainment." "How does one become the victor?"

Bram laughed and clapped Saphritte on the back. "Why, it's whoever catches the *griss*, of course!" He cupped his hands and shouted to the men, who were plainly ready to begin. "Good hunting, my friends!"

And with that, the boy stripped the cloth from the bundle to reveal a sturdy, wiggling piglet that leapt from his arms and took off like a shot.

Screams echoed up and down the hall as the chase began. The young men in pursuit took it dead serious, clearing any and all things from their path to get their slippery hands on the creature. Tables were bumped, drinks spilled, and chairs upended.

It wasn't till a flying cup of ale just barely missed my head that I finally ducked beneath the table, where I was fairly sure I'd be safe. To keep me sustained, I took a sweet dish—some Thorvald apple bread—and sat to have a think in the middle of all the noise.

Ever since news of the burning in Bellsbrake came, it felt as if I'd been hiding under a table, just waiting for something to happen. I had no idea how Lady Folque's plan to talk the king from his throne was going—or even *if* it was going. Had she abandoned the effort when Renart's wits got muddled? And I hated the thought that those muddled wits were all that stood between the indentures and the angry city, who bayed for their blood.

The man who was the key to it all—the man with the port-wine stain on his arm—was still as mysterious as he'd been months ago when Jon first told me about him. Why would he want to frame the Ordish? Was he behind the burnings as well?

The tablecloth suddenly lifted and a white blur slid underneath it. Even in the gloom, I was surprised to find myself sitting next to Saphritte, who started when she noticed me.

"Only!" she exclaimed. "This isn't . . . that is to say . . ."

"It's okay, Highness. I'm surprised there aren't *more* palace folk who've come looking for a place to hide."

The princess's face twisted in embarrassment. I offered her the dish. "Try some of this, ma'am. Apples are a bit tart, but it's not half bad."

Saphritte broke off a piece. "I suppose if anyone were to know whether something made with apples was good, it'd be you." She took a bite and chewed thoughtfully. "You're right. Not too sweet. The Thorvald word for apple is *epli*, by the way."

I picked another piece off the sweet bread and let the taste of the sour northern *epli* dance on my tongue. "This sure ain't like any marriage feast *I* ever been to. Papa's foreman, Hewe, got wed a few summers back. One of his mates tried to dress a horse in a gown for a laugh and got kicked into the millpond, but that's about the worst of it."

Over the ruckus, there was the sound of someone being loudly sick in the corner. Saphritte put her hand on my knee. "This really isn't the place for a child. I'm not sure it's entirely the place for *me*, and it's my wedding feast."

She gestured to the chaos on the other side of the tablecloth.

"It's not because of any of this that I'm not keen to marry, mind you—all folk have their own traditions, but . . ." Her eyes grew sad. "Perhaps it would have been best if my only love was for Orstral."

"What do you mean, ma'am?"

Saphritte snapped out of whatever daydream she'd be lost in and rubbed her eyes. "That wasn't a fitting thing to say. Forgive me. I'm not one for strong drink."

If at harvesttime, some cut-wise had told me I'd be hiding under a table with a princess during a Thorvald wedding feast, I would've laughed them out of the yard. But there we were—the daughter of the orchard and the daughter of a king—both trying to find a few seconds of peace to be alone with our sorrows.

"How's the king, ma'am?"

"On the mend." The answer was one the princess had practiced, and not actually true to boot. Her face told me so just as plainly as the blue-green glow that lit up the underside of the dark table.

"Mistress Devi has kept him full of sleeping draft," she amended, realizing her mistake, "in case it's some sort of brain fever. When he wakes, he has moments when he seems as well as he ever was, but then . . ." She shook her head. "The scale always tends to tip toward madness."

"I'm sorry . . ." I thought hard on what words to use—I sure couldn't summon any sympathy for the king, but for his daughter, about to marry into a pack of rowdy Thorvald for the good of Orstral, I could find a bit. "I'm sorry it's come at such a hard time, Highness."

The princess gave a huff. "I certainly don't deserve any sympathy from you."

"I don't think it's a matter of deserving it, Highness, but you got it all the same."

Saphritte patted my knee. "Let's see if we can slip away long enough to take you back to your chamber before something more untoward happens. I could use a few moments to collect my head."

I poked my head out the back of the table, between two chairs. "I think we're clear, ma'am."

Saphritte pushed the chairs apart and the two of us slid out from under the cloth. The princess adjusted the pine crown on her head and took my hand to lead me out of the hall.

"*Isabrot!*"

The shout of her soon-to-be husband rang to the rafters, even over the sound of twelve grown, shirtless men chasing a greased pig. Before the princess could even turn, she was swept off her feet by the greasy Orrad and delivered back to Hauk on the other side of the hall, where he stood waiting with two earthen cups.

"*Skal!*" shouted the Thorvald, rushing to pick up their glasses for the toast.

"Oh, another?" Saphritte said weakly as Hauk pushed the cup into her hands.

"Friends!" Orrad declared, hoisting his own cup in the air. "Drain your bowls for the *ulfrlitt* of Thorvald and his bride! May they live long enough and well enough to grow old and fat together!"

If Hauk's face was anything to go by, he wasn't best pleased to be called by his nickname in front of the assembled company.

Or maybe he didn't like the suggestion that he'd grow old and fat. But he shouted *"Skal!"* along with the rest of them and drank deeply. Saphritte sipped politely from hers.

It was at that moment the pig, which'd found a spot to hide, decided to go hell for leather and escape. It darted out from behind a stack of wood and raced, squealing, for the door. The shirtless fellows, who'd been distracted by the toast, hollered in delight and dove at the terrified animal as it wove its way between the forest of legs and toward freedom. Two of the pig chasers collided, sending one crashing into the tall stack of casks containing the Thorvald bridal ale. The whole assembly watched as the top cask wobbled and began its slow tip over the side.

Time slowed down, like when Papa once tried to fell a tree in the garden. He made the careful first cuts, to make sure the thing'd fall away from the house, but he didn't know the inside had been et by termites. On the third cut, there was a loud *crack*, and we all watched as the tree fell right onto the kitchen. It was just like that with the cask, everyone watching and waiting for the moment when it hit the stone floor. And when it did, it went off like a cannon.

There wasn't a soul in forty feet of that cask not covered head to toe in the sweet honey ale. The Thorvald roared their approval. The palace folk were not quite as pleased and stood, shocked and soaking. My rough yellow skirts began thirstily drinking the stuff up as it spread out in a sticky pool. It soaked through my slippers and began to seep between my toes. Saphritte's and Hauk's clothes weren't white anymore, but a dull brown.

Just then, a familiar cry came from the doorway.

"Make way for the king!"

The whole court turned, horrified to see His Majesty standing in the doorway of the hall in just his nightshirt. His legs and feet were bare and his mane of white hair floated round him, wild and unkempt. No one but the princess and Lady Folque had seen him since he was put in the care of the healers after the Day of Misrule, so his appearance was all the more unexpected. Adria stood behind him wearing a face that was trying to tell everyone present she'd nothing to do with any of it.

Stranger still, the king was carrying a cat. Bonnet, one of the palace mousers, was caught fast in His Majesty's grip. It'd clearly been a struggle—long scratches covered the king's forearms and hands. All knew how the old man was able to lay hands on the beast in the first place.

The sodden princess quickly picked her way through the crowd and stepped in front of her father, as if hiding him from the gawking court could make everyone forget what they'd just seen. "Majesty, you should be resting. Come, let me help you back—"

But the king pushed past her as if she wasn't there. "I am glad you are all gathered together," he announced in a wavering voice, "for I have an announcement that you must have the hearing of."

Saphritte stepped in his path once again. "Father, you're ill and—"

Alphonse Renart sidestepped her once again. "This kingdom is in peril and I am weak of spirit. And that is why today, before the Mother and all of you"—the king hoisted the animal above his head—"I hereby relinquish my throne and do anoint my only daughter, Saphritte Bethan Fisroy D'Abreu Renart, Queen of all Orstral!"

Gasps echoed round the room as the old man tried to crown the unwilling princess with the furious housecat. She managed to dodge several swipes of Bonnet's claws before a very anxious Vasha Devi burst through the door, followed by three members of the king's guard.

"Oh, Your Majesty, you had us all worried to death!" she cried.

"I am not His Majesty! Not anymore!" Renart warbled gleefully, still waving the hissing creature in the air. "Come, come! My lords, my ladies, bow before your queen!"

The Thorvald stood openmouthed in surprise. The rest of the court, trying hard not to squirm in their ale-soaked garments, stared at one another in disbelief.

"What are you waiting for?" roared the old man. "Bow!"

Slowly, both ladies and gentlemen, Thorvald and servants bent their knees, keeping a wary watch on the king—he'd sunk into a very low bow himself, seeming not to notice the cat was doing its best to shred what little clothing he was wearing.

"N-no, no, please," stammered Saphritte, her cheeks burning red, "please, good guests, don't, I beg you. Please rise, there's no need—"

"Long live the queen!" shouted Alphonse Renart, springing to his feet. "Long live the queen!"

The princess rounded on the guards and Mistress Devi. "Get him out of here."

In a swish of tunics, the king was swiftly taken from the room, although his cries of "long live the queen" could still be heard in the corridor for some moments after. Bonnet, who'd managed to make her escape in the confusion, shot off into the dark corners of the palace, where she may or may not have encountered the pig.

The *fyrstagildi*, a scene of chaos just a moment before, was now quiet as a dark morning before second bell. The Thorvald were the first to break the silence with fierce chatter in their native tongue. The rest of the Orstralian court erupted only seconds after.

"Is she really queen?"

"Mother's breath, why weren't we told he was so affected?"

"That wasn't legal, was it?"

"What is to be done with His Majesty?"

Sometimes, I dreamed of falling—out of trees, into wells, or off the city walls into the River. There was always the feeling, just before I hit the ground, that I *knew* I was dreaming and I'd wake up any second to find myself in my own bed. As I slipped from the room, mayhem at my back, I hoped to All I was in a dream, 'cause I could tell there wouldn't be any soft landing.

Open are our hearts,
Open are our doors,
Come, Stranger, and rest here until night is past.

—Words for the lighting of the Stranger's candle

Once, when I was just a grasshopper who dreaded the last lamp of the evening being blown out, I asked Non why the dark had to be so *dark*.

She stroked my brow. "The dark ain't so bad. Besides, if we didn't have the dark, we wouldn't appreciate the light so much."

I burrowed under my quilt. "I wish it could be light all the time."

"Well, day and night, they're a bit like life, ain't they? It'd be nice if it was all sunshine and lavender, but sometimes it's gonna be midnight and spiders."

I shivered, not over keen on spiders, but Non pulled the quilt from my head. "But even when it's black as pitch, we always know the light's gonna come back. Think about when we light the candle for the Stranger on Long Night. That light's a promise to anyone out there in the darkness. It tells 'em they got a place they can come where they can wait out the night, until morning comes."

The fourth afternoon bell had only just rung, but the winter sun had already begun to set on Long Night in Bellskeep. As Lark dozed on my great bed (now without the hateful canopy), I took a match from the silver dish on my study desk and lit the new candle I'd begged from the castle store, one tall enough to burn all the way through the night till sunrise. I carried it to the window so its flame might shine out over the mountains and the dark sea beyond—a tiny sentinel to keep watch on the darkest night of the year.

In Presston, they'd be making the great bonfire on the village green. With every window in the village ablaze, folks would gather—their breath filling the air as they greeted one another over cups of mulled wine and spiced bread. Whelps would proudly show off new trinkets they'd got before dinner and run to beg sweets from Mistress Coomey, the confectioner. And then, at twelfth bell, a great cheer would rise up for the new day, which was finally on its way.

But it was the dead of night in my heart. After the earlier scene at the *fyrstagildi*, there was no doubt the king was truly well separated from his wits. In front of hundreds of nobles, he'd given up his crown—but news had quickly spread round the castle that the princess hadn't any intention of accepting. Me and the indentures were so close to freedom, I could almost taste it. I hadn't hoped for the king's madness, of course, but a wheel doesn't complain about a road, long as it gets the wagon where it's going.

A quiet knock upon my chamber door tore me away from thoughts of darkness and light.

Lark's eyes popped open and she was instantly on her feet. "Is that Master Iordan already? I thought we couldn't look through his telly-scoop till it was dark!"

I shook my head and smoothed down my untidy hair. "Come in," I called hesitantly.

The door opened to reveal Lamia Folque. The lady was more splendid than I'd ever seen her before, in a gown and cloak of cloth-of-gold and dozens of crimson rosettes in her hair, each with a glittering ruby at its heart. The great jewel at her breast with its blue-green fire stuck out sorely among the rest of the finery, but I'd grown so used to seeing it, it hardly mattered.

"A good Long Night to you, ma'am," I said, bobbing a little curtsy.

"And to you, my dear. I wanted to make sure you were well after the chaos this afternoon."

"I'm not sure I'll ever get the smell of ale out of my nose, lady, but I'm well. How's the princess?"

"The princess has withdrawn to her chambers and made it clear she'll admit no one—not even Prince Hauk. The Thorvald, as you can imagine, are in quite an uproar after the king's appearance at the bride feast."

"They probably want her to take the throne, don't they?" I asked.

"But of course! They were as deeply concerned as the rest of us by the king's behavior. They want their son to marry into a strong kingdom—not one ruled by a man who can't tell a cat from a crown!"

"Are you going to speak with her, ma'am? Try to convince her to accept?"

Lamia sat gracefully upon the chair by the window, the dancing light of the Stranger's candle catching the facets of the rubies in her dark hair. "I don't expect I would make it through the door. The princess and I have never been peaceable companions. But coming from your lips, the argument might hold more weight."

It took a moment for Lamia's words to trickle through me. "Wait . . . you want *me* to talk to the princess?"

"Her Highness has always had a fondness for you. And a good deal of sympathy, too, considering how you've been treated by her father."

"B-but, ma'am," I stammered, "you know I can't lie!"

Lamia shook her head. "Who said anything about lying? Surely you can see the need for her to do her duty by Orstral?"

"But—" *But she knows I have something to gain from it!* is what I wanted to say, but I couldn't bring myself to reveal Saphritte's promise to free me to Lady Folque.

"My dear, it is precisely because you cannot lie that your words will hold more weight." The councilwoman leaned forward. "You told me once in a letter that you chose Orstral. Orstral now waits for you to make good on that promise."

The candle in the window flickered against the dying light outside. Was I going to let the sun set on the kingdom without at least trying to save it?

"All right," I said finally, a swarm of butterflies beating their wings in my belly. "I'll talk to her if she'll see me."

Lamia rose from the chair, took my face in her hands, and kissed my cheek. "History will look most kindly upon you, Only Fallow, that you did this thing when no one else was able."

The idea of history looking over my shoulder while I was talking to the princess made me want to bring up all that *epli* bread I'd scoffed under the table.

Lamia made to go, but at the last moment, she turned, a question unasked.

"I nearly forgot. This seems such a petty thing when so much is at stake, but your girl—she's good with a needle and thread?"

"Her name is Lark, ma'am," I said a little irritably, looking back to where the Ordish girl was standing. "And yes, she is."

Lamia didn't acknowledge my scolding, but turned to address Lark directly. "The seamstress is terribly busy and some of the stitching on Adalise's gown for this evening's revels has come undone. Would you mind awfully seeing to it? My daughter would be much obliged."

The look on Lark's face said, *I'd rather lick the bottom of a bilge*, but her mouth was more mindful of its manners. "As you wish, lady."

"My thanks." Lamia turned the handle to my chamber door. "Good fortune go with you, child."

"Thank you, ma'am," I answered, knowing it would take more than good fortune to put the crown of Orstral on the head of an unwilling princess.

I'D NEVER BEEN to the royal suites before.

The princess's day room, where I'd been escorted, was three times the size of my chamber, but almost as plain—her life in the palace looked a bit like her life out in the field with the king's guard. The only decoration, other than the Renart-blue drapery, was an entire wall of custom weaponry. Upon it hung a collection of beautifully made swords, daggers, and bows, all of which she was probably very good at using. I wondered what went through Prince Hauk's mind the first time *he* walked in. *Probably that he shouldn't ever think about crossing his fiancée,* I thought.

A guardsman marched smartly through the door, Saphritte following behind. The princess, unlike Lady Folque, was not yet dressed for the Long Night revels and instead wore a heavy coat in midnight blue with silver trim.

"Good evening, Highness," I said. "A good Long Night to you."

Saphritte waved the guard from the room. "And to you. I must admit, I hadn't thought to see anyone, but I was told you wished to speak with me."

"I did, Highness. I mean, I do." I looked round, trying to

think of a way into the conversation. "That's a fancy collection of arms you've got, ma'am."

The princess raised an eyebrow, taking in the wall with all its edges gleaming in the lantern light. "Most were gifts. Some have sentimental value."

It was hard for me to imagine having soft feelings for something so sharp. "Which one's your favorite?"

"I don't know if I could call it a favorite, per se, but I often look to the bow when I'm faced with a difficult decision."

The wood of the weapon had a rich, dark stain with silver inlay on the grip. "Why's that, ma'am?"

"I used it the first time I ever took a life," the princess answered. "A hare, when I was ten. Mistress Coppervale praised me for my aim, but I wept for the beast for an hour after. I like to consider that moment whenever I weigh matters of great importance."

How lucky is Orstral that she'll be queen someday! I thought. *If only I could hurry that day along a little.*

Saphritte gazed out the window, where a servant had already lit the Stranger's candle. "But I'm certain you didn't come to discuss armaments. Why are you here, Only?"

It was the question I'd been dreading. "Ma'am . . . my papa, he's a canny orchardman."

The princess looked confused. "Yes, I imagine he is."

"He manages all of it, from the picking to the pressing to the coin. There ain't a thing that goes on that don't depend on him."

Saphritte smiled sadly. "I'm sure he's an excellent overseer."

"But, Highness . . . if he suddenly started firing the men from the pressing sheds, or . . . throwing out the good apples along with the bad, or sowing the wrong seeds in the lavender fields—"

"You would feel that he was no longer able to do his job and would take over the running of the orchard, I expect," interrupted the princess. "I know what you're trying to say. It's the same thing everyone else has been trying to tell me all afternoon."

Drat! "I know you must think it's because I'm eager to get home, and . . . well, I can't say I'm not. But, ma'am, I ain't asking for me, but for Orstral. And for the indentures. After all the burnings, this city's fit to be tied, and the whelps belowstairs aren't safe no more, not even inside the palace."

The princess cleared her throat. "I understand your concern and it's a credit to you, but—"

There had to be some way to find a crack in Saphritte's armor! Without warning, I blurted out the only thing I could think of whose point might fly true to her heart.

"I'll stay."

The princess's head turned slightly. "You don't mean that."

"I couldn't say it if I didn't, Highness. If you take the throne . . . I'll stay."

"Only—" Saphritte began gently.

"No! I swear it, Highness, just let the indentures go free and I'll help you make peace with the Ordish. I'll . . . I'll help you and Prince Hauk be the best rulers Orstral ever saw! By the Mother, I'll even help with the royal whelps when they come along, just—"

"Only, stop!"

I was surprised to find myself shaking. I *did* mean it. Even with the sweet promise of a return to the orchard slipping through my fingers, I meant every word. Even if it meant I couldn't smell the summer lavender, shinny up the branches of apple trees, or sit down to supper with Mama, Papa, Non, and Ether, I wanted to see Saphritte Renart sitting on the throne and know my friends were safe.

The princess took me by the hand and led me to the window seat. A simple candle burned there—same as the one in my chamber.

"Who lights the Stranger's candle at your house?" she asked.

It was a peculiar question, considering the speech I'd just given. "Non, usually," I answered shakily. "Sometimes Mama."

Saphritte ran her finger round the base of the candlestick. "My father used to be quite a different man. He was kind. Patient. I miss that."

She stared out over the city, where tiny lights were beginning to appear in windows as far as the eye could see. "And perhaps, just perhaps, if the healers can do their work, he can leave a legacy besides his madness."

"You told me the night I arrived that the kingdom was like the pines of the Wood—that it was bigger than any one man!" I protested.

The princess's face hardened, not best pleased to have her own words thrown back at her, but she answered me calmly. "This year, my father is the stranger lost in the dark, and while there is still hope of his recovery, I will leave the light of the throne burning for him. I can do nothing less."

I knew her tone all too well—it was the same one Mama used when she declared, "And that's that!" There was no moving her.

I'd failed. I'd failed the indentures, Bellskeep, and Orstral. *What gave Lady Folque the fool notion I could do this?* I thought bitterly, holding back tears. And worse, what made me believe her?

Saphritte reached up to brush an escaped hair off my forehead. "Don't take it so. Yours is a good argument, and well made. And when the time *does* come, I will keep to my promise—you'll see the orchard once more."

"Yes, ma'am," I mumbled miserably.

"Now," remarked the princess, rising from the seat, "I'd like to be alone, and you have revels to attend. But don't think I haven't heard you—I'll see to the safety of the indentures."

I got to my feet and made a half-hearted curtsy. "Thank you, Highness. A good Long Night to you."

Saphritte opened her chamber door to see me out. "And to you, Only Fallow. I hope the light of First Day will bring an answer to all of our troubles."

LAMIA WAS WAITING right outside my chamber door. My king's guard escort snapped a quick salute before returning the way he came.

The great stone round her neck blazed in the lantern light of the corridor, as if it were as eager for an answer as she was.

"Well?" she said, in a low voice. "Did she agree?"

"I tried, ma'am, honest I did," I told her earnestly, "but her mind is already made up. She believes the king can get better and . . ." I hung my head. "I'm sorry, ma'am."

After a pause that felt longer than Long Night itself, Lamia finally spoke, though I couldn't for the life of me tell what she meant by it.

"So am I, child. So am I."

9

The constellation of Helvia Hyalus, *visible in the north-western quadrant of the sky at the winter solstice, consists of nine bright stars that form an irregular oval shape. Its name stems from the legend of Queen Helvia, who was said to possess a magic glass which she often consulted on matters of principle. If a decision was true to her heart, she would see her face reflected in all its natural beauty. But if she strayed from her conscience, the glass would show nothing at all, as if no one stood before it.*

—From *A Guide to Observing the Heavens*, by Aloycious Barrat, royal astronomer under Queen Fulvia Lamblin

The hallsroom looked awful different at night.

One of the large windows was thrown open when I arrived, letting in an icy draft from outside. Before it was an enormous, wonderful contraption made of shining brass. It stood on four legs and a cross-shaped base with small wheels. It had a large stand in the center with screws and swivels, which Master Iordan was fiddling with. Mounted at the top was a long tube made up of five other tubes, each smaller than the next, till it ended in a small, round piece of glass at the end. The light from Iordan's lantern slid over the metal, which glistened in the dark of the room.

I moved closer, not daring to touch it but wanting to with every one of my itchy fingers. "Is *this* a telly-scoop, master?"

"A *telescope*, yes," he sighed.

"Could I see?" I asked eagerly.

The inquisitor lowered his eye to the narrow end of the glass. "Patience, child. I'm just making adjustments—ah!"

He stepped back, motioning for me to take his place. "Quickly, now—celestial bodies don't stay still."

I peered into the glass. A small, bluish blob appeared, a thin line running through its center. The thing was moving slowly across the tiny tunnel of the scope, like a stray bit of summer milkweed.

"I don't understand, master. I thought this contraption was supposed to make things in the sky *clearer*. All I see is a tiny smudge."

The inquisitor's old, haughty tones met my findings. "Child, you're observing a *planet*, which is farther away than either of our imaginations can fathom. The fact that we can see it at *all* is nothing short of miraculous."

My breath caught in my throat. "That's . . . that's a planet?"

"It is indeed—the planet Sythea." He looked into the scope again, fiddling with the knobs once more. "It is particularly clear tonight. Even the rings are visible."

He let me have another look. Still small and fuzzy, the speck of light now made me think of the Stranger's candle once again, but one that burned far beyond the reach of any whose feet were planted on the ground. A terrible wave of homesickness swamped me.

"Master, if this thing can see all the way to Sythea . . . d'you suppose we could have a look at the orchard? I mean, it ain't half so far away."

"*Isn't* . . . ," Master Iordan began to correct, but he stopped, putting a hand upon my shoulder. "I'm afraid this device isn't designed for earthly observations, my dear, or I should be happy to."

A quiet *click* of the door handle declared Lark's arrival. She hugged herself tight, caught out by the cold air.

"Did you get Adalise's gown fixed?" I asked as she came to join us.

"After all that trudging round the castle, it was barely two stitches to the bodice," Lark grumbled. "*And* it was under her arm. No one'd've even noticed, unless that Thorvald fella got *real* friendly."

"Ladies, less chatter, more attentiveness, please," chastened Iordan. "Now, if you're ready to begin, we'll turn our attention to the northwest—"

All at once, the door to the hallsroom slammed open, admitting a gasping Gareth, who nearly fell to the floor with the effort.

"Good heavens, young man!" scolded Iordan. "Is that any way to enter a room—unannounced and with such violence?"

"Only . . . I mean . . . the Mayquin . . . is needed at . . . council," he wheezed.

The inquisitor's bushy brows crimpled in disbelief. "What business could the council possibly have at *this* hour? On Long Night?"

The answer was *no business*. Whatever had pushed Gareth up the long flight of stairs like all seven hells were behind him, it had nothing to do with the council. The fearful green fire of the lie licked at him from his temples to his toenails, and my heart quailed to see it.

"Princess's orders," he gulped, hoping Saphritte's name would make the dour inquisitor less likely to question him.

His gamble worked. Master Iordan gave a bone-deep sigh, wheeled the telescope back from the open window, and replaced the cap. "I look forward to the day that matters of education are given the same respect as matters of state. Go, then."

Gareth motioned frantically to me and was away down the stair. Lark looked to me, confused—she didn't need a cunning to tell something was wrong.

"Go on," I told her. "I'm right behind you."

I'm not sure what made me hang back, but I didn't feel I could just leave Iordan without some sort of farewell—not if something terrible were about to happen.

"Master?"

"Yes, child?"

"Thank you very much for all the learning. A good Long Night to you."

"Why . . . I . . . ," stammered the surprised inquisitor, "thank you kindly. A good Long Night to you as well."

I don't know how long he stood there, pondering my unasked-for thanks, because I was out the hallsroom door like a shot, following the sound of Gareth's and Lark's frantic footsteps ahead of me on the stair. I caught up two-thirds of the way down, running into Lark so fast, the three of us nearly toppled like ivory gaming tiles.

"What in the name of All is going on?" I demanded, but Gareth lifted an urgent finger to his lips to shush me.

"First, I get you to safety, then we talk," he hissed. "You stay here. I'm going to make sure there's no one in the hallway below."

Without any further explanation, he disappeared down the spiral.

A shiver ran through Lark that even I could feel. "What does he mean, get us to safety? What's happening?"

"I don't know, but he's spooked as a horse near flashfire." The dread I'd been feeling since the *fyrstagildi* threatened to swallow me whole.

The light tapping of Gareth's leather-soled boots got louder as he made his way back up to us.

"Quick! The way's clear."

The three of us emerged into the hallway only to hear the far-off clap of footsteps drawing closer.

"All take it!" Gareth swore. "Back up the stairs!"

Lark and me didn't need asking twice. Hiking our skirts, we skittered back the way we'd come, only stopping when we'd twisted up and out of sight. But even from round the bend of the stair, we could hear shouting—it seemed to be coming from everywhere. The footsteps we heard grew louder until we could hear the jangle of a guardsman's scabbard.

"Farway!" the guard barked. "I thought you'd gone for the evening!"

"I was just about to, sir, when the news came. I . . . I decided to join the search instead."

"I was just going to have a look in the hallsroom tower—"

"I just came from there, sir," Gareth said quickly. "Master Iordan said the Mayquin and her girl had already left for the revels. Maybe check her chamber again? I'll head down toward the kitchens."

"All take that pair of witches!" roared the guard, storming off down the hallway.

They're looking for us! I realized with a start.

The panting steward appeared round the bend in the stair once more, motioning for us to follow.

We flew through corridors I'd never seen before—ducked and dodged into alcoves and down stairways I didn't even know existed, in spite of my exploring. The air round us got colder as we descended. *We must be getting close to the cellars,* I thought. Finally, we came to a door where Gareth fumbled a key into the lock and shoved it open.

It turned out to be a large closet, filled to the brim with buckets, pails, brooms, brushes, and the remains of a hastily abandoned game of Deuces.

Gareth kicked the cards to one side and swung open the door of a long wardrobe, filled with neatly pressed tunics, dresses, and all manner of serving apparel.

"Get in."

Neither of us was impatient to be shut up in a wardrobe, but everything we'd seen on our fraught journey from the hallsroom made us keener to follow Gareth's lead. Lark climbed in first and I followed, settling behind a set of starched aprons.

"Gareth," I pleaded, "we're as safe as we're like to get stuffed in the back of a closet in—where exactly are we?"

"Servants' cupboard."

"In the servants' cupboard, then—will you *please* just tell us what's going on? Why are they looking for us?"

The steward leaned heavily on the hanging rail, his head bowed in exhaustion.

"Gareth?" Lark prodded.

The boy finally looked up, grim as the grave.

"The king is dead. And you're the ones who killed him."

For a moment, it felt like I couldn't breathe—like the starched aprons and tunics we were hiding behind were trying to smother us. My mouth was so dry, my voice was nothing but a rusty squeak.

"What?"

Gareth held up his hands. "I mean, *I* know you didn't, but he is. The king. Dead, that is." He groaned, rubbing his eyes. "Oh, this isn't coming out right."

"He's *dead*?" moaned Lark. "How?"

"And why in All's name do they think *we* did it?"

The steward shushed us again. "All I know is what I've over-heard. When Mistress Devi went in to give him his evening sleeping draft tonight, the guards outside the door were insensible—their ale had been drugged. And the king . . . well, he was already gone."

"How did he die?" I asked, not really wanting to know.

"He had these dark streaks around his mouth, and his eyes were yellow as a buttercup. Mistress Devi said it was a poison." He hesitated. "An Ordish poison."

"Green Man's fingers," gasped Lark. "I must've heard a dozen tales about it!"

"But that's not all," Gareth said. "Lying on his chest, they found this . . . this little doll, I suppose. The princess said it belonged to you, Only."

"The Jack! That's what got stolen from my nameday box!" I tried to scoot out of the wardrobe. "Gareth, I've gotta speak with Her Highness—I've got to tell her—"

The steward put out his hands and pushed me back in. "The princess also said you tried to talk her into taking the crown just three-quarters of an hour before. And witnesses saw Lark near the royal chambers not fifteen minutes before the king was discovered!"

Me and Lark burst out angrily at the same time.

"Only 'cause Lady Folque asked me to!"

"I was only there because Lady Folque wanted—"

We both broke off and looked at each other through the aprons.

"Lady Folque," we said together.

It felt like the time Waymer kicked me in the stomach for being daft enough to walk too close behind him.

"Oh, Lark," I whispered. "You were right."

"That book! The book we got her from the library—it had all sorts in it. That must be where she learned to make Green Man's fingers!"

"Wait, wait," Gareth exclaimed. "Are you saying all of this is *Lady Folque's* doing?" He blew out a breath. "This is worse than I thought."

"How could it possibly be *worse*?" I exploded.

"Because of all the burnings and all the unrest in the city, she's been bringing in more and more of her own men. I reckon Folquesmen probably outnumber the king's guard three to one by now!"

"What is she aiming to do?" asked Lark.

I rested my head in my hands. "My cunning ain't never been wrong before. How did she . . . ? I . . . I thought I was helping!"

Exasperated, Gareth gave me a sharp poke. "I didn't bring you down here to feel sorry for yourself! We need to get you both out of this castle."

I grabbed his sleeve. "If I could just talk to the princess—"

The steward cut me off. "I promise, if you show your face anywhere in these halls, you will be cut down before you have a chance to speak at all."

Lark's fingers snaked between mine and squeezed hard. "What about Ro? I can't just leave him!"

"The indentures belowstairs are safe—under guard for their own protection. But the only way the two of you are going to be as safe is to leave."

"This place must be locked up tighter than a treasure house right now!" I fretted.

Gareth gave a sly smile. "Remember you said rabbits didn't care much for walls and would always find their way into a garden?" He leaned in closer. "It just so happens I know a rabbit who can get you out."

IT WAS HARD to tell how much time passed after Gareth left, promising to come back as soon as he was able. I was so shocked and blindsided, I couldn't be sure time inside the wardrobe wasn't just standing still. Lark cast tiny, sad glamours in the palm of her hand—little flames to break up the darkness—but her heart was so heavy, they fizzled out almost as soon as they flared to life.

I thought of the princess's face when she told me she hoped for her father's recovery, and how grieved she must be now that he was gone. Shame flooded my heart—in my darkest moments, I'd never wished the old man dead, and I definitely didn't want *Saphritte* thinking I'd anything to do with killing him. Nor Lady Mollier nor Lords Sandkin and Dorvan.

As for Lady Folque—I didn't know enough curses to fit what she'd done. Cozy teas, library errands, and secret notes—all so she could pin the blame for her foul business on me and Lark!

In spite of what she'd said the morning of our tea with the king, she *must* have been responsible for his madness. I'd *felt* her cunning—if she did that every morning during their meetings, was it any wonder he'd finally got parted from his reason?

I just *had* to tell the princess. But even if I got her alone for five minutes without a guardsman trying to lop my head off, what would I say? It sure didn't seem likely Lamia was planning to retire to her estate like she said, but what *was* her plan?

But through all my anger and shame, I felt even worse for Lark, having to leave Rowan behind in an angry palace. She'd tried to be brave before Gareth, poor thing, but the moment he was gone, she wept as if her heart would break.

"P-Papa'll never f-forgive me," she sobbed, "if I c-come back without h-him!"

I did my best to comfort her, but it was hard, there in the musty cloth of that wardrobe, not to feel like much more than two lost little girls.

"D'you s'pose it's First Day already?" she asked hoarsely, after some time had passed.

"I'm not even sure last *night* happened yet," I told her, tugging absently on an apron string.

She laid her head on my shoulder. "What'll we do if Gareth gets caught? Or if he can't get back to us? What do we do then?"

"Let's try not to think about that. He's not been gone so long."

"Hasn't he?" she asked. "It feels like days."

"It feels like five minutes ago."

The doors to the wardrobe were suddenly flung open. Lark and I grabbed hold of each other with a frightened squeal.

"It feels like you should have a little more faith in me than that," quipped Gareth, peering in at us. "Especially after all I've been through in the last few hours!"

"You donkey!" I shouted, aiming a kick at him. "I almost went straight to the Mother!"

He dodged to avoid my foot and swung open the second door of the wardrobe. "Sweet All, some thanks for finding you a way out of palace! But quick now—let's find you some togs that fit." He rummaged through the forest of fabric, pulling out one of the light blue gowns that the kitchen girls wore along with one of the stiff serving aprons. "This should be all right."

I knew I couldn't very well go swanning around the city in the ceremonial clothes of the Mayquin, but my arms broke out in gooseflesh at the thought of taking them off. I unpinned the great brooch at my throat, unbuckled the belt, and shrugged off the beautifully warm salmon greatcoat of my office, feeling chilled but strangely lighter. Lark helped me button the gown I shrugged over my shift and tie the apron I threw over both. White kerchiefs covered our hair, just as an extra measure of disguise. As an afterthought, I dropped the brooch deep into one of the apron's pockets.

"Have we got far to go?" Lark asked.

"By the luck of the Mother, it's just the next door over but one," he said. "Come on, quietly now."

Gareth opened the door to the servants' cupboard to peep

into the hall. Seeing no one about, he slipped through, us close behind. As he promised, just two doors to the left, he brought out his ring of keys once more.

The door opened, then closed and locked behind us; Gareth stopped short in the dark and rummaged in his pocket. A moment later, a tiny flame burst forth from a match struck on the wall. As if in answer, hundreds more ignited, reflected in rows upon rows of bottles resting on racks higher than our heads. The shelving stretched in both directions, farther than we could see by the light of the small lantern Gareth coaxed to life.

I stared up at the gleaming bottles. "Is this . . . the wine cellar? How're we supposed to get out through *here*?"

"Everybody's got secrets," the steward answered, "even the palace. Follow me, and try not to bump into anything. Some of these wines are worth more than my house."

Gareth led us on a twisting, turning path through the shelves, stacked full of bottles, until we finally came to the far end of the store. In the corner sat a low, mostly empty rack with only a few bottles resting in their cradles. It looked out of place after all the other ones we'd passed.

The steward put the lantern down and set to work clearing off the rack, placing each bottle carefully on the stone floor. Once it was empty, he pulled the rack away from the wall. Satisfied the space was bare, he dusted his hands and leaned against the wall.

"What do we do now?" I asked.

"We wait," he said. "But not long."

"Gareth," Lark began, trying to steady her shaking voice.

"Could you please look after Ro? Tell him to keep his head and his hackles down and tell him—" She swallowed hard. "Tell him I'll be back for him. No matter what."

"I will," he said earnestly. "I swear."

"And keep a hawk's watch on Lady Folque," I added. "If she was willing to have the king killed, she must've had a reason for it."

Suddenly, there was a grinding noise somewhere by our feet.

Gareth bent down to pick up the lantern. "I'll say one thing for him—he *is* punctual."

The grinding got louder, and we could see in the dim lantern light that the second stone from the corner was *moving*— disappearing backward into the wall.

Lark and I backed away.

"What's that?"

"The rabbit," Gareth answered.

The stone retreated farther into the blackness until it disappeared altogether and was replaced by a face that was more than passing familiar.

"I never thought I'd live to see the day you'd actually *ask* me to break into the castle!" said the young man, looking us up and down. "Well, they don't look like king-killers to me, baby brother."

Gable Farway was the spit of Gareth—if Gareth had been over a foot taller and hadn't the luxury of taking most of his meals in the palace. Gable was leaner, dirtier, and hungrier, but shared the same twinkle of mischief in his eye as his younger brother.

"That's because they're not," answered Gareth irritably. "I told you as much."

"Good met, Master Farway," I said, crouching down to peer into the blackness that half of Gareth's brother was still lost in. "Where does your . . . rabbit hole go, exactly?"

Gable began to wriggle backward. "Someplace where no one's much troubled about a dead king. Come on, then, before someone abovestairs decides they need a bottle of Acherian red to drown their sorrows!"

His answer didn't give me a warm feeling, but Gareth was already gently pushing Lark toward the opening. I stood up again, lost for words.

"Gareth, I don't know how I'll ever—"

"You can pay me back by getting out of the city tonight," the steward insisted.

I grabbed him round the neck and squeezed tight before he could go on. His wiry arms slipped round my shoulders and squeezed back.

"Be careful," I told him. "Something rotten's going on."

He released me, winking. "I'll keep my eyes open and my napkins sharpened to a deadly point."

"Cheeky," I said fondly.

"Pain in the backside," he answered. He bent over, squinting into the dark. "You'll look after them?"

Gable's arm emerged from the tunnel in a three-finger promise. "Like they were our own sisters."

The steward nodded sharply and, with a sad little wave, took his lantern and began the winding journey back through the wine cellar.

But I didn't have time be sorrowful. The sound of a match flared and Gable lit a candle stub to show us an object he'd dragged from the tunnel. It was a long, flat, dirty cart with small wheels.

"So, this is the way of it," Gable said, pulling the cart out. "We lie down and leg our way through."

I frowned. "What d'you mean, 'leg'?"

He sat on the edge of the cart. "We lie on our backs, put our boots to the top of the tunnel, and push till we get to the other end."

"Wait, we can't walk?" Lark asked in alarm.

"Not unless you're just under four feet tall, no." Gable pulled three handkerchiefs out of his pocket and handed one each to me and Lark. "Here, tie this round your nose and mouth. Otherwise, you're going to be tasting dirt for the next fortnight."

I shook my head, looking at the cart. "I don't understand—we're going to—?"

Gable blew out an exasperated breath and counted the steps aloud on his fingers. "Look—tunnel, lying on our backs, legs in the air, pushing us along. Now, we can stand here jawing about it or we can get to it."

I took the kerchief and tied it behind my head. "You're a lot bossier than your brother."

"You don't see *me* laying anyone's dinner settings, do you?" he snorted as he shoved both himself and the cart into the tunnel, leaving the longer end sticking out into the well. "Now, let's leg it."

Full of misgivings, Lark and I settled ourselves on the cart and took one last breath of the cool cellar air before Gable's feet pulled us and all our doubts into the smothering dark.

10

Down the dark
A dark that's deeper
Down-a-down
The midnight creeper
Watch-y wait-y
Catchy feet
In the dark
The dark so deep.

—Orstralian children's hand-clapping rhyme

Over the past months, I'd spent a lot more time than was good for a whelp of my years thinking about how I might meet my end—attackers in the Wood, a villain at the gates of the city, or the palace guard for the murder of the king. But being smothered while lying on my back on a handcart inside an earthen tunnel had never really crossed my mind.

It'd only been about ten minutes, but it seemed hours. My legs, though they'd got used to the strange feeling of pushing earth above my head rather than below it, were crying for mercy like I'd run from Presston to Lochery and back. It was also no help I'd never known such a darkness in my life—being in the tunnel felt like being buried in the earth before your time. The only thing that kept the panic in my chest from roaring up and choking me was the sound of my companions' voices, even if they were tight with toil.

"How come no one's ever found this tunnel?" Lark panted, muffled by the handkerchief.

"Oh, there are plenty of folks in the castle who know it's here," he grunted, "but it suits them well enough to keep it quiet."

"What d'you mean?"

"If they want something bringing in or out, of course! There's an old steward who's got light fingers—sometimes he sends little bits and pieces to be sold. A duke that often visits likes to make wagers at gambling dens, but doesn't want the duchess to know. The herbs mistress pays to have tincture of Acherian tigerweed brought in, 'cause the curate had it outlawed in Bellskeep."

I tried to forget the burning ache in my thighs. "Who dug it?"

Gable snorted as a rain of dirt covered his face. "This whole passage comes out at the bottom of a dried-up well. From what I've heard, some clever sod had it in mind to dig into the counting-house on the other side of the alley. Turns out he wasn't as clever as he thought and ended up going in completely the wrong direction. Must have had the luck of the Mother, though, 'cause after a year or two, he dug straight into the palace wine cellar."

My foot dislodged a rock in the tunnel's ceiling and it tumbled down, bouncing off my forehead. I swore, feeling my heart begin to speed up again, as I was reminded where I was.

"Nearly there, nearly there," Gable huffed under his handkerchief, picking up on my panic. "You're doing better than I did my first time down here."

"Why?" I squeaked, furiously rubbing my sore head. "What happened to you?"

"Got into a nervous flap and passed out. Lucky I was with Big Ford, really. He had to leg my sorry backside all the way through to the palace."

There was a hollow, wooden thud as the cart stopped sharp.

"See, what'd I tell you?" Gable crowed.

There was a sound in the dark of a latch being lifted, then the squeak of hinges. A cold rush of air swept into the cramped passage, chilling the sweat on my neck. Gable gave a last shove and the cart rolled out into the open. We found ourselves blinking up at a crescent-shaped sliver of dim light about forty feet above our heads.

Gable jumped straight to his feet, but Lark and I only had the strength to roll off the sides of the wheeled wooden plank. We pulled off the kerchiefs, glad for even the little fresh air at the bottom of the well.

"Ugh!" Lark coughed, brushing soil from her hair. "I feel like a living dirt clod."

I sneezed and blew my nose on the already filthy kerchief. "I think I inhaled half of Bellskeep."

"Normally, I wouldn't hurry a pair of ladies that've had the sort of evening you have, but the sooner we get you outside the city walls, the better." Gable dusted off his breeches and retrieved his coat from a rusty hook beside the tunnel. "Have you thought to where you're headed?"

The words didn't even make sense to me for a moment. After months of having my days measured in council meetings, dinners, and lessons, I hardly knew how to answer the simple question *Where do you want to go?* Though every part of me longed for the orchard, I knew I couldn't lay my new troubles on my family's doorstep. But Lark had an answer all prepared.

"Farrier's Bay. My folk'll keep us safe till we figure out what to do." Her mouth twisted. "Though I don't suppose there's many that'd be willing to help us get there."

Gable laughed wryly. "I think you'd be surprised."

THE SHALLOWS, LIKE Gareth had said, weren't a place respectable folk wanted to be caught, and it was easy to see why.

At the top of the ladder of iron rungs, Gable muscled the well cover to one side and climbed out into the open air, me and Lark just behind him, fingers numb and legs like jelly after the long slog through the tunnel.

We found ourselves at the back of a tavern, whose sign declared it the Iron Glove, and whose scent was none too kind on the nose. The privy, set far too close to the back door, desperately needed redigging. Even in the cold, the smell of the rotting entrails in the corner of the yard was near unbearable.

Even in the early-morning dark, I could tell the tavern itself was a mess of mold-covered exposed beams, and the daub, which once might have been white, was a sullied gray. The windows were blackened with years of grime and pipe smoke. It certainly wasn't the Bird in'th Hand.

"We're not going in there, are we?"

Gable raised a freckled brow. "You're the two most-wanted souls in Bellskeep. You're looking sideways at a *pub*?"

"Well, it don't look terrible friendly," I huffed.

Gable rolled his eyes and, with no further ado, pushed open the back door and plunged into the gloom.

If I thought the outside of the tavern looked unfriendly, it was nothing compared to the inside. The floor was actually dirt and straw, though it was hard to tell one from another. All manner of malodors sat just below the haze of tobacco that kept the patrons hidden under its cloak. For a moment, I was afeared we'd lost Gable, but I spotted him by the bar and quickly hurried to his side, trying not to breathe too deeply.

The fellow he was jawing with looked like he'd not been cleaned any more recently than the building. His bald head bore several long, suspicious scars, and the collar of his tunic was stained yellow with smoke and sweat.

"What's the word, Hugo?"

Hugo spat in a glass and began wiping it with a dirty cloth. "King's dead."

"Yeah, everyone with a pair of ears knows that by now—they've been ringing the bells all night."

The barman sneered, revealing a few brown teeth. "What d'you want, Farway?"

"Someone to get something out of the city."

Hugo's bloodshot eyes landed on us. "Some*thing* or some*one*?"

Gable shrugged. "It all goes out the same gate, doesn't it?"

"You know the lot in here." Hugo waved a crooked hand at

the people-shaped forms in the tavern's thick air. "They'll do just about anything if there's enough coin in it."

The mention of coin perked up a few ears. In the shadows, heads turned slightly, hoping to catch wind of the opportunity.

"We haven't got any coin!" Lark whispered close to my ear. "How're we supposed to get anyone to take us?"

I didn't have a chance to answer as a figure loomed toward us out of the grimy recesses. He looked to be one muscle stacked upon another—even his face and his neck seemed to be in disagreement as to where one ended and the other began. His thinning brown hair was slicked back hard with goose grease, and he wore a cold look in his milk-tea eyes.

"You have something that needs moving?" he grunted.

Gable looked like the handle to the other fellow's butter-churn, but didn't seem alarmed by his demeanor. "Two parcels to Farrier's Bay."

The brute's lip twisted. "That's a long way. What's the pay like?"

"I reckon you could name your price to the Ordish once you get their girl here back to 'em."

"Ah," said another voice from the side of the bar. "Well, you see, you *could*, iffen the Ordish was still there."

All eyes turned to a small man with a feathered brown hat whose brim drooped low over his right eye.

The brute gave a contemptuous snort. "I wouldn't listen to ol' Doddy if I was you, but I know *I* don't work without money on the table." He spat on the floor and clumped back into the haze.

Lark, who'd been holding on to the strings of my apron, peered round my shoulder at the fellow in the hat. "What do you mean," she said boldly, "*if* they were still there? It's winter. Where else would they be?"

"That's a very good question, my dear, a very good question indeed." He rapped his knuckles on the bar. "And one that might require a little refreshment in payment for the answer."

"But we haven't got any—"

Two coins from Gable's pocket sang on the wood. I tugged at his sleeve, but he waved me off with a wink. "I'll put it on Gareth's tab." Turning to the fellow in the hat, he jerked a thumb back at the bartender. "Choose your poison and we'll have our answer."

"You're too kind, too kind, master, but as you can see, my friend's parched as well, and I'm not one to leave a man thirsty while I drink myself."

"What frie—" began Gable, but just then, the thing we'd all taken for a pile of laundry at the bar next to the man suddenly straightened up. The tall, lanky fellow looked as if he'd run full pelt into a washing line and then collapsed facedown on the bar. He was wearing a pair of long breeches as a tunic, with his arms shoved through the leg holes and his head through a rip in the gusset. He'd also a pair of ladies' stockings upon his head and several scarves wound round his long face.

"Beer," demanded the pile of clothes, before falling heavily back to sleep on the bartop.

Gable reluctantly drew out another two coins, casting an eye round the rest of the bar stools to make sure the fellow hadn't any *more* friends hidden in the woodwork. "Right. Have your drink and loosen your tongue."

The man with the hat pointed to a bottle of foul-looking aniseed liquor. Hugo took it from its shelf and poured a stingy measure into the glass he'd just spat in before sliding it down the way. The man drained the glass with a great lip smacking and motioned to the beer keg for his friend.

"Oh, that hit the spot, I don't mind telling you," he said, wiping his mouth on his sleeves.

"Maybe you also wouldn't mind telling us where the Ordish have gone, then," prompted Lark boldly.

The man's eyebrow shot up under the brim of his hat. "You're a curious one, aren't you? But ol' Dodd, he keeps his promises, he does." He swabbed the inside of the glass with his finger, licking off the remains of the liquor. "It so happens the folk of Farrier's Bay got wind of what befell the town of Bellsbrake and decided to take matters into their own hands before it could happen to them."

"What do you mean, took matters into their own hands?" I asked warily. Taking matters into their own hands is precisely what the people of Bellsbrake had wanted when their alderman came to visit the princess. And it sure didn't bode well for the Ordish.

Lark stepped out from behind me and walked very slowly across the bar to stand in front of the man—close enough to stare right up under the brim of his hat.

"*What . . . happened?*" she asked, in a low, dangerous voice.

The fellow, Dodd, presumably, wasn't half spooked by the Ordish girl with the guts to belly up to a stranger in a tavern in the Shallows. "Steady on, my dear, steady on, no need for any unpleasantness. There wasn't no killin' from what I heard, but the wintering sheds were set alight. And the barges themselves were chased out to sea. They ain't been seen since."

Lark looked to me to confirm the terrible truth. Peculiar as the fellow was, he was honest. I shook my head sadly.

I don't know what I'd've done if someone'd told me my family'd been chased out of the orchard. Would Saphritte do that, I wondered fretfully, now that I was thought to have helped do in the king? But Lark was made of strong stuff. She held Dodd's eye for a moment before coming back to us, a mission in her steps.

"We're not gonna find what we need here," she declared.

"What *do* we need?" asked Gable.

"A boat. A seagoing one. I know where they've gone."

She began to make for the front door. Gable, trying not to lose control of the rescue operation, ran to catch up. But not as quick as the man in the feathered hat.

"Not so fast, my dears, not so fast. My dainty ears couldn't help overhearing talk of a boat."

Lark made to step round him. "Unless you've got one, you can get out of the way."

The fellow put himself in the middle of her path again. "Well, that's the thing, my dear—it just so happens I do."

Gable wriggled his way between them. "A real boat?"

The boat owner looked offended. "Well, it isn't a toy!"

"An oceangoing one?" I added, just to make sure.

"As sure as the tides, my dear, as sure as the tides. Perhaps you'd like to enlist the help of myself and my esteemed colleague over there?" He swept the hat from his head. "Warin and Dodd, at your service. You're a lucky bunch, as you've caught us at a loose end. As you can see, our last job"—he gestured at the pile of scarves and bonnets still flat on the bar—"did not go as planned. And you are?"

Gable spoke up. "Two young ladies who need to make a quick and quiet exit from Bellskeep. What's your price?"

"Well, as we're in a bit of a spot, I think we can bargain." He rubbed his fingers together. "But a little coin on the table wouldn't go amiss."

I didn't know how much more coin Gable could part with. Out of habit, I shoved my hands into the pockets of the apron, expecting to come up empty, but my fingers closed round the answer to our problems.

"Will this be enough?"

I opened my palm to reveal the great golden-eye brooch with the cold jewel in the middle. Dodd's eyes almost dropped out of his head, but he clasped my hand shut with both of his.

"Are you mad, my girl? Flashing something like that around in a wolf den like this?" He leaned close—close enough I could still smell the aniseed. "Is it real?"

"I swear on the Mother. And it's yours when you get us . . ." I realized I had no idea where we were headed. I looked to Lark.

"We'll come to that once we get to the boat," she declared.

The fellow tapped my closed fist. "For *that*, I'd gladly sail every one of these blackguards to the southern tip of Achery and back. You got a bargain."

Gable folded his arms. "That's all well and good, but how do you intend to get them out of the city?"

Dodd put a finger aside his nose. "You leave that to ol' Warin and Dodd—ready to execute an artful plan at a moment's notice!"

A loud snore sounded from the bar.

"Just as soon as I wake him up."

11

The night is gone at last—
The darkest hour passed.
With smoke and cheer,
And wine and beer,
The shadows dwindle fast.
The dawn, it breaks so bright,
The morning bird takes flight.
Let hearts be kind,
Leave cares behind,
You children of the light!

—"Children of the Light," traditional Orstralian First Day carol

The smell of hot coffee and rum buns made my belly rumble. Gable had offered to buy us a slice of bread and butter at the tavern before he departed, but neither me nor Lark wanted to eat anything Hugo might have touched. Now that we were abroad in the streets, with the spices and flavors of First Day in the air, I wished I'd taken him up on his offer. But I kept my head down under my cloak hood, a silent shade behind the chipper Dodd and silent Warin.

My ears were hungry, too, for snippets of conversation as we wove through the crowds, all achatter with the events of the night before.

"Why aren't they saying how it happened is what I want to know!" said a man with a cup of ale.

"So soon before his daughter's wedding!" wept a well-dressed girl to her friend.

"His Majesty should have heeded Curate Heyman," sniffed a mother carrying a babe in her arms, "and not brought that little witch into the palace."

I shuddered beneath my cloak and pulled my hood down further.

"Don't take no notice of those clotbrains," Lark said, grabbing hold of my hand. "People don't know for sure what happened. Wonder how it's not got out yet?"

"The princess probably made sure it hasn't. I know you're worried over Ro, but she really *does* want to protect the indentures, even now—I'm sure of it!"

Lark nodded, but didn't look convinced, as the two scoundrels led us through winding alleys and crowded thoroughfares. Though I knew the chances of anyone recognizing us were next to none, it didn't keep me from casting distrustful glances at the guards that walked among the worried citizens of Bellskeep, hands poised on swords. The more we passed, the more soldiers I noticed wearing the Folque rosette of crimson and gold on their uniforms. Gareth was right—Lamia had made sure the city was chock-full of her own men. The question was *why?*

The street was near a standstill as we came up on the barbican.

I couldn't see a thing through the forest of bodies ahead of me. The slight Dodd stood on his toes to peer over the crowd before prodding the gentleman next to him.

"What's the news, friend?"

"Waiting to hear if the wedding's still going to happen at week's end," the elder man replied gruffly. "I hope to All it is—I brought my wares all the way from Timberwick to sell. Had to get lodging at the Mother's Arms and all!" He scratched his peppered beard. "S'pose there's always the funeral, but folk are less like to part with coin when the occasion's not a merry one. Maybe if there's a hanging . . ."

There was a sudden rumble from the crowd and the press of bodies got tighter. I clung to Lark's arm. "What's going on?"

"The crier's come out," Dodd told me, craning his neck.

A hush fell over the assembled bodies as one of the palace criers mounted the tower of the barbican. His face was drawn and weary and a single black feather stood out somberly in his blue cap.

"Her Royal Majesty Saphritte Renart sends these words to be read before her subjects," began the crier, unrolling a short scroll. "'My good people—my heart, as yours, is heavy this day. I thank you for your kind thoughts and beseechments for my family in our grief.'"

It was almost more than I could take, knowing Lamia Folque sat safe and blameless in the palace while we were forced to scuttle through the streets like rats.

"'But it is my belief that my father, Alphonse Renart, would want me to think of you, the people of Orstral, even in this dark hour. Therefore, the nuptials between myself and Prince Hauk Eydisson of Thorvald will take place as arranged in four days' time. As the Mother says, *In your sadness, turn to one another in comfort—and in your love for each other, you will find my love for you.*

"'Let it be known,'" the crier continued, "'that in the early hours of the morning, I have taken the solemn vows of state. Rest assured, the throne of Orstral is safe in my hands. So therefore, go and make ready to celebrate—for we shall have joy today, even in our sorrow.'"

The man rolled the proclamation and shouted, "The king is dead! Long live the queen!"

"Long live the queen!" answered Bellskeep. "Long live the queen!"

"A new backside upon the throne, then, Warin, my lad, a brand-new backside!" Dodd exclaimed, putting his shoulder into the crowd. "Business as usual, then."

"You don't care," I asked, "that the king's dead?"

"King or queen, princess or prince, fairy or changeling, it don't mean nothing to us, so long as they don't poke any royal noses too far into our affairs."

"And what *are* your affairs, master?"

"Fish," grunted Warin.

Lark wrinkled her nose. "Your affairs are . . . fish?"

Dodd straightened his collar as we crossed into the crowds of the market. "Well, not precisely, my dear, but it happens our friends from the sea provide us with a little cover to explore . . . other interests."

My stomach let out another grumble as we passed by a

woman roasting chestnuts, hoping some of their other interests might involve food—the last time I'd eaten had been at the *fyrstagildi*. The feeling grew as we wove through the tight-packed stalls, but I couldn't help noticing there were some not-terribly-friendly glances thrown our way from the folk behind them. I took a few large steps to catch up to Dodd.

"Master, I don't mean to talk out of turn," I began, hoping he could hear me under the hat, "but it don't look like we're appreciated here."

"Jealousy's an ugly thing, poppet," he replied, cheerfully tipping his brim at a scowling pieman. I bit my lip as a ferocious display of color broke out round the blackguard's head. I couldn't challenge the fellow without giving away who we were—for all his good humor, he seemed like the sort who'd be happy to hand us straight to the palace guard if the price was right. I hoped the promise of the brooch with its enormous sapphire would be enough to keep him and the silent brute at his side friendly.

We came to a ramshackle stall with cracked and faded lettering on the sign, which swung from rusty chain from its roof: WARIN AND DODD, FISHMONGERS.

Behind the stand was a boy of about Gareth's years, leaning against a post and practicing his charm on a well-dressed kitchen mistress. It didn't seem to be working.

"I'm telling you, my dear lady, a finer cut of lake perch will not be found in this whole market. Caught just a day ago and brought on ice with all haste to the city!"

The woman peered closer at the fish, sniffed, and wrinkled her nose. "It's greenfin from the stream or I'm the Mother—you should be ashamed of yourself, trying to take advantage of honest folk!" She lifted up that selfsame nose and strode off.

"How dare you impugn the good name of Warin and Dodd, madam?" Dodd exclaimed to the woman's retreating back. "We're as honest a couple of fellows as you ever will meet!"

Once the kitchen mistress was safely out of sight, Dodd turned to the boy. "What is it actually?"

"Not even greenfin," the boy said. "It's leftover bait."

Dodd grimaced. "Mark it to move. It's a bit past prime, son, a bit past its prime."

More folk, out early to buy First Day supper, stared at us with distaste. I caught the man's sleeve once more. "Excuse me, master, but my friend and I really are in a hurry and we'd be grateful for a little less attention."

"Ooh, mum's the word, my dear," Dodd assured us, pretending to zip his lips. "Master Warin's fetching the wagon as we speak."

He leaned against the stall as the boy began trying to lure customers back with the promise of deeply discounted lake perch. The man pointed to my pocket, where the brooch still lay, a heavy reminder of what we were running from. "What's your tale of woe, then? Thought to make off with some of the old man's royal trinkets before they're missed?"

"Keep your voice down!" hissed Lark. "And it's no business of yours. If your boat's seaworthy and we get where we're going, you'll be paid."

"Don't lose your head, my girl, I was only asking! And I ain't one to judge—things should belong to them that needs 'em.

What do the dead need with a few baubles? Why, nothin' at all, that's what!"

The rumble of cart wheels through the narrow market saved us from any further talk of grave-robbing. Warin, sitting tall and menacing in the driver's seat, drew the rickety wagon up beside the stall. The speckled horse pulling the cart looked as if its best cart-pulling days were behind it, but it stood patiently as Warin jumped down and unloaded a huge cask from the back. The big fellow pushed the cask behind the stall, where a few strips of sackcloth made for a little bit of private space in the bustling market.

There was something about the cask that made me not want to ask the question, but I still turned to Dodd.

"Master, could I ask how we'll be getting out of the city?"

"Barrel," grunted Warin.

With a quick twist of his iron bar, the brute popped the lid open, letting out a whiff I could nearly *taste* from a few feet away. I forced myself closer, to look over the lip—though it was clean, the years of fish it'd held left behind their stink.

"In that?" I asked. "Masters, that's one of the worst things I ever smelt—and I been down a privy!"

Dodd's mustache twitched. "Are you in a rush or ain't you?"

"Yes," said Lark, grabbing my wrist. "Yes, we are. Help us in."

Without ceremony, Warin grasped me under the arms and dropped me into the rancid-smelling barrel. I choked back the bile in my throat and shrunk down inside as Lark climbed in beside me.

"I don't care how much the princess wants to keep the way the king died a secret," she whispered as we huddled in the fishy stench together. "It'll get out, if it hasn't already. And when it does, we need to be as far away from here as we can get."

Dodd peered over the lip at us. "Won't be too long, ladies, not too long. We'll be out of the city gates in half an hour. Until then—" He tipped his hat at us. "Enjoy your trip."

The light was snuffed out from above by Warin, fitting in what looked like a shallow trough, the same shape as the barrel, to the top, pressing our heads down farther.

"Hey!" I protested from one of the very small knotholes, but Dodd's eye appeared, small and beady, outside.

"Nothing to be worried about, my dears, nothing to be worried about—it's a false lid. Just to warn you, though, it, ah, may get a bit riper in there."

I was about to ask him what he meant, but I was answered with the nauseating sound of wet, slippery bodies being dumped into the trough above us. Slimy muck almost immediately began to run into the barrel.

"Great Deep!" Lark gagged.

Over the sound of our own retching, I could hear Dodd remarking, "Try not to breathe too deep, my dears!"

The barrel wobbled and Lark and I were tossed into the slimy walls, hands grasping for a hold that wasn't there as we were loaded onto the back of the wagon.

"Oh, All," I gagged. "We might have been better off taking our chances with the king's guard!"

The wheels beneath us began to rumble, and me and Lark grabbed on to each other, winding arms and legs into knots so that neither of us had to put too much of our bodies against the slippery sides. I buried my nose in my friend's cloak.

"I'm sorry about your folk," I said after a moment. "And I'm sorry I trusted Lamia." Real shame at our predicament turned to tears that squeezed out the corners of my eyes.

"They brought you here 'cause they wanted you to use your cunning," Lark answered, her voice muffled in my collar. "It ain't your fault you didn't know how it worked yet."

"I don't understand! No one has ever been able to lie to me before, not even the tiniest fib, without me seeing it. So, how did *she* do it?"

"Don't suppose it matters now, as we're stuffed in a barrel of fish," Lark muttered gloomily.

"But it *does* matter, Lark!" I insisted. "You heard the crier—the princess is queen now. She might actually free the rest of the indentures and stop the kidnappings for good. What if . . ." A thought less appealing than the goo dripping down the walls of our tiny prison popped into my head. "What if Lady Folque's got something in mind? Something worse?"

"Worse than killing the king?"

"I . . . I don't know. But she's planning something, I just know it!"

The cart moved downward through the underpassages and finally clattered to a halt at what I hoped was the Rivergate.

The voice of a watchman sounded outside. "Papers, please."

There was a rustle from the front as Dodd handed over his documents. "There you are, gentlemen, there you are. I trust it's all in order?"

But there was a sudden bark. "Oy! I know you! You sold me a bracelet for my wife—said it was real silver, but it turned her wrist green in a few days!"

Dodd laughed nervously. "Master, you've mistaken me for someone else. I wouldn't ever *dream* of swindling a city watchman, wouldn't dream of it!"

"No, it *is* you—I'd know that silly hat anywhere!" said the other voice. "I bought a hair tonic off you not two months back, and I'm *still* bald as an egg!"

"Oh, good sirs, I'm sure you must be thinking of someone else! We're honest businessmen, and no mistake!"

The first watchman spoke up again angrily. "Well, if you're so honest, you won't mind if we have a look at your cargo, to make sure everything's on the level."

"Well, I'm afraid it's just the one today," said Dodd, "but I don't think you'll find anything to your liking."

The cart dipped with the weight of one of the watchmen. Lark and I held on to each other tighter as the wood above squealed under the force of an iron bar. The true lid came open with a *pop*, followed by a disgusted exclamation.

"Oh, Mother's milk!" coughed the man through his sleeve, slamming the lid back atop the barrel.

"You see," said Dodd, like butter wouldn't melt in his mouth, "good citizens that we are, we have refrained from dumping fish guts into the city sewer and are instead taking them out to be slurried."

"All's breath!" cried the second man. "I don't care what you're doing with them—just get out of here!"

"All too glad to, masters, all too glad. Come on, then, my lad, let's offend these gentlemen's noses no longer!"

The cart moved forward with a jerk, and a moment later, the wheels beneath us went from a weighty clatter to a dull drone.

We were outside the city.

Warin and Dodd, the not-exactly-fishmongers, waited till we were nearly three miles outside the city before opening the barrel to let us out.

After what seemed like forever in our reeking tomb of fish guts, that first glimpse of gray winter sky above our heads was the most beautiful thing I'd ever seen. Even Warin's face, with all its pockmarks, looked sweeter than the Mother's as I let him lift me out, weak as a babe, into the fresh air. But Lark, her dander up, climbed out and planted herself square in Dodd's face.

"White Lady's knuckles, why'd you leave us in there so long?" she shouted.

Dodd backed away, wrong-footed by her ire. "Calmly now, my dear! We had to make sure no one'd be about to see!"

I was just as cross to have been trapped for so long with only a few tiny knotholes for air, but I'd heard some of the talk of the travelers around us as we'd rolled out the Rivergate and into the countryside. Lark was right—news was getting out.

"You'll not believe this," one woman standing next to the cart had said to another in a low voice, "but I heard from my cousin who's got a sweetheart working in the kitchens that it was murder."

"It never was!" gasped her friend.

"Hand to my heart! The girl said they weren't to tell anyone, but it was one of those indentured wetcollars. And the Mayquin helped her!" She sniffed haughtily. "I don't know why the queen's bent on protecting those rats. If it were *my* father, I wouldn't be so quiet about it!"

"If it were *my* father," replied her friend, "I'd hang the lot of them!"

I just hoped Dodd and Warin had been too busy with the watchmen to have heard, or if they had, too dim to connect it to me and Lark.

Dodd was still poised as if he was expecting my friend to challenge him to fisticuffs, but with his ridiculous hat flopped down over his eye, he had all the menace of a pup with one ear that won't stand up straight.

"Now, if you're finished squawkin', maybe you wouldn't mind telling us where we're bound for, eh?" he said.

Lark looked round and sniffed the air. The two men had pulled the wagon into a small copse of trees just off the road. "We're not heading toward the sea—we're going inland," she said, mistrustful.

"And just how do you know that, girl?"

"You think I don't know the difference between the smell

of the ocean and the river? We're definitely headed *away* from the sea." She poked Dodd in the shoulder. "You said you've got a seagoing boat."

"So we do, dear, so we do," answered the scoundrel, with no hint of a lie. "But you see, it ain't *on* the sea."

It may have been all the time in the barrel, but I was feeling mightily befuddled. "If it's not on the sea . . . where is it?"

"Lake," grunted Warin, tightening the cart horse's tack.

"Oh!" Whatever the fellow meant, it improved Lark's mood. "That's all right, then."

"Glad you approve, my chuck, but where, may I ask, are we bound for?" asked Dodd.

"We'll speak on it when we get there," she told him. "If you don't know, you can't tell no one else along the way."

"Speaking of along the way, we don't have to get back in the barrel, do we?" I asked, fearful of the answer.

Dodd sighed. "There's some straw and extra 'orse blankets in the back, but what with the king being dead and the queen about to wed, I don't s'pose anyone's gonna be looking for a stolen trinket." His eyes glinted like the sapphire in my pocket. "Even iffen it's a real shiny one."

I put my hand in my apron, just to make sure.

"Come on, Only," said Lark, leaping up into the wagon and extending her hand down to me. "I don't know about you, but I'd be happy to put my head down a bit."

All at once, I was nearly as tired as I'd been on the day I arrived in Bellskeep—and wasn't so sure I wanted to close my eyes round Warin and Dodd.

"Do you swear you'll not do anything to us as we sleep?" I asked, keeping a keen eye on the two scoundrels.

Dodd laid a hand upon his breast. "You cut me to the quick, my dear, right to the quick! We ain't cutthroats. We're honest villains, we are—a danger to no one but the purses of foolish men. Young ladies, their virtue, and their pockets are as safe wif' us as they'd be wif' their own mothers."

The man seemed to be telling the truth, but my misadventure with Lady Folque put a tiny seed of doubt in my heart. If she could hide her wickedness from me, maybe others could, too. But I didn't have a lot of choice—spending the night crawling through the belly of Bellskeep had left me spent.

I grasped Lark's hand and let her pull me up into the back of the wagon. Warin took the false top of the barrel off and threw the reeking fish parts into the trees. The smell still clung to us, but it wasn't enough to keep us from burrowing into the thin layer of straw at the bottom of the cart and throwing the itchy weight of the horse blanket on top of us. I rolled up my apron tight, guarding the brooch, just in case.

Lark turned her sleepy eyes toward me with a sad smile on her face.

"I can smell the water. I can smell home."

I couldn't help smiling back.

THE AIR HAD changed when we woke, from the dry frost of Bellskeep to the damp kind of cold that gnaws you right to your bones. Even huddled under the thick blanket with Lark, I could feel it sneaking through the weave, trying to get at us.

A mournful-sounding bell clanged in the distance as the wheels clattered on the cobbles at the edge of a town, stirring us roughly.

Being covered in straw and smelling like fish isn't the best way of waking up, but I tried to remember it was better than being locked in a cell in the palace, and poked my head over the side of the wagon just in time to see a damp wooden sign declaring the town of Ebbeshore.

The name stirred memories of an old hearth story—Caol and Ebbe were twin giants who battled in the heavens. They were so set on harm to each other, they didn't notice they'd strayed too close to the edge. Both of them fell to earth and left the holes that became the lakes of the Great Wood, named for them and their foolishness. Ebbe's Mouth led southward, becoming the Hush, which flowed down the country until it came to the orchard. Ebbe's Foot, at the bottom of the lake, flowed out into the sea.

A seagoing boat on a lake! I understood then that we were coming up on the shores of Lake Ebbe. I gave my groggy friend a shake.

"I think we made it."

Lark was awake in a blink, her eyes so wide, her pupils near covered the silvery-green color of them.

Ebbeshore was a bustling little harbor town with rows upon rows of wood-sided houses, smoke curling from their chimneys in lazy spirals. The small village square was abuzz with First Day revels, even late in the afternoon, but as we drew closer to the docks, there was hardly a soul to be seen. A huge portmaster's house sat at the edge of the water, where small fishing boats and larger ships bobbed gently, side by side. It was the most water I'd ever seen, in fact, stretching far into the distance, where it stopped at the base of the mountains.

The wagon drew to a halt. Dodd snagged Warin's collar to bring him down to his level. "You go work your magic, my son," he said in a low voice.

The big man looked at his tiny companion in confusion for a moment. Then he reached his giant hand behind Dodd's ear and came out with a coin. He grinned, waiting for approval.

Dodd slapped the copper from his hand. "Not actual magic, you clot! The other thing! The thing we discussed along the way that might ease our passage from the harbor!"

Warin's enormous ears flushed, realizing his mistake. As he turned to slink away, I caught his sleeve.

"I thought it was a good trick, master."

I was rewarded with a shy, crooked-toothed smile as he disappeared in the direction of the docks.

The harbor was eerie and quiet—only the sound of the buoy bell rang out across the water.

"Is everyone in the square celebrating First Day, master?"

"They certainly are, my chuck, they certainly are." Under his breath, I could have sworn he mumbled, "Lucky for us."

Lark had already climbed out of the wagon and was standing a little way off, staring at the tiny waves lapping at the docks. I expected her to be wild with glee at the sight, but she just stood for a moment in a sanctuary hush on the shore. Then she bent slowly, unlaced her boots, stripped her socks, and waded out into the cold lake. Her reflection stretched on the surface of the water in the afternoon sun.

"We ain't really got time for a swim, my dear," called Dodd, slinging a bag over his shoulder.

But Lark dipped her fingers in, raised her dripping arms to the sky, and began to sing.

Return we to the river,
Its water calls to mine,
Too long, too long, from clear and sweet
And brackish and the brine.
We have this winter weathered
Storms bearing cold and dread,
Too long, too long, 'neath ice you slept
And dreamed of warmth ahead.
Pour into me, O Mother,
And drown my soul in you.
Too long, too long, from your deep heart,
Now I am washed anew.

The sweet sound of her voice brought tears to my eyes, thinking of all the other whelps that should be here, singing their own greeting and feeling the cold water dripping from their fingers. I feel sure the rough dockmen, were they there, would have stopped to listen—even Dodd was struck still by the melody.

The little man wiped away a tear at the corner of his eye. "Now, if that ain't a tune to warm a cold heart, I don't know what is."

I slipped down from the wagon to join my friend on the bank.

"It's what's sung every spring when we head north from Farrier's Bay," Lark said, looking out on the clear lake. "Though I've never been so glad to sing it as now. I just wish . . ." She swallowed her sorrow. "I wish Ro were here."

"I reckon that's the song I'll feel when I see the orchard again," I told her, the music still in my bones.

"Come on, then, my dears, feet dry, socks on, come this way," chivvied Dodd. A grin bunched his cheeks as he pointed to the end of the dock. "There she is, my poppies, there she is. And don't she look fine?"

Lark gave a gasp of delight. "It's a flyboat! Oh, Ro'd give his eyeteeth for a journey on one of these."

I didn't know one sort of boat from another, but the one moored at the dock's end was a handsome craft. It was the smaller kin of the great sailing ships I'd learned about that were built in Dorvan Bay—but this one looked fast and sleek, with its name writ in dark red across the prow.

"Your boat's called . . . *Falda's Drawers*?" I asked hesitantly.

"It is indeed, my girl, it is indeed. My mum, Falda, you see, she was a washerwoman. Took in clothes to keep bread and meat on the table." He patted the hull fondly. "Think she would've liked this beauty."

I couldn't help wondering how proud the scoundrel's mama would be if she knew the boat was named after her underthings.

Or if she knew about the false barrels of fish, counterfeit silver bracelets, and useless hair tonic. Still, it *was* a fine boat. Its rigging was well kept and the white sails were rolled neatly onto the main- and foremast.

With the help of his bigger companion, the smaller fellow hoisted himself over the handrail and landed lightly upon the deck. He flicked an anxious glance toward the harbormaster's house. "Let's be going, then, my dears. A little rush wouldn't go amiss."

Warin cupped his hands to give me a boost over the rail. "Why?" I asked, pulling myself over. "Why've we got to rush?"

Dodd laughed nervously. "Well, the sooner we're under way, the sooner we can get where we're going, of course!"

A halo of blue shimmered to life round his head as his shifty look fell on Lark. "We'll be needing our directions now, my girl."

Lark leapt over the rail without any help from the giant Warin, color bleeding back into her cheeks to be afloat once more. "We're headed to the Hatchings," she declared.

Dodd's eyebrows bunched. "The Hatchings? But there ain't nothing there!"

"Except all my folk," Lark added definitively. "This ain't the first time we've been chased off by landwalkers. Everyone knows: If all goes to pieces, we meet at the Hatchings."

"The Hatchings it is, then, my dear, the Hatchings it is. You heard the lady, Warin. Cast us off, will you?"

I caught Lark's sleeve, watching the lie round Dodd fade. It was like the night back at the river with Toly all over again—my cunning trying to warn me of danger, but not being able to say anything for fear of giving myself away.

"Master, is there . . . any *other* reason that we need to be under way so quick?"

Dodd laughed, high and quivery, as he pulled in the mooring rope Warin had just undone. "Course not, my dear, why you asking?"

The lie shone darker this time. It followed him as he shinnied up the foremast to undo the sails just at his partner gave the craft a great shove from the dock, clinging on to the bowspirit. The big man swung himself up, shuffled along the length, and climbed into the forepeak. Dodd freed the ropes that held the sails, and right away, the cold little breeze filled their bellies, tugging the eager craft forward into the water.

"Ho there!"

The shout bounced off the water from the door of the harbormaster's house. An older man stood there, festive tankard in hand and his great silvery beard quivering with outrage.

Warin, from his place behind the wheel, bellowed up at his friend in the rigging.

"Trouble!"

Dodd shouted down to Lark, "If you're any good with a sail, my dear, now might be a good time to prove it!"

Throwing off her cloak, the Ordish girl scrambled up the mainmast, quick as a squirrel, her nimble fingers making short work of the tight knots. There was more shouting from the docks now—a few men and women had joined the harbormaster in his stew of furious gesturing at our departing bow.

"You said this boat was yours!" I shouted up to Dodd.

"It is, my girl, it is! It's just been, er . . . temporarily impounded for nonpayment of dock fees."

I slapped the mast in frustration. "Mother's milk, you mean we're *stealing* it?"

"You can't steal what's yours, my poppet! Besides, I'm sure old Master Dumphrey won't mind when we come back with the coin from that trinket you got!"

Maybe the scoundrel was right, but at that moment, Master Dumphrey minded very much indeed. Feet clattered on the wood of the dock as about six young men and the harbormaster himself hurried to crew a slim, fast-looking craft.

"You mudheaded eel!" shouted Lark, freeing the last knot on the boom. "We said we needed to make a *quiet* escape! There's no way this ship outruns that caravel!"

"Ah!" said Dodd, with a smug grin upon his face. "You would be right, my dear, you would be right, but for the fact Warin here has done a little *repair work* on the caravel before we shoved off, didn't you, my son?"

For the first time since we met them in the city, the scoundrel's large partner looked something other than surly. His big, pitted face was twisted with repentance—a fact that wasn't lost on the little man up the foremast.

"Warin?" Dodd called down nervously. "You cut the caravel's rudder, didn't you, my boy?"

"Forgot," grimaced Warin. "'Cause of the magic."

Dodd almost fell off the foremast in his ire. "By the Mother, this is exactly how you ended up with a pair of trousers on your head not twelve hours ago! I don't know why I bother telling you anything—it just drifts in one of your great pancake ears and straight out the other!"

The little man dropped down to the deck, removed his hat, and began thrashing Warin with it, but it was really no more bother for the big man than a horsefly is to a bull, so he bore it patiently. When Dodd's rage was spent, he jammed the hat back upon his head and rolled up his sleeves.

"Not to worry, my chits, not to worry," he said through gritted teeth. "I got no intention of getting caught."

It might not have been Dodd's intention, but though we'd got a head start on Master Dumphrey and his crew, the quick little boat was gaining on *Falda's Drawers* at a fair old clip. I groaned. *Why did we have to choose these two clods to help us make our escape?* If we were taken, then what? How long could me and Lark hide who we were before someone figured us out and sent us back to Bellskeep?

As we approached the lake bend, the harbormaster put a piece of leather shaped like a cone to his mouth. It carried his voice across the water to us as if he were standing right on the deck.

"All right, you scoundrels!" he bellowed. "Stop and be boarded and I'll not ask the magistrate for the rope!"

"Oh, now, Master Dumphrey, that's a bit harsh, don't you think? Just a bit harsh!" Dodd shouted back.

"You owe me twenty gold coins!" roared the harbormaster. "If you think you can just sail off with— *Sweet All!*"

The man dropped the leather cone in surprise. The other men on board stopped their tacking and turning to gape in horror at what was coming round the bend of the lake—four Ordish barges at full sail.

I didn't even see Lark move, but suddenly she was atop the mainmast again, whistling and screaming with all her might and waving her arms. Down on the deck, Dodd peered over the rail in wonder.

"Now, *that's* a sight you don't see every day," he said, smoothing down his mustache. "I ain't never seen a barge on the lake in my life."

My heart grew three sizes to see them. "The princess—I mean, the queen—said there haven't been any barges south of Timberwick in three hundred years!"

The moment the words rolled off my tongue, I wished I could take them back. The one eye that could be seen under Dodd's enormous hat swiveled in my direction.

"Now, when would a little kitchen dolly like yourself have spoken to the queen, I wonder?"

I felt like I'd swallowed a too-big chunk of apple. *Only Fallow, you goose!* But lucky for me, I was saved from giving Dodd an answer by Lark's joyful shriek from the top of the mast.

"They've seen us! By Deep, they've seen us!"

My friend was right—cries and whistles answering Lark's had broken out aboard the barges and the four vessels had slowly turned our way, red sails billowing.

"Oy!"

We all turned to where Warin was pointing behind us—the caravel had turned around and was heading back with all haste. Dodd punched the air and did a little jig in place on the deck.

"Oh, my lad!" he cried, leaping up to the wheel and hugging his partner's enormous arm. "The Mother's smiling on us today, she is!"

I hung over the rail, trying to get a better look at the approaching boats. As the lead barge came closer, my spirits were flung straight into the heavens.

"It's the *Briar!*"

But Lark had already seen and was hanging from one of the *Falda*'s shrouds, tears running down her cheeks and her long, dark hair, free from its prim palace bun.

"Papa!"

And for just one moment—the moment when Bula Fairweather laid eyes on his daughter's face for the first time in months—everything was right with the world.

13

The sea, my dears, to the sea!
To the rolling waves go we!
The gulls in the sky,
We'll dig as they cry,
For cockles all buried below.
And if there's a boat,
We shall go for a float.
The sea, my dears, to the sea!

—Orstralian seaside rhyme

"You need to keep your eyes on the horizon."

"It's too dark," I moaned. "I can't even *see* the horizon."

There'd been a good many hands on my back since we sailed out of the wide channel of the Ebbe estuary and into ocean waters, but as my head'd been over the side of *Falda's Drawers*, I'd no idea who they belonged to. But Dodd came once, giving me a hearty slap that nearly knocked me over the rail.

"It ain't the best season to be introduced to the big blue, my dear." He chuckled. "But never you mind—we'll be there by the morrow!"

A gurgling sound was all I could make in reply. Me and the ocean weren't going to be good companions.

I tried to steady my belly with the memory of joy on the lake as the four barges surrounded us, the Ordish on them crying and shouting at the sight of one of their lost whelps. Lark didn't even wait for the *Briar* to butt up against the larger ship before she launched herself onto the roof, ducking sails and masts to throw herself into Bula's arms behind the tiller.

Later, after Dodd had invited the clansmen and -women from the other barges aboard the *Drawers*, it was my turn to be caught up in the Ordishman's embrace.

"Jack's beard, Only Fallow, I didn't expect to see your face, but I certainly am glad of it!" he said, his voice shaking with feeling. "And there'll be others just as glad as I!"

"Jon?" I asked, hardly daring to hope. "He made it back?"

"Him and the rest, with such a tale to tell! You—a heartseeker!" Bula shook his head. "I'm sorry the bit of our blood that runs through your veins has been such a trial to you."

"It ain't nothing to the trials your folk've been through, master. But what are you doing here? Lark said you were all at the Hatchings!"

"Aye, we are." The man's face grew solemn. "But it's time to put an end to this. We've been too much abused—first our children stolen, now driven out of our wintering grounds! The council decided it was time to treat with the king, no matter what the risk."

"I'm afraid you're a little too late for that, master."

"Why? What do you mean?"

Lark came from behind to nestle beneath her father's arm. "What Only means, Papa, is that there ain't a king no more."

"No king? The White Lady's heard our beseechments, then!"

I turned toward the familiar voice. "Mauralee!"

My brother's sweetheart embraced me, laughing. "Such a blessing to see your face! I don't know how I'll ever be able to thank you for all you've done, but I suppose now that we're sisters, I got plenty of time."

"Sisters?"

Maura grinned and pushed back her hair. Just behind her ear, a perfect, complicated knot had been tied in one of her long locks, held in with two golden beads.

"Tides!" Lark cried. "A love knot!"

"What does it mean?" I asked, still confused.

My friend grabbed my arm, all giddy. "It means she and Jon got fasted!"

"Just after he and the rest of them got back. We wanted to wait and do it proper next harvest at the orchard, but I near lost him once. I didn't intend to again." She ran her fingers over the knot. "I hope you and your folk ain't sore."

A mix of feelings chased their tails round me—I wished I'd been able to be there for Jon's happy day. And now he was wedded, I knew he was never coming back to the orchard, not to stay. But in a way, he'd wedded all the Fallows to the river, making us part of a bigger family—one where I had a sister. *A sister!*

I grinned. "Does this mean you'll help me make Ether's life a misery next time we all meet?"

"You can count on it," she replied, kissing me on the cheek.

———

171

Lark seized me by the hands and twirled me round. "That practically makes us cousins! Oh, Only, ain't that a fine thing?"

Bula put his hands on Lark's shoulders. "There'll be time for our joys later, but for now there are things that should be known."

And so began an hour of questions and answers. Lark and I explained the goings-on in Bellskeep—the king's madness, the burning in Bellsbrake, our betrayal by Lady Folque, and Saphritte's new crown. The Ordish listened, their concern growing by the moment as we spoke. Dodd and Warin were listening, too—I could see the smaller man's one eyebrow rising and falling in surprise under the brim of his hat. I had to hope they were more honorable than I took them for, and I could buy their silence with the rich jewel in my apron pocket.

After some time, the scoundrel spoke up.

"My good ladies and gents, my fine friends—while it's been an honor to host you aboard our esteemed vessel, I believe the time 'as come where we must move one way or t'other."

He raised a finger for silence. In the distance, more bells of alarum were ringing in the port of Ebbeshore. "As you can hear, we've caused a bit of a stir."

Bula looked round to the three other clan leaders— a handsome, older woman, Gully Slowcreek, from the Blue; a steely-eyed girl, Sorrel Rimedell, from the Lannock; and the stout Fisher Moor from the Rill. "What say you, friends?"

"If the city is mourning a king they believe we had a hand in killing," began Gully Slowcreek, "it seems a poor moment to bring a suit."

"No matter who sits on the throne, they still got our whelps!" argued Fisher Moor.

Sorrel Rimedell's eyes flashed fire. "Queen or king—makes no difference! Bellskeep took what's ours!"

"But what good'll it do us getting strung up as soon as we step through the gates? Bellskeep'll *still* have what's ours, and we don't live to see those beloved faces again!" Bula countered. He held his hands out to Sorrel. "Your brother. My son. Gully's granddaughter. Fisher's nephew—all our whelps, in the belly of that castle. If we ain't careful, we put them in even more danger."

The three other leaders looked toward the racket on the shore.

"We retreat," said Mistress Slowcreek. "Just for a time—until some of the anger dies down."

Fisher Moor's frown spoke loud, but he nodded in agreement. Sorrel Rimedell folded her arms and set her jaw, ready to argue her case, but I decided to put in my two coppers.

"Mistress, I know you have no reason to trust the crown, but the queen—she's not her papa. She's protected your whelps before from folk that wished them ill, and, even though she's sore, I know she'll do it again."

The young woman's gaze went straight to my marrow, but she finally looked to Bula.

"We wait. But not for long, Fairweather."

Dodd clapped his hands together. "It's settled, then. We sail for the Hatchings."

He was roundly ignored by the Ordish, but Lark and I

exchanged glances. I put my hand in my apron pocket and pulled out the golden eye.

"A bargain's a bargain, master. You got us to Lark's folk. I reckon you and Master Warin can go where you like now."

Dodd stared hungrily at the brooch but made no move to take it. He straightened to his full height and hooked his short thumbs through the buttonholes of his greatcoat.

"A bargain *is* a bargain, my girl, a bargain was made. We'll see you to the Hatchings or we ain't got enough honor between us to blow out a candle."

"Right," grunted Warin.

"Haven't you got some . . . fish to catch or . . . something?" I asked.

"Pssht! There's real villainy about, my dear, real, proper villainy! That Folque woman ain't gonna get away with it so easy neither. We petty scoundrels can do a good turn when the kingdom's at stake."

Lark perched her hands on her hips. "And you're also a little afraid of Master Dumphrey."

Dodd's cheeks reddened. "I admit that I am also a little afraid of Master Dumphrey."

Back on the sea, *Falda's Drawers* gave a mighty heave. I hung, limp as a fish and green as an onion, over the ship's rail, doing some heaving of my own. The sea spray was cold and soaking, but I couldn't move. I could just make out the four barges behind us, their red sails dipping and swaying in the waves. Lark was aboard the *Briar* with Bula. The Ordishman thought the crossing'd be easier on me in the flyboat, but there was nothing easy about it.

"Only, honestly, you gotta look up. You won't feel near so sick if you do."

I swatted at the advice giver with the hand that wasn't wound so tight round the rail it'd almost gone numb. Truth is, I'd tried looking up, down, and sideways. I've even tried not looking at all, but my belly'd got caught up in the roll of the gray-green waves and there would be no peace for it till we were on dry land again.

"Oh, don't be like that." Maura patted the top of my head. She'd been next to me a good half hour, slicking the salt water from my forehead. "I know it's right miserable, but it won't be long now."

I felt shameful to be so foul, especially after all the Ordish had been through—driven out of their wintering grounds to make a rough sea-crossing to a cold piece of rock. It vexed me so that I spat over the side.

"I'm sorry," I mumbled to my new sister. "I don't mean to be horrid. I just . . ." Bile rose up in my throat again, choking off words.

Maura rubbed a soothing circle on my back. "Honest, I went gray as a porpoise out of Farrier's Bay. For all of us to have made it the islands, Mama Deep must have carried us in her own hands."

My stomach churned again, wishing I could feel the Mother's hands round me as the chill, dark waves broke against the side of the ship.

"Shall we pass the time with a tale?" Maura asked. "Old Llyr Sparrowbrooke was spinning one the other night—one about the first Mayquin, it happens."

"Non told me how that one ends," I said miserably. "She

served the queen and all that came after her to the end of her days."

"Not this tale," Maura promised. "This one's got a happy ending."

Hanging over the side of a rolling ship in the dark of the night made me long for a happy ending. I gave a weak nod. "All right, then."

Maura patted me between my shoulder blades. "That's the spirit! So, this is the tale of the Liar's Pearl."

AN OLD WIDOWER *by the name of Heywood went to Bellskeep. Though he was possessed of a goodly barge, he wanted to buy a small scrap of land from a duke near Farrier's Bay to build a barn, where his clan could keep wintering supplies. In those days, a body would have to ask permission of the throne before making such a purchase from a nobleman, so off to the capital he went.*

Now, the king who sat on that throne was a new one, and still tasting his oats. His mother, the queen, was scarce cold in her tomb, but he had made a house of merriment and excess of the palace. Advisors quailed and the council balked as they watched the funds of the royal treasury shrink under his gambling and entertainments. And it was this king Heywood came before to plead his suit.

The king could hardly be bothered to hear petitions. He approved Heywood's purchase and waved him off, but Heywood was loath to depart. For standing behind the king's throne was a beautiful clanswoman who he recognized as his own daughter, Makeen, lost many seasons before in the bustle of Bellskeep. Though the years had been long, there was no mistaking his girl, and he could see by the joy on her face that she knew him, too. He'd heard tell of the king's heartseeker and knew of her power and her obligation to the crown, but he resolved then and there to return with a plan to bring her back to her people.

Heywood hurried back to his clan and went straight to the cunning woman, who was called Jesset.

"Good Jesset," he said, "I'm joyful, for I've found my daughter, but heartsick, for I don't know how to free her from servitude!"

The cunning woman consulted with the stars, the bones, and the tea leaves. Then she said to Heywood, "There is a stream in the north where the redjack go to spawn. During the next new moon, catch one in a pail and offer it a piece of gold. It will give you what you seek."

Though it sounded like a strange plan, Heywood knew cunning women weren't to be questioned, so he journeyed north to the redjack stream. On the night of the new moon, he dipped his pail into the stream and brought out a magnificent fish. Heywood offered it a gold coin, and to his surprise, the fish greedily plucked it from his fingers, spat a stone out into the bucket, then leapt clean across the bank and back into the stream. The stone was a fine and bewitching thing, full of lustrous blue and green fire.

Heywood took the stone back to Jesset. The cunning woman consulted with the river mud, some egg yolks, and the afternoon wind. Then she said, "This stone will allow you to lie to your daughter without her knowing. Your deceit will mean her freedom."

"But how can lying to her set her free?" asked Heywood.

The cunning woman consulted with the cards, the needles, and the currents. Then she said, "The king likes a game of chance. Make him a bet he cannot refuse."

With a plan forming in his head, Heywood made the long journey to Bellskeep once again. When he arrived, the weight of the stone heavy in his pocket, things were worse than before. Revelers roamed the halls of the castle at all hours. The king could hardly be persuaded away from his gaming to hear Heywood's suit, but when he finally did come, he looked on the old man with scorn.

"I gave you the dispensation you asked to buy your land. Why do you trouble me again?"

"Sire," said Heywood, "I have come to offer you a wager."

The king was tempted, for he did like a good wager. "What do you want? And what have you to offer me?"

"Your heartseeker is my daughter and I have come to take her home. If I can lie to her three times without her knowing, she is the boon that I ask. If I fail, all my goods and my life are forfeit to your crown."

"This is a foolish wager, riverman," scoffed the king. "No one can lie to my Mayquin. And she can lie to no one. But if you are determined to try, I will accept your wager. How shall we test this matter?"

Heywood pointed to the court entertainer, who had a bucket full of juggling balls, all of which were different colors. "Have my daughter turn around."

The king's Mayquin turned from the court, her heart hopeful that her father knew what he was doing.

Heywood picked up a red ball, showed it to the court, and then hid it behind his back. "Turn and see me, daughter."

The Mayquin turned to look upon her father's face.

"In my hand, I hold a ball that is green. It is green as the grass in summer, as the first buds on the willow, as the algae on the hull of a barge. I tell you, this ball is green. Am I lying, or am I telling the truth?"

"You are telling the truth," she answered. And everyone knew the Mayquin could not lie.

Heywood showed the red ball to the astonished Mayquin. The king gave a careless smile. "Pure luck. I'm sure it will not happen again. Turn around," he ordered the Mayquin.

Heywood picked up a white ball. "Turn and see me, daughter."

The Mayquin turned to look upon her father's face.

"In my hand, I hold a ball that is yellow. It is yellow as the sun, as the fields of wheat, as the dust of buttercups. I tell you, this ball is yellow. Am I lying or am I telling the truth?"

"You are telling the truth," she answered. And everyone knew the Mayquin could not lie.

Heywood showed the white ball to the astonished Mayquin. The king pursed his lips. "I have never seen such a thing. I'm sure it will not happen again. Turn around," he ordered the Mayquin.

Heywood picked up an orange ball. "Turn and see me, daughter."

The Mayquin turned to look upon her father's face.

"In my hand, I hold a ball that is black. It is black as the night, as the dark of the bilge, as the depths of a shadow. I tell you, this ball is black. Am I lying or am I telling the truth?"

"You are telling the truth," she answered. And everyone knew the Mayquin could not lie.

Heywood had won his wager.

Mayquin—Makeen once more—flew to her father and embraced him while the king fumed from his throne, all of his advisors chiding him at once for having lost such a treasure of the kingdom.

IF I THOUGHT my belly was upset before, it was nothing to how it felt after hearing old Llyr Sparrowbrooke's yarn. That great stone, glittering round Lady Folque's neck—the thing I'd took for some family legacy! I'd seen it every day, admiring its fire and never knowing it kept her wicked lies hidden.

I noisily retched nothing into the ocean below, again and again.

"Only? Only, what's the matter?" asked Maura, concerned over my new bout of sickness.

The ship rolled on through the night.

I was jolted awake by a shout of "Anchor away!" and a tremendous splash.

The world was still waving about, but now I was looking up at it, watching the mast swinging to and fro like a sword fighting against the heavy sky, lightening to dawn. Some kind soul had stowed me in the middle of a large rope coil after I'd dropped off, so it was that I found myself tangled in when I tried to scramble to my feet. My belly and my head were strangely calm, as if I'd become part of the ship and its wild dance with the water. The bow dipped as the heavy anchor struck bottom, but I hardly noticed.

Before us stood towering cliffs, white as the Cathedra and ten times as tall. No light from the rising sun could break through the thick carpet of cloud, but they still seemed to glow like some sort of palace made of alabaster.

"Sweet All," I whispered to myself.

"It's a sight, ain't it?"

Maura swung down from the shroud to sit beside the rope. "Mama always told me stories of when she and some other whelps stole a barge and sailed out here one summer. Said the cliffs were like mountains of snow in the middle of the sea. I always thought she was telling tall tales, but . . ." She spread her arms before the magnificent scene before us.

"Master Iordan gave me a lesson on them once," I said, not able to take my eyes from the cliffs. I could almost hear his haughty voice inside my head. *Now, Mayquin, attend, if you please. The Hatchings are a small outcropping of chalk islands off the western coast whose only inhabitants are wild sheep and rock screets, a variety of bird whose guano is used for—*

I shook my head to banish the inquisitor from it—just one more inhabitant of the palace that now thought the worst of me because of Lady Folque. "They're beautiful."

Maura reached down to help me to my feet. "Come on. This great floating brick can't get too close to shore without running aground. We'll take the barges."

The *Briar* was butted up alongside *Falda's Drawers*. As soon as my face appeared over the railing, Lark leapt up from her spot on the roof. Even though neither of us had got near enough winks, she was fresh in Ordish clothes, her eyes kohled and glorious metal beads in her hair. She was home. And I had to admit I was just a little bit envious.

"It wasn't half a wild ride, was it?" she said excitedly. "Papa made me go in for the worst of it, but he let me take the tiller awhile during the calm bits."

"There were calm bits?"

Maura draped an arm round my shoulders. "Our poor land-walker spent a lot of time calling to the Deep." Her nose wrinkled in distaste. "The whiff of these clothes isn't helping matters any. Let's get you cleaned up."

Carefully scaling the rail with Maura's steady hands to guide me, I dropped down to the roof of the *Briar*, where Lark was waiting.

"What'd you do with your dress?" I asked.

"Threw it over the side. It might have been wasteful, but I don't care." She tossed her head, beads clicking. "I'm no servant anymore. And neither are you, Only Fallow."

My spirit lifted to match hers *after* I'd scrubbed the filthy fish stink from my skin in a bucket of cold water and borrowed a thick red woolen gown from Lark's cousin, along with her third-best coat. By the time I was done, we were near the shore, but Lark opened one of the barge's small ports.

"Go on, then," she said with a grin.

I shoved the hateful blue dress and apron out into the sea. A cry of protest went up nearby.

"I hope you remembered to take that trinket out of your apron, my girl!"

"Your payment's safe and well, Master Dodd," I called back, tucking the jewel carefully into the pocket of my coat.

We both stumbled forward as the *Briar* hit the sand of the

shore. Lark raced to open the stable doors so we could watch the men and women at the ropes dragging the barge farther up toward the cliffs and the hundreds of other barges already beached there. Large wedges of wood were hammered underneath the hull so the boat would sit steady on her new home upon the chalk.

A huge crowd had gathered to see why the four barges that had only set sail the day before had returned so soon. Lark's appearance on the bow was met with gasps and cries of delight—half a hundred hands reached for her at once, and she fell joyfully into them.

I was feeling a little sorry for myself, longing for the arms of Mama, Papa, and Non, when my new sister reached up to help me off the deck.

"I know you must be missing your folk," she said, hugging me tight, "but don't forget, you've got all of us now, too."

"Maura!"

A young man shoved his way through the crowd on the beach. The last I'd seen his face, it'd been dirty and bruised on a dark night in Bellskeep. I'd only been able to hope I'd see it again, and now here it was.

Jonquin threw his arms round his wife. His hair, now long and sandy like Mama's, was wild and windswept, with a love knot behind an ear.

"Sweet All, why're you back already? You only just left— what's happened?"

Maura kissed his cheek. "We ran into some friends bearing news."

"Friends?" huffed Jon. "We've got no friends anym—"

He spotted me over Maura's shoulder. I suppose I must have looked different to him, too, dressed as I was—it took a moment before the light of understanding flickered in those eyes that looked so like mine. And before I knew it, I was crushed to my brother's chest.

"Mother's breath, Pip!" he cried. "I can't believe . . . There ain't been a day gone by I haven't beseeched the Mother that old wretch'd let you go, but I never expected—" He broke off, swallowed up with emotion. "No harm came to you, did it? For what you did in freeing us? Or to your friend the steward?"

"No," I said, laughing, wiping away a few joyful tears. "No, but, Jon, so much's happened since!"

Maura put her arms round both of us. "Bula's going to call the whole Southmeet together again. Things have changed."

"Changed? Changed how?"

"It's best you come and listen," she told him. "The story's long."

Jon put a gentle hand to her cheek. "I'll be along by and by. It's my turn to attend to our guest."

"You have a guest?" I asked. "Here on the Hatchings?"

"Oh!" Jon seized me by the shoulders. "We caught him, Pip—we caught the snake!"

"You caught *who*?"

"The man from the Southmeet! The one who sent us to the Wood after the coach!"

"The one with the port-wine stain on his arm?"

"The very same!" crowed my brother. "Before we got chased

from the Bay, the Driftgrass sisters from the Rill went up to Whiteburn Watch to sell some dyed wool, and there he was. They knew his face right away, so Lilla knocked him down and sat on him while Yara and Willow tied him up." He shuddered. "Almost felt sorry for the fellow. Lilla's over six feet tall and could probably pull a barge all by her lonesome—I'd not like to have her sit on *me*."

"Who is he?" I demanded. "What's the fellow's name?"

Jon shook his head. "He keeps insisting he's a 'friend of the river,' though on the matter of his name, his mouth's been sealed tighter than a duck's backside. We thought we might offer him to the king, though, as evidence."

I grasped my brother's sleeve. "Jon, take me to him. I ain't got much to offer, but my cunning might be of some help!"

Not wasting a moment, Jon took my hand and led me up the beach through the crush of bodies. Large chalk pebbles were scattered at our feet like snowballs, leaving white streaks behind on my battered boots. We trudged up toward the base of the mighty cliffs, where I could see a few different hollows.

"Thank All the weather's been mostly good since we came," said Jon, pointing ahead of us. "Still, we've sheltered in the caves once or twice, when the wind's been fierce."

"Have you heard from Mama and Papa?" I asked.

A guilty look crossed his face. "I tried to write a couple times after I left, but I couldn't think of the words. And then I went with the men to the Wood . . ." He looked down at the pebbles on the beach. "You think they'll forgive me? For leaving?"

I thought on it—Mama's rage the morning he disappeared and the sad days after, just before Bellskeep came to our door. "You know how Non says good and ill share a table sometimes?"

"I've heard her say so."

"Non says a lot of things I understand better'n I used to." I picked up a small chalk pebble and a big one. "I think this little one is gonna be the hurt they feel, but this other one's how happy they'll be to see you again and to know you're happy, too."

Jon tousled my hair with a grateful grin. "When'd you get so wise, Pip?"

I didn't feel very wise—the sting of being fooled by the Lady of Folquemotte was still lodged under my skin, burning me every chance it got.

We reached one of the smaller caves at the foot of the cliffs and ducked inside. Jon led me straight to a clever cell made from wooden barge planks. Buried deep in the chalk at the top and bottom, the planks were thick and unshiftable, but during the day, they allowed the weak sunlight from outside the cave in, so as not to keep the prisoner in total darkness. The Ordish had been more charitable to the villain than I'd've been—his lies had led to desperate men dying at the hands of the king's guard.

A man lay with his back to us, on a bed of straw and furs—another comfort Jon and the Ordish prisoners'd been denied in the palace dungeon. Jon rapped sharply at a hinged panel set into the door of the cell.

"Your plate and cup," he barked.

The fellow didn't stir, so Jon rapped again louder.

"You plate and cup or you'll not have any more vittles today."

Led by Jon's threat to his stomach, the fellow slowly pushed himself upright and turned to scowl at the disturbance of his nap.

It was Maddock Beir.

15

I once got my fingers caught in the stable door to the kitchen when I was small. I uttered a curse I'd no doubt heard one of my brothers say, but was unlucky enough Mama had the hearing of it. I had to sit for five minutes with bitter greenroot on my tongue as my penance. As I spat and spat in the yard after, Non took me aside and told me it was best to save up my curses for a time I might really want 'em to work.

I must've had more curses stored up than I thought, 'cause I let every one of them go at Lady Folque's proctor. I even used some of the ones I'd overheard the pressmen mutter in the sheds where they made the cider—ones I didn't even know the meaning of, but probably weren't fit for respectable company. Both my brother and Master Beir were shocked senseless as I made a poem of my profanity, unleashing verse after verse at the man in the cell.

Jon finally put a halt to my cussing. "All's teeth, Pip!" he cried.

"Have you been hanging around with sailors as well as with lords and ladies? You *know* this scoundrel?"

Master Beir was now on his feet with his face pressed to the wooden slats of his cell. "What in all the seven hells are *you* doing here?"

"I'm here no thanks to you, your rotten mistress, and her rotten pearl!" I shouted. "She only went and did away with the king and blamed it on me and Lark!" I grabbed hold of the slats. "Why'd she do it? Why's she filled the city with her men? And why did she send *you* to hoodwink the Ordish?"

Beir stepped back nervously. "I'm sure you must be mistaken on all counts, Mayquin."

The lie was ugly and spread round him like a bruise, filling up the tiny cell. I could see it, even in the dark.

"How is it you remembered that I'm the Mayquin but forgot what it is I can do?" I growled. "I'm not mistaken."

The proctor's lip twisted and he retreated back to the straw bales, where he sat, hunched like an ill-tempered crab.

"Who is he?" begged Jon.

I scowled at the man in the cell. "The proctor of Lady Folque. Jon, I don't like this one bit. If he's the one who sent the Ordish against the coach in the Wood, it means . . ."

Truth was, I didn't know what it meant, but it was certain whatever Lamia Folque had planned was bigger than just clearing the way for Saphritte to take the throne.

I turned to my brother. "Did he have anything with him when he was took?"

"Aye, a traveling bag with a change of clothes and a few papers, but no one here's been able to make heads or tails of them."

Something seized hold of me. It felt like squinting at a figure on a faraway hill but not being able to get any closer to make out their face.

"Has someone still got them?" I asked. "Could I see?"

Beir's back stiffened at that, as if he wanted to make an objection, but he kept his mouth shut.

Jon nodded. "I think the Driftgrasses have it. We might be able to catch them before the council meets, if we're lucky."

"Let's go, then! Lead the way."

My brother ducked out of the cave, but I hesitated, staring back at the man in the cell.

"You caused a lot of harm here, master. I aim to make sure you can't cause any more."

THERE WERE MORE barges than I'd ever seen in one place pulled up on the beach. The endless line stretched as far as the eye could see, until it disappeared round the opposite side of the island. Every Ordish man, woman, and child—save for those indentured in Bellskeep—all exiled together. It made me even more sore at Maddock Beir, and more wild to know what he was up to.

My brother and me walked a good half mile up the beach, passing folk gathering what little wood they could find from the island's few tough, scraggly trees and carrying buckets of freshwater from a spring that pooled deep in one of the caves. "I know they're round this way somewhere," muttered Jon, peering at each bow we passed. "*The Gray Swan* . . . *The Cliffwalker* . . . *Deep's Heart* . . . oh, here we are, *Star of the Low East.*"

My brother climbed up a small rigged ladder on the side of the barge and knocked on the front stable doors. After a moment, the top door opened and the head of a tall woman poked out.

"Good day, Master . . . Fallow, isn't it?"

Jon nodded politely. "It is, mistress, and a good day to you. Me and my sister are sorry to disturb your family if you were at table."

"We're just doing something light for tea. Would you like to come and join us?"

Apart from a measly few strips of dried beef I'd begged off Dodd aboard *Falda's Drawers* (which I lost straight away once we hit the ocean), my belly hadn't seen proper food in two days.

I may have accidentally made a mewling noise, because the woman smiled kindly.

"It sounds like your sister might be in need of feeding. Please, come in."

The inside of the barge was warm. A fat-bellied iron wood-stove burned in the corner and lanterns lit the walls. In the small galley kitchen, two other women climbed over and under each other, each helping to prepare the midday meal.

The head of the tall, strong woman who'd seen us in just barely brushed the top of the low roof. I expected she was Lilla Driftgrass, and I had to agree with Jon—being sat upon by her must have been an experience Master Beir would sooner like to forget. The two women nattering in the kitchen were smaller, and they all three had deep-honey-brown hair and high cheekbones.

"Adda, Willow, we got some guests."

"Hope they like clams," said one of the women, trying to force a knife into the shell of one of the tight-lipped devils. "'Cause it's all we got."

The other made a face. "They look like something that dropped from a horse's nose, but we can't be ungrateful. Not out here."

The first sister raised a clam to her eye level and tapped it. "But what I wouldn't do if you had a good joint of lamb hidden inside!"

"Mistresses," I said, "it's awful kind of you to invite us in, but we were wondering if we could see the bag."

"Oh, the one from that rogue in the cave? Aye, you sit down and I'll find it."

Jon and I settled ourselves on two cushions round a low table. One of the women brought a loaf of soft, thick bread and some salted oil. I'm ashamed to say I filled my face with it before Lilla returned with the bag.

"I don't know what good it'll do, master," she said, dropping the leather satchel upon the table. "The council's already had a gander."

"But the council didn't *know* the scoundrel," Jon told her as I undid the straps and began rummaging around inside. "Only *does*."

One of the women from the kitchen came to join us at the table. "Of course! You're the heartseeker, aren't you? Heard 'em talking about you on the beach!"

There were a few things in Beir's bag any fellow on a journey might have. A comb and brush, a blade for shaving, a change of clothes. But at the bottom was a leather roll with parchment inside. I untied the laces and let it fall open.

The large piece of parchment at the top curled stubbornly, but I smoothed its edges so I could see it. At the top of the page, there was a short message. The writing was so flowery, so full of curls and loops, I had to read slowly, like a whelp on their first primer.

To the Most Excellent Lady:

I hope this little exercise is completed to your satisfaction.

Yours, most humbly,
Godfrey Noble,
Master Herald

Beneath was a coat of arms. It had been done in haste—the marks of the artist's pencil hadn't even been erased after the ink had dried. To the right of the crest reared the red Eydisson stag on a cream-colored field, proud and wild with its enormous rack of antlers. To the left pranced the white Folque rabbit on red and gold, its pickax slung over its shoulder. And in the middle, between them, was a crown.

"The art of heraldry," Master Iordan told me once, "is about trying to tell the story of a family without words. Coats of arms are meant to show strengths and alliances." He pointed to the banner of the Molliers, hung in one corner of the hallsroom. "On the left is a bunch of grapes on a blue field, representing their vineyards and the sky, which brings them warmth to grow. On the right are two geese on purple and green checks. The colors represent the grapes, while the geese represent persistence and courage. In addition, the Molliers have always used geese to keep their vines free of pests, so it has a double meaning."

"Can you put anything you want on your coat of arms?" I asked.

"Within reason," the inquisitor replied. "Apart from a crown. Only the ruling monarch is allowed to use that particular symbol."

I blinked at the parchment, trying to make out the meaning of it.

"Lady Folque's daughter was sure friendly with Prince Orrad," I said slowly. "Maybe she's trying to marry her off. It'd sure be handy to be head of a council in one country and the mother of a queen in another."

"There was this, too," said Lilla, pulling an envelope from under the parchment. "It was right mysterious."

The envelope was addressed to Master Beir in a sharp hand, care of the waystation in Whiteburn Watch. The paper inside was rough made—bits of bark visible in the weave of the fibers. I pulled it out carefully.

To my disappointment, there wasn't much written on it. And what there *was* didn't make much sense.

> Mother's arms
> 25
> 3 bell
> Yewheart, 3 red fletch
> I take 200 gc, as agreed
> Safe passage
> Roysa Beale

I shook my head. "Does anyone know Roysa Beale?"

"No one here has heard of her." Jon pointed to the paper. "This part makes a little sense, see? 'Yewheart, three red fletch.' The Ordish use yewheart bows and arrows fletched with red."

"'Three bell' might be third bell. And the 'two hundred gc' is probably two hundred gold coins," added Lilla.

"Think how many lamb joints that could buy!" said Willow dreamily from the kitchen.

Lilla sat down on a cushion beside me. "But the other bits—something about Mother's arms? The number twenty-five?"

The face on the hill was still maddeningly out of focus. *Only Fallow, if you ever needed that thing between your ears, it's now. Think!*

I tapped a finger on the table. "'Safe passage.' Is Roysa Beale wishing *Master Beir* a safe passage, or is she *asking* for safe passage? If Lady Folque is paying her two hundred gold coins to do something, it might be a dangerous something. Something she'd need safe passage for after she did it."

Jon blanched. "Something with an Ordish bow. At third bell."

Mother's arms. Where had I heard that before? It had only been in the last day—how could I have forgot so fast?

There was a cry outside the barge.

"All those wishing to attend the Meet will convene at the Forks at sundown!"

"Well, at least the clams'll have time to cook," groused Willow, stirring the pot. "If we're to stand in a full Meet for hours, I'd at least like to fill our stomachs first!"

The shout outside stirred something itchy between my ears, just like during my tea with Lady Folque and the king. But it wasn't a real itch—just a feeling like something was about to reveal itself. Something like . . .

I leapt to my feet, knocking Jon and Lilla off their pillows. "Mother's arms!"

My brother righted himself. "Sweet All, Pip! What's the matter?"

"She doesn't mean 'Mother's arms' like the arms of your mama or of *the* Mother—it's an inn! The biggest in Bellskeep, right in the Cathedra Square. Before the crier came out, a fella outside the castle said he was staying there to sell his wares for the wedding."

Jon put his finger to the paper again. "What about the twenty-five?"

"A room number, it's got to be!" I exclaimed. I'd passed by the Mother's Arms on the way to the Cathedra every Matins. It was a tall, white stone building—its front covered in narrow, diamond-paned windows. "I think it's got about thirty rooms, so number twenty-five'd be near the top."

"So, doing something with an Ordish bow at an inn in the Cathedra Square at third bell that would need safe passage after," said Lilla. "That don't sound like it could be anything good."

A fella outside the castle said he was staying there to sell his wares for . . .

"The wedding."

A wave of fear, cold as the ones on the ocean crossing, crested and broke over my body. *Mother's breath, the wedding!*

"Jon, someone needs to get Proctor Beir and bring him to the Meet," I said, rolling up the crest and the letter in the leather case.

Worried lines creased my brother's forehead. "Why? What are you going to do?"

That far-off figure on the hill had suddenly got a lot closer.

"I'm gonna be the Mayquin," I declared. "Just one more time."

16

High saileth the moon and three times must the nightjar cry
Before we can our mischief make. The hour cometh!
O most unholy hour!

—From the virtue play *A Caution to Witches*, author unknown

I always thought it was quite something that I knew every soul in Presston. A little over four hundred folk seemed a lot of folk to know.

But it was nothing compared with the Ordish Southmeet. Lark hadn't been telling tall tales when she'd said that near ten thousand souls gathered every year. And every one of them was headed for the Forks.

The largest cave on the island had three entrances, each leading into one great chamber in the middle. While it couldn't hold nearly everyone, it was certainly the best place to gather in and around so as many folk who wanted could have their say.

Even with the crowds, it didn't take long for me and Jon to find Lark. She was at the center of chattering cousins and playmates by a fire, telling the wide-eyed whelps of her time in the palace. For the first time since we'd met, I felt shy. Everything'd been so different in Bellskeep. What if, now that she was among her folk again, she didn't really care for my company?

The thought was more than I could bear, but it vanished when she looked up to see me. She broke through the circle to pull me into it.

"And since Only's Jon's sister, that makes her part of the clan, too!" she announced, continuing some conversation that'd been going on before I arrived.

Some of the littler ones tugged at my skirts and my hands with a dozen questions all at once.

"Are you really a heartseeker?"

"Are you gonna live with us from now on, like Jon?"

"You could get fasted to my brother!"

"No! My sister!"

Jon stood next to the fire, grinning at my predicament, but Lark rescued me.

"All right, it's near time for the Meet. You go find your mamas and papas, go on, now!"

The whelps groaned, but did as they were bid, scattering into the darkness toward their barges.

"Where've you been?" my friend asked. "I haven't seen you since we stepped ashore!"

I grabbed hold of her hands, warm from the fire. "Oh, you wouldn't believe what we've found out, Lark Fairweather! And I got an idea to find out more, but I need your help. Your papa's and Warin's and Dodd's, too, but we've already spoken to them. You're the one I really need to see this through."

Jon hoisted his lantern. "I'll go fetch the villain. You sure you know what you're doing, Pip?"

"No," I said honestly, "but it's all I can think to do." I held out the leather roll to Lark. "Come on. I'll tell you about it on the way."

We wove through the throng of bodies that got denser the closer we got to one of the cave's openings. The going was slow, but it gave me time to tell Lark about Maddock Beir, the crest, the letter, and, most important, what I had in mind to drag the whole tale from him.

She gave a low whistle as we finally made it to the cave mouth. "I'll sure do my best, but that fella don't seem like one who scares easy. Remember who he works for!"

"He might not be afeared of much in a fancy castle, but he ain't in one *now*, is he? He's stuck out in the middle of the ocean with the whole Ordish Southmeet who hates him. He's pro'bly wondering why no one's dumped him over the side of a barge with rocks in his pockets yet!"

"The folk at this Meet who lost men in the Wood are prob'ly wondering the same thing," Lark said darkly.

Inside the cave mouth, bodies were packed shoulder to shoulder, but they parted before Lark, knowing her to be Bula's whelp. We crept forward inch by inch till we finally broke through into the main chamber.

The large cavern was lit with torches and held two hundred folk, easy, but more were crammed in for the big Meet. The cold of outside was nothing but a memory so deep inside the cliff—sweat beaded on my neck as we wove through the throng to find the council. Bula's broad shoulders finally appeared toward the center of the chamber.

"Ah! Just in time," he said, clapping me on the shoulder. "I've shared your scheme with the council. They're willing to give it a try."

"I think if we want to know how to go about getting the whelps back, we need to know what's *really* going on in the city," I said. "And Master Beir might be the only one who can tell us."

A grumble of discontent surged forward from one of the three passages leading into the chamber.

"You two, make yourselves scarce," Bula ordered. "Sounds like the villain's on his way now."

Lark and I ducked into the crowd, listening to the jeers and curses as they made their way forward, till finally the crowd moved aside to admit Jon, leading the bound Maddock Beir ahead of him.

An angry rumble filled the cavern as a space cleared in the center. The proctor didn't look so stubborn now, surrounded on all sides and protected only by my brother. The clan council—Bula, Gully Slowcreek, Fisher Moor, and Sorrel Rimedell—moved to meet them.

"Thanks to Deep!" bellowed Bula, ending all the chatter.

"Thanks to Deep!" echoed the Meet.

"Some of you may know and some may not that we received news yesterday of the death of the king." Scattered cheers rang out through the Forks, but Bula held up his hands. "It's ill to rejoice in a death! Do not give the White Lady reason to knock next upon your door!"

The cheers were silenced.

"If we wish to treat for the release of our kin, we walk into a city at a restless, changeable hour. But before we come to that, we would once more question the wretch who sent our good men to their graves in the north." Bula held the letter in the air for all to see. "This was found among your things," he said gravely.

"As I've told you, a letter, nothing more," grumbled Beir.

"A letter signed by one 'Roysa Beale.'"

"A correspondence with my sister!" the proctor lied.

"Not *the* Roysa Beale?"

The shocked voice echoed around the chamber. Bula craned his neck to see where it'd come from.

"Who speaks?"

Folk parted to reveal Dodd, who swaggered to the center of the cave like he was taking the stage at one of the city's great theaters.

"I tell you, friends, that lady's name is enough to put needles down any man's spine, yes, any man!" He stopped short of Beir. "Growing up with her must've been a fearful trial, sir, a fearful trial! It's a wonder you made it this ripe old age!"

"I'm only nine and twenty!"

"That's what I mean, sir, that's what I mean!"

Beir glared at the dapper scoundrel, who didn't wait for an answer before addressing the crowd.

"I only say it because, well, I've got some little knowledge of

Miss Roysa Beale." Making sure he'd everyone in the cave leaning forward to catch his words, he made them all leap with a shout.

"A most fearful assassin, this fella's sister is, with a heart of coal and the temper of a badger caught in a trap! Why, I once watched her cut a fella's head clean off in a tavern, just for spilling her drink! And before both bits of the man hit the floor, the taverner begged her pardon and brought her another!"

Behind him, Warin drew his long finger across his throat.

I wondered if Master Beir would have alarmed to see the display of billowing flashfire rocketing out from behind the head of the petty scoundrel as he wove his tale. In truth, Dodd *had* heard of Roysa Beale through whispers round the Shallows—a hired sword (or bow) that'd take care of anyone causing you trouble. "But don't you worry none, my girl, don't you worry," he told me. "I'll sell the tale and he'll buy it."

Dodd leaned closer to the bound man, the shadows from the fire gathering under his hat. "I don't suppose someone like Mistress Beale would take too kindly to a . . . personal bit of family business falling into the wrong hands, would she?"

Master Beir gulped. He was definitely buying what Dodd was selling.

"But," the little man continued airily, "maybe she don't have to know. Maybe after all this is over, you disappear. Scuttle off into some little hole, like a good little rat, where sister dearest can't find you."

A spark of hope kindled in the proctor. He looked round to the clan leaders. "You'll . . . you'll let me go?"

Gully Slowcreek crossed her arms, staring daggers at him. "We'll see if your answers are to our liking."

"Or, more to the point, to the heartseeker's liking," Fisher Moor added. "It's her you have to worry about."

Beir gave a dismissive huff. "I'm not worried about a child."

"Perhaps you should be," warned Bula.

Lark stepped out from behind her father's shadow. "Maybe you should have been listening in Cathedra rather than plotting with Lady Folque. Curate Heyman tried to warn you."

Now the proctor laughed out loud. "That superstitious old blowhard, with all his warnings about devilry?"

Sorrel Rimedell cocked her head. "Who says devils ain't real?"

Some of Beir's bluster melted away as I finally stepped out of the crowd.

"Glamours are tricky," Lark had told me on the way to the cave. "To glamour another person, I usually gotta be touching them. Like when I made your hairpins glow back at the palace."

I leaned toward her and the little knife she pulled from her pocket. "But you think this'll do?"

She snicked off a small lock of my hair and held it tight between her fingers. "It should. Let me try—hold out your hand."

I turned my palm faceup, and to my surprise, a pale green nightmoth appeared, its long, lazy wings opening and closing.

"It's the shine on the apple! But I don't reckon that villain is going to be frighted by a moth."

Lark puffed up proudly. "Oh, I can conjure up more than moths."

So, as I approached Master Beir, I wondered what Lark had in mind. Whatever it was, I could tell from the proctor's face that it was unsettling. Even some of the clan leaders took an unwitting step backward. I took the letter from Dodd's hand as I passed and held it in front of Beir's face.

"Lady Folque hired Roysa Beale for two hundred gold pieces. At the third bell, she'll be at the Mother's Arms in room twenty-five with an Ordish bow and three red-fletched arrows. After she's done what she's been paid for, she'll get safe passage from the city."

I leaned closer. My reflection in Beir's pupils showed me I'd a pair of burning red eyes, so I widened them further.

"What's Roysa Beale going to do?"

Beir's lip quivered but stayed shut. I had to keep from shrieking when the letter in my hand suddenly erupted in flames—the same ones I'd seen a thousand times round the acorn in the beloved Jack's belly.

"What's she going to do?" I shouted.

"The queen!" cried the terrified man. "She's going to kill the queen after the wedding!"

I tried my best to swallow my horror as it all unspooled in my head: Saphritte, gasping her last on the steps of the Cathedra, a clutch of arrows through her chest. *That's why Lady Folque had to kill the king,* I realized. *Saphritte wouldn't take the crown on her own! And now, if she's killed after she marries Hauk, he's got a claim to the throne and an empty seat beside him.* From the pocket of my coat, I pulled the scroll with the crest, which also immediately set to burning.

"And that has to do with this?"

"Yes, yes, of course!"

An enraged Fisher Moor stepped forward to give the proctor a shove that knocked him to the ground. "Why did she need involve *us*? What wrong have we ever done her?"

Beir looked up from the rocky cave floor. "Don't you see? She needed Orstral to have an enemy—one she could save them from and be loved for it! So she convinced the king to start the abductions to give folks a reason to suspect your revenge." Even through the man's fear, a wry smile came to his lips. "When you've got people afraid of the wolves at the walls, they're less likely to notice the cat in the pantry, stealing the cream."

"And the burnings?" I pressed. "Those were her doing, too, weren't they?"

Glamoured flames licked the tips of my hair. Beir shrunk back.

"Yes! Yes, it was her men in disguise!" he gibbered.

Fire shot from the tips of my fingers, Lark's rage pouring out through the glamour. "Lamia Folque committed murder, slandered the Ordish, and let the country go hungry just to *put her daughter on the throne?*"

For the first time since I started my questioning, the proctor looked confused. "You think she wants to put *Adalise* on the throne?"

"This crest," I said, brandishing the parchment like the Mother herself had written on it. "It's got the Folque and Eydisson symbols on it with a crown in between!"

The exhausted man shook his head. "Do you really think

a woman like Lady Folque went through all the trouble to gain power just to give it away? She's young yet—only eight and thirty. If she can talk a king into madness, she can certainly talk a widowed prince into love. But the crest will do just as well for two nations as it will for one."

"So . . . she's going to marry Hauk herself!" I exclaimed. *"And wed her daughter to his brother, who's the heir of Thorvald!"*

Gully Slowcreek shook her head in disbelief. "Two countries, ruled by the same family."

"And us despised in both of them," added Fisher Moor.

Sorrel Rimedell made a noise of disgust. "I've heard enough. Take the eel back to his cell."

Shouting erupted in the cavern. Shells, pebbles, and moldy clams flew at Beir. My brother, still tasked with guarding the villain, had to duck so as not to be hit by any of the missiles. As Jon shoved him out through the crowd, Master Beir's face twisted, realizing his days of proctoring for the Folques had just come to an end.

17

Each soul shall have their say,
Should Meet night turn to day.

—Ordish saying, on the subject of Meets

No matter what anyone else can say about the Ordish, it sure can't be said they're not fair.

After Bula settled the riled crowd, the council began calling on folk. I was keen to stay up and hear what the decision would be, but Lark led me out of the cave, past an orderly line of folk, and back to the *Briar.*

"A full Meet only happens when there's something big to jaw on. And they'll be jawing for a long while yet."

"How long?" I asked.

"Some folk have their say, go to bed, get up the next morning with something else on their mind, and get in line all over again."

"But . . ." I heaved myself up the ladder, protesting. "Now we know Lady Folque's going to try to kill the queen. We even got proof! Someone's gotta stop it . . . don't they?"

Lark shrugged, climbing up after me. "There's a lot of folk here that wouldn't've crossed the street to spit on the king if he was alight. I don't know how they'll feel about sticking out their necks for his daughter."

"But Saphritte said *she* wanted an Orstral that belonged to everyone. If we just let it happen, Orstral won't be for no one but Lady Folque!"

Lark pushed open the stable door. "That's awful well put. It's a shame you've got to have sixteen harvests under your belt in order to speak, or I'd say it to the council myself."

I looked despairingly at the lines that stretched out of all three of the cave entrances.

My friend took me by the hand. "Come on, there's enough room in my bunk for us to sleep top to toe. Hope you don't mind snoring—my cousin Reed sounds like a pig with a stopped-up nose."

Lark's bunk was soft and warm, and her cousin Reed *did* sound like a pig with a stopped-up nose, but the last hopes I had before drifting off—that the Meet would come to a decision— were dashed the next morning, when I poked my head back out those same stable doors and saw the lines of folk still hovering round the caves.

"There're only two days after this till the wedding!" I told Lark as we sat on a little plateau just above the beach to watch the flurry of activity below. The sun had poked its nose out from the blanket of cloud that'd lain across the Hatchings since we arrived, turning the dingy wool white of the cliffs to brilliant ivory.

"The Meet's the Meet," Lark replied, spinning part of a screet eggshell on her finger. "It's the way we always done things."

Frustrated, I pulled my coat tight around myself and flopped back onto the stubbly grass, staring up at the cliff. In two days, the queen would walk out of the Great Cathedra with her new husband, insensible to the fact that in room twenty-five of the Mother's Arms, Roysa Beale would be nocking an arrow to put through her heart—the heart that loved Orstral above all else.

Lark lay down beside me. The yellow-legged screets wheeled high above our heads and clung sideways to the soft chalk, squawking out their opinions as if they were having their own noisy Meet on the cliffs.

"I wish Ro were here."

The sadness in Lark's voice put a crack in my heart. I'd been so tangled in my worry over the queen, I'd near forgot Lark and Bula were grief-soaked missing Rowan.

"We're gonna get him back, Lark. I swear on the Mother."

A strange noise rose up the cliffs. It was a sound made by voices—almost a song, but deeper and stranger. Its harmonies stretched out like a beautifully woven piece of cloth, covering the whole of the island. The screets abandoned their perches and took to the air, *screet*-ing a complaint.

I sat up. "What *is* that?"

"It's the Meet!" Lark beamed, leaping to her feet. "They've finished!"

I scrambled up and we both half ran, half slid down the chalky slope toward the beach to join the rest of the Ordish, poking their heads from barge doors at the sound.

"How're they doing that?" I asked, trying to keep up with my friend. "Making that noise?"

"Gully's got a bit of a cunning with sound," she explained.

"Can make it go farther than it normally would. It's dead handy here, isn't it?"

We were some of the first to gather in the big cavern, so we were forced to wait, nervous and impatient, while the space filled up around us. The council was still singing their call to gather, which, slow but sure, drew all those who wanted to hear the Meet's outcome. Finally satisfied the cave and its entrances were full enough, the song ended and Bula shouted, "Thanks to Deep!"

"Thanks to Deep!" came the reply from everywhere.

"It's been a long night," said Fisher Moor.

"And we've listened to your voices," added Sorrel Rimedell.

"And so, we now deliver the outcome of that hearing," declared Gully Slowcreek.

Bula stepped to the front of the council and began to speak, his voice projected beyond the caves to those on the beach, unable to squeeze in.

"You've spoken with many voices," he said. "We've heard anger and worry. We've heard calls for forgiveness and those for revenge. We've heard suggestions that are canny and others that throw caution to the wind. Some are thinking of the past, and others of the future. We have heard you all, and from that hearing, we have decided the best way forward"—he held up an envelope—"is a letter."

"A *letter*?" I whispered, hardly able to believe my ears.

"A letter that our new friends, Masters Warin and Dodd, have agreed to deliver."

In the corner of the cave, Warin gave Dodd, who was asleep

beneath his hat, a sharp poke. The little man sprung up, bowing deeply as he did.

"In this letter," Bula continued, "we have included the evidence gathered against Master Beir and Lady Folque. We have also included a warning of the threat we believe to be against the queen's life. And in conclusion, we beg for a hearing so that our stolen whelps might be returned and that we ourselves might be safe to travel the rivers once more."

"We thank you all for your wisdom," concluded Fisher Moor. "Now go gently till we Meet again."

Voices surged upward in the cave in agreement and dissent as the bodies began to clear from the cavern. Me and Lark ran forward, my friend staring at her father in disbelief.

"We ain't gonna try to get Ro?" Lark asked.

"And begging your pardon, master, but do you know how many hands a letter's got to pass through before it gets to the queen? There's no way it'll get to her in time, if it gets to her at *all*!" I said.

Bula put a hand to both our shoulders, dark circles standing out beneath his eyes. "I understand it's not what you wanted to hear. And if it's any comfort, I'm of your mind—our people would have a chance to live peaceably in Saphritte Renart's kingdom. Lamia Folque's already shown the only thing she thinks we're good for is blaming her evils on."

"But you're the head of the council!" I complained. "Can't you just—?"

"It's *because* I'm the head of the council that I can't 'just' do anything, child. I'm not a king or a queen—governing how we do means sometimes you don't get your own way." He held his hands up in surrender. "And this time, I didn't. So we wrote a letter. If the queen lives, we treat with her. If she dies . . ." A weariness greater than a night's lost sleep fell upon him. "If she dies, we bargain for our whelps and quit Orstral."

"Quit Orstral?" Lark said in a small voice.

"Master Iordan said as long as there's been an Orstral, there's been Ordish!" I exclaimed. "You can't just . . . go!"

Bula's eyes went hard. "Little landwalker, I don't say this to be unkind, but you never really knew fear before the king's inquisitor came to your door. You grew up safe behind respectable walls. I wager your pa was never cheated at market and afraid to ask for justice. Your brothers never needed to fear a beating from a stranger, nor your mother fear bawdy jests in the street. Lark, what were the first lessons I taught you about land folk?"

"Keep my eyes down," she said quietly.

"And?"

"Always say 'yes, mistress' and 'no, master.'"

"What else?"

Tears pooled in my friend's eyes. "Don't go to town in groups bigger than three 'cause folk get nervous. Never cheek the watch or ask 'em for help. Don't laugh too loud. And words are just words, no matter how ugly they are—they ain't worth trouble over."

Master Fairweather took in my thunderstruck silence. "Do you see now?"

I bowed my head shamefully. "Yes, master."

"I think you should go and say your farewells to the fellows who brought you. Though they've not asked, I know they were promised payment, and now that they've agreed to do this thing for us, they're owed doubly."

I reached glumly into the pocket of my borrowed coat. The great jeweled eye of the brooch seemed to be mocking me with a hundred glittering might-have-beens.

Bula knelt down. "You know you've a place with us for as long as you need, child. Our clan is your clan."

I nodded, regretful at my thoughtlessness. "I'll take this to Warin and Dodd, master."

Lark sniffled. "I'll go, too, Papa, to give 'em my thanks."

Master Fairweather stood. "That's a fine idea. When you're back, go find your auntie Maven and she'll teach you two how to dig for clams." He made a clucking sound at the back of his throat. "They ain't the best tasting, but there seem to be plenty of 'em to keep us fed."

"Aye, Papa, we will."

The walk from the cave to the beach was one of the longest I ever took. Lark was downhearted and silent beside me, our feet dragging harder than ever on the soft white pebbles.

I kicked one of them so far, it rattled all the way down the shore to the edge of the water. *All take Lamia Folque!* The devious councilwoman had taken the king, and she was only a heartbeat from taking the queen, the throne, and the Ordish's home.

And I could've stopped it. Just a word to the queen after Lamia first confided the secret of her cunning and her plan to use it—I could've stopped it, but I didn't.

Maybe, said a tiny voice in my head, *but who says you can't stop it now?*

I skidded to a stop on the beach. Could I? I'd got out of the palace, after all, right under the noses of the king's guard. And out of the city, right by the watch. Why couldn't I just . . . get back in?

Look at you, Pip, Non's voice answered across an ocean of months, *wanting to move mountains.*

I started running without even noticing I was doing it. Lark trailed behind me, baffled at my haste and struggling to keep up. Finally, I spotted the two men I was looking for.

"Master Warin! Master Dodd!"

The short man and his tall companion looked up from where they were preparing a small rowboat to cast off.

"Ah, you're just in time, my dears, just in time to see us off!" said Dodd. He gave a sheepish shrug and pulled the letter from his satchel. "We got this to deliver, I s'pose." He poked Warin in the arm. "Say goodbye to the young ladies, my lad."

Warin turned, his face probably as close to sorrowful as it ever got. He reached behind my ear and plucked out a copper, offering it to me with a crooked little smile.

I thrust my hand out with the jewel. "I ain't here to say goodbye, masters. I'm coming with you."

Dodd looked at me blankly. "I'm sorry, I might need to clean out my ears, my girl. Did you say you—?"

"Want to come with you, yes, master."

Lark grasped the sleeve of my coat. "Only, what're you doing?"

I pointed to the envelope in Dodd's hand. "You know as well as I do this won't get there in time. I'm gonna try to get to her, Lark—I'm going to try to get to the queen."

"Poppet," Dodd began, "it ain't like we can smuggle you into the *palace* in a barrel of fish."

"No more barrels, no more fish," I put in hastily.

"But even if you leave now, you won't get back into the city until the day of the wedding!" Lark protested.

"I'll sneak through the front doors of the Cathedra if I have to!" I pulled the leather roll out of my coat. "Her Majesty's gonna see these or I'm gonna get took by the king's guard—"

"*Queen's* guard now, if you want to get technical about it, my dear. Queen's guard," interrupted Dodd.

"Or I'll get took by the *queen's* guard trying!" I finished.

It dawned on Lark that I was dead set on my path. "Only, you don't have to do that 'cause of what Papa said. He was—"

"He was right, that's what he was! Your folk shouldn't have to do this alone. I should've done something about Lamia Folque before everything got so far. I'll not let her chase you out of Orstral."

"But—"

"Because if she's allowed to chase *your* folk off, who'll she blame the next time she wants to do something foul? And the next? And what about the folk in Thorvald who'll have to live under Adalise? She can't be allowed to take the crown, Lark, she just *can't*!"

I hadn't realized how loud I'd got till I heard the silence I left behind. Dodd, Warin, and Lark were all regarding me with a mix of shock and wonderment, but I didn't want to waste another second. I shoved the brooch into Dodd's hand.

"Are we going, or aren't we?"

The small man looked at his enormous friend, who shrugged.

"We got room," the big man said.

"Have it your way, then, my dear, have it your way," Dodd said with a sigh, motioning for me to hop aboard the small boat. I'd just put a foot in the stern when Lark spoke up.

"You got room for two?"

I turned around. "You can't."

She put her hands on her hips defiantly. "Says who?"

"Your papa will—"

"My papa'll understand after I get my brother back. I don't care what the council says—I ain't leaving him to Lady Folque."

"So, are we a party of four, then, my dears?"

Lark took a last, long look toward the shore, where her people were talking and singing while going about their chores, and then stepped into the boat.

"We are."

18

In Blessing now there lives a maid
(Mark well what I say!)
With coal-black hair in a shining braid
(Oh, sailor, stay!)
Oh, ho, Blessing Belle,
Save a dance for me,
And don't you wink at other lads
When I've gone off to sea!
When I get home, we'll married be
(Mark well what I say!)
And nevermore I'll go to sea
(Oh, sailor, stay!)
Oh, ho, Blessing Belle,
Save a dance for me,
One day I'll take your pretty hand
And pledge my life to thee!

—Traditional Orstralian sea shanty

To be truthful, I think I was dreading the passage more than
the idea of trying to turn up unannounced at a royal wedding,

but thanks to the Mother, or Mama Deep, or even the merfolk who were said to live under the sea, my belly had settled its quarrel with rolling waves.

And it was a good thing it had.

"Since we have a difference of opinion as to the ownership of this here vessel," Dodd said as the white cliffs fell away behind *Falda's Drawers*, "returning to the port of Ebbeshore would not be, shall we say, in our best interests."

"The rope," Warin reminded him from behind the wheel.

Dodd put a nervous hand to his neck. "Too right, my lad, too right. You do go straight to the heart of the matter."

"So, where're we headed, then, masters?"

The slight man curled the ends of his mustache thoughtfully. "I hate to say it, my dears, but I think if we're to turn up on time for Her Majesty's nuptials, we've got to make Bellskeep Port."

"Mad!" barked Warin.

Dodd waved him off. "Keep your socks on, my boy, keep your socks on. Near six years have passed since that business with the molasses. I'm sure they've forgot all about it."

Warin didn't look convinced in the slightest.

"Don't you worry, my lad! Set us a course round the top."

He licked his finger and stuck it in the air. "If the winds hold fair, we should get there early Matins."

"But that's the day of the wedding!" I protested.

"If you want to speed us along, my girl, you can beseech the Mother for a good breeze, but otherwise, the morning of the wedding it is!"

Having exhausted that matter, I joined Lark in the stern,

where she was watching the spot on the horizon where the Hatchings had been.

"You haven't changed your mind, have you?"

She pulled her billowing hair to one side. "No. I just know how angry Papa'll be when he finds out we've gone."

"I think he'll know why you went. Mama and Papa were furious when Jon upped and ran off, but they knew he only did it 'cause he loved Maura. They'll be happy enough to jump over the moon when he comes back at harvest."

The unpleasant thought popped into my head that if Lamia Folque got her way, the Ordish might not *be* back for harvest, but I kept it to myself.

Night falls thick on the ocean—darker than the sticky black mud at the bottom of the river. I s'pose I must not have noticed on the first crossing, lost in my haze of sick, dizzy misery, but that night I marveled at it, and at the brightness of the heavens. *If only Master Iordan could bring his telly-scoop out here!* I thought.

As we dropped anchor in a shallow cove, Warin, in his mostly wordless way, showed me and Lark how to use a sextant and the stars to find your way on water. He even laid out a map of the heavens on the tiny chart table belowdecks. It was just as beautiful as the ones in Master Iordan's hallsroom, and according to Lark, you could decipher it with a compass and a ruler. Above deck, Master Dodd reclined on the coil of rope, smoking a small clay pipe, and pointed out a few of the more interesting constellations.

"An' that one, my dears, with the six stars, is Anax the Cat. Can you see his tail just there? I named me own moggie after him when I was a lad. Old Mum didn't want him in the house, but I snuck him in all the same. 'Wildibald!' she'd cry. 'What did I tell you about—?'"

"Your name is Wildibald?" I interrupted, with a snort of laughter, before I could mind my manners.

"'S an old family name!" the little man answered proudly. "Besides, you ain't one to talk about names, my girl! How'd you come to get saddled with a moniker like 'Only'?"

"Oh, that's not much of a tale, sir. My papa wanted a big brood. He's got eight brothers and sisters still living and three that have gone on. The orchard's big, so he wanted more hands." I smiled to think of Papa telling the story whenever I'd sit on his knee and ask. "But Mama came from a quieter house, just her and my auntie Rya, and I think she liked it that way, so after Ether was born, she told Papa, 'Only one more!'"

Dodd chuckled. "Well, there sure ain't much 'only' about you, my dear, not much at all."

In the morning, we broke our fast with stale bread, dried venison, and cold clams, though the clams were quickly tossed overboard.

"Those slimy little devils are hardly to be stomached hot, my dears!" Dodd said as we all spat over the side.

Lark scraped at her tongue. "I ate a worm once 'cause Ro dared me to. I'd rather eat a dozen of 'em than one more of those!"

That day, as Dodd and Warin took their turns at the wheel and at the sails, Lark and I talked round our plan below, though it was less of a plan and more a jumble of questions we hadn't got any answers to. Our ne'er-do-well friends had promised they could get us back into the city in a manner not involving fish. But once we were there, we'd go our separate ways—them to deliver the Ordish letter to the palace as they'd promised, and us to stop the queen from falling prey to Lamia Folque. Secretly, I'd hoped they'd offer to help us with some cunning scheme that would get us to Her Majesty, but Dodd had shaken his head.

"I fear, my dear, the time is coming soon that me and my esteemed associate must bid you farewell."

I tried not to let the hurt show through on my face. "Oh, I see."

I guess I'm not the best at hiding how I feel, 'cause the little man ruffled my hair. "Oh, don't take it so, my girl, don't take it so. Me and Warin aren't the sort of fellows to get ourselves tangled up in castle politics, are we, my lad?"

Warin gave a scornful snort and a shake of his head. "Politics."

So, with that settled, me and Lark went back to our thinking. But even after hours talking it over, the only thing we could agree upon was that we should probably try to look as little like ourselves as possible. We'd no way of knowing how far or how fast news out of the palace would travel. Lark found a sharp scissors used for cutting sailcloth and, without hesitation, began snipping at her long locks.

"Oh, Lark, you only just got all your lovely beads back!" I moaned, picking up a thick bound strand.

She shrugged, another lock falling to the deck. "Hair grows back, but we might not have another chance to stop Lady Folque."

After she finished with us, our heads cropped short as any

fieldboy, we studied ourselves in a small, cloudy glass in the cabin of *Falda's Drawers*.

My throat got tight. *Don't be stupid,* I told myself. *You're not one of those swollen-headed girls who fuss over a little something like a haircut.*

We were ready for Bellskeep.

THE FIRST SIGN that Dodd'd been as wrong about the Port of Bellskeep as he had about Ebbeshore was the harbormaster grabbing him by the throat and pinning him to the mast. It turned out that *no one* had forgot about the business with the molasses. Lark and I peeped up from the cabin stair, careful to stay out of sight.

"It was the summer!" shouted the man, blood vessels in his neck standing out thick as snakes in the early dawn. "When those barrels exploded, the whole port smelt for months! Not to mention the legion of flies and bees that came from all over Orstral to help themselves to a mess so sticky, not even seawater could shift it!"

Warin gave a warning rumble deep in his throat, but Dodd held out the hand he wasn't using to keep from being throttled.

"Now, now, my lad, Master Philbin is quite right, you know, quite right," he gurgled. "We did leave him with an awful mess. Perhaps this might go some way toward making it up?"

The brooch glinted in his fingers, and the ones round his neck loosed instantly. Eyes greedy, the harbormaster reached for it, but Dodd pulled it away.

"Not so fast, my good sir, not so fast. This little treasure's worth more than most of the ships in this yard. But after it's sold, you'll get your share."

Dark greens and blues circled round him, but I didn't have any time to waste wondering what sort of swindle the fellow had planned.

Master Philbin was rightly suspicious. "How can I be sure you'll be back?"

"Why, you've got my boat, of course!" Dodd grinned. "All tied up snug and safe in the harbor."

"I'll bet Master Dumphrey thought the same thing," whispered Lark.

Looking for a hole in the little man's tale and finding none, the harbormaster crossed his arms. "I s'pose I do."

"There now, we've an understanding, my good sir, we've got an understanding. And since we've got such an understanding, I wonder if we might add something to our tab?"

Not half an hour later, with me and Lark outfitted in dock boy's clothes, the grumpy harbormaster pulled round a wagon—a fancy one, with the name of one of the most respectable fishmongers in Bellskeep market on the side.

"I had to pay off the driver to let you take this run, so that's more you'll owe me," Philbin said, stepping down from the driver's seat. "I'm assuming you know where this goes."

"I should think we did, sir, I should think we did! Now, come on, my lads, it's time we were going!"

Lark pulled her cap down so no one'd take too close a look at her face and helped me into the back of the wagon with the barrels. We were both sore grateful not to be inside one.

"If you boys had any brains in your heads, you'd not take up with these fellas," the harbormaster muttered. "They'll lead you nowhere good."

"Thanks kindly for the advice, Master Philbin," Lark said, giving Dodd the stink eye. "It ain't for long—just till we can get better work."

"You wound me, my boy, you really do wound me!" said Dodd, pretending to take exception. He doffed his hat to the harbormaster, the feather tickling the end of the man's nose. "May the Mother bless you for your generosity, my good sir."

"*You'd* better bless me with the gold you owe, and sharpish," Master Philbin grumbled. "Now shove off out of my yard."

Warin snapped the reins and the strong cart horse had us on our way, rolling out of the shipyard.

The moment the harbormaster was out of sight, Dodd rubbed his hands together and gave his partner a friendly punch on the arm. "Ooh, my boy, just think how well this wagon'll look with *Warin and Dodd* painted on the side!"

I peered back at the dock. "Is there anyone in this city you *haven't* swindled?"

"You two must have the worst reputation of any crooks in Bellskeep!" exclaimed Lark.

"Oh, that's not fair, my dear, not fair at all! Ludo Brewster's got a far worse reputation, hasn't he, Warin, my son?"

Warin nodded in agreement. "Much worse," he rumbled.

We joined the procession of goods carts on the road from the docks, all the carters hallooing one another in the sunrise. (Though none, I noticed, wanted to speak to Warin and Dodd.)

In a journey of only a few miles, the walls of the city once again rose large in front of me. This time, I wouldn't be afraid. This time, there'd be no feasts or lessons or council meetings.

This time, I'm the rabbit sneaking in under the wall.

To our good fortune, the watchmen at the gate had never bought anything from our compatriots and gave only a glance at the inventory before waving us on our way. The River was crowded with merchants and visitors, making the going slow—it took a good three-quarters of an hour to travel its length to the market.

Warin halted the cart just outside the confusing warren of stalls. It was the end of the road.

Me and Lark hopped down from the back. I double-checked the inside of my docker's coat for the leather roll containing the crest and the letter from Roysa Beale. Finding everything in order, I looked up at the men in the front. Dodd put his hand to his chest dramatically.

"So this is where we part, then? I must say, I think I've got a lump in my throat, my dears, a big old lump."

I felt warm to see no trace of a lie round him. "Thank you, master, for everything you and Master Warin have done for us."

"You're most welcome, my dears, most welcome. And iffen you're ever in Bellskeep again and need anything, you just be sure to ask around after old Warin and Dodd, and we'll set you up proper." He cleared his throat. "Unless it's hair tonic or silver jewelry, in which case, we might send you elsewhere."

Warin tapped him on the shoulder and leaned down to whisper in his ear.

"Oh yes! My esteemed colleague wanted me to tell you we just happened to think of a way of getting Her Majesty's attention before the wedding."

"Really?" asked Lark.

"It's a tradition, my girls, a tradition, you see. When royals or any of the great families marry, the bride always comes into the Cathedra Square to hand out coins to the children before the ceremony."

Hope swelled up in my chest, which before felt so empty. "So we might be able to warn her!"

"If you get a good spot, you just might. Now, if you ladies will excuse us, we've got some fish to sell cheap before we deliver that letter."

Warin snapped the horse to a trot, and we watched the fine wagon disappear into the maze of market stalls.

"They're going to end the day in a dungeon," Lark declared, shaking her head.

I knew there was no one around to recognize us, especially disguised as we were, but I was eager to get moving.

"Let's just make sure we're not in there with them." I linked my arm through hers. "Come on. We've got a long walk to the Cathedra Square."

19

Two come, one goes.
With you goes Siv.
With you goes Sivgar.
With you goes gladness.
With you goes life, waiting to begin again.

—Thorvald wedding blessing

The echoes of the first afternoon bell were just dying in my ears as we made our way down the long, broad vestry road that led to the Cathedra Square.

The merchants who'd hoped the marriage would still go ahead lined the street, the crowds gathered round the stalls to buy flags, wooden mementos, horns and antlers that could be worn on your head, metal tokens, garlands of winter flowers, and blue sugar drops. Whelps waved white-and-blue kerchiefs while their parents clung tight to their hands, fearful of getting separated in the crush.

But even for such an exciting occasion, folk were moving a little slower than they were before. Clothes hung a little looser and cheeks were a little more sunken. Rage burned my throat—all that grain that was burned, just to make people fear the Ordish! It made me want to push my way through the crowd, kick open the doors of the Cathedra, and shake Lady Folque till the teeth rattled in her head.

But we kept our heads down and followed the crowd. I'd never seen so many folk all in one place in my life. I reached out for Lark's hand to hold and found hers already on the way to mine. Even with her hat pulled down over her eyes, she was still afraid of being twigged. We clung tight, even after we ran into a thin whelp who was being steered through all the bodies by his own mama. He dropped his kerchief, but quick snatched it from the ground before it was trodden on.

"Keep hold of that," his mother scolded gently. "The queen'll only give coins to the children waving her colors, so you don't want to lose it!"

"Did you hear that?" Lark whispered. "She'll only give us a coin if we've got something with her colors on it!"

The crowd came to a complete halt just before the square, and we found ourselves trapped and looking desperately for something, *anything* with a bit of blue and silver on it. Stalls in the marketplace were selling all sorts of banners and handkerchiefs, but both of us had empty pockets.

"I say, what is taking so *long*? We were meant to be in our seats a quarter of an hour ago!"

The cross voice came from behind us, and we were rudely shoved to one side as a rich merchant and his wife parted the crowd only to find themselves just as stuck as we were.

"I told you this way would be too crowded, didn't I?" scolded the woman. "I told you we should have spent the coin to hire a carriage!"

"You're *wearing* a third of the coin we took in last month, Viella, so don't lecture me about a carriage!"

Viella's clothes *were* terrible fine. Her ironed blond curls spilled over the blue-and-silver cape trimmed with white fur that covered a gown of deep blue, woven through with white flowers. The Renart colors swayed tantalizingly in front of our faces.

Lark's hand dove into her pocket and came out with the sail scissors she'd used to cut our hair aboard *Falda's Drawers*.

"Auntie Maven says it's always a boon to carry a pair of scissors," she said, smirking.

"Oh, Lark, you wouldn't."

"You are a skinflint, Ilbert Hodgekin, and no mistake!" Viella shrilled.

Snip! Snip! Snip! The material came away in my friend's hand.

"Would, will, did," Lark declared.

The crowd chose that very moment to begin moving forward again, leaving me and Lark to duck round Ilbert and Viella and push our way to the square.

It was a strange mood Bellskeep was in. The joys of Yule, Long Night, and First Day were still humming in the air along with the promise of the wedding. But every few moments, it's as if the city remembered it was missing its king and that its bellies were empty. Then everyone would go quiet for a spell before excitement swelled again. It was like living two different days at the same time.

The Cathedra Square was already heaving with whelps, excitedly waving banners and kerchiefs, and their parents in the crowd behind. It'd taken us longer than we'd hoped to get there, so I knew we hadn't got much time to fight our way to the front. But as we reached the farthest circle of youngsters, there was barely a needle's width between their shoulders.

Lark's brows bunched together and she stuck her hands in her coat dispiritedly. "We'll never get through there, not in a million years!"

I rolled up my sleeves, determined. "I can. I know I can. Wish me luck!"

Without waiting for her to answer, I dropped to the ground, tucked the piece of Viella's cape between my teeth for safekeeping, and began to crawl. Knees bashed the sides of my head, feet stomped on my fingers, and hands slapped at me for my cheek, but there was nothing that was going to keep me from the front of that crowd. I wedged my way through until I thought I could see a clearing between the hems of dresses and heels of boots. I gathered the blue-and-white cloth and stood quickly, just in time.

The queen's guard were marching solemnly down the steps of the Cathedra in a protective circle, their charge in the middle of them. Folk stood on tiptoe and craned their necks to catch a glimpse of the royal bride, but the soldiers didn't part until they reached the square.

The sight of Saphritte near took my breath.

In spite of the cold, the queen wasn't wearing a cloak, allowing everyone in the crowd to admire her bridal finery. Her gown was a waterfall of cornflower-blue silk that clung to the curves of her body and was covered from bodice to thigh in tiny, glittering jewels. A gauzy cape spilled over her arms and shoulders, with more gems glinting against bare skin. Her raven hair was swept up and pinned carefully at the sides with two delicate silver antlers—a tribute to the Eydissons. At her throat was a great necklace of diamonds and Renart sapphires that glittered like the meeting of frost and winter sky.

But for all her radiance, there was no light in her eyes—only determination. Her knuckles were white round the bend of the coin basket, as if they'd rather be stretched round the grip of a sword. And even though I knew she probably hated me for what she thought I'd done, I wanted her fire and spirit back worse than just about anything in the world.

I dug my elbows into a few rowdy whelps around me, trying to push through the crowd of hopeful, open hands. At last, I broke through to the front, waving the kerchief with all my might as Saphritte came ever closer.

"Majesty!" I shouted, along with the rest of the whelps. "Majesty! Over here!"

And then she was directly in front of me, her smile thin, as she dropped coin after coin into small, waiting hands. Straining, I thrust my hand out toward her, hoping to snag the edge of her sleeve . . .

"Out of the way!"

A vicious fist connected with my side, doubling me over. It took the wind out of me a moment, but by the time I straightened, the queen had passed and only the large ginger-haired boy who'd knuckled me was left behind.

"Sorry, dock rat," he sneered, flipping the silver coin neatly with his thumb. "Guess this just isn't your day." Laughing, he turned to go, his boots throwing up cold dust from the cobbles.

I wanted to cry. Just sit down in the middle of the square and wail like a whelp till I was stepped on, questioned, or caught. After everything, I didn't move any mountains. I'd barely even shoveled a bit of dirt.

Lark came up behind me as the square began to clear.

"I suppose it don't make you feel any better to know I just bumped into that mudlicker and glamoured the coin to look like a hairy, great beetle?"

I wiped my nose on my sleeve. "Maybe a little."

She squatted down on the cobbles next to me. "Come on, now. We didn't sneak back into this city for nothing. We'll find another way."

I nodded, sorry for my moment of despair.

We took to the streets and alleys that led round the rear of the Cathedra. On most, we ran into regiments of guard and city watch, forcing us to double back and try another route. Finally, a tiny passage behind a tailor's proved to be our lucky path.

The alley it intersected was mostly empty, apart from a huge crate of white doves just in front of us, and two dovekeepers to the left, caught up in a game of Royal Bones. To the right, the alley continued on only a few more feet before dead-ending in one of the Cathedra's far corners, where a row of blue-robed men and women were filing in an open side door.

Standing next to the door was a soldier, his Folque rosette

crying his loyalties atop the royal colors. Getting into the Cathedra behind the robed men and women without being noticed was hopeless unless we could lure the Folquesman from his post.

Lark looked to the dove crate and back to the door, where the last few folk were disappearing into the darkness of the Cathedra.

"I reckon those birds are meant for *after* the wedding, don't you?"

I nodded. "It'd be awful distracting if they got out before, wouldn't it?"

"Terrible distracting," Lark agreed, pointing to the soldier. "Let's hope it's distracting enough for *that* fellow."

Keeping careful watch on the dicing men, Lark reached out of the alley and flicked the catch atop the crate with her thumb. The door flipped down, landed on the cobbles with a crack, and the cloud of spooked doves exploded into the air, both tickled and terrified by their new freedom.

The men, startled from their game, leapt up, mouths open in surprise.

"Oh, Mother's milk, no!" the older of the two men shouted, cuffing his young apprentice. "You didn't latch the crate proper, you dolt!"

Both fellows sprinted off to give chase, but by that time, the birds had already risen up as a beautiful white cloud over the Cathedra Square. The soldier from the door took a few long strides toward the commotion, peering down the other side of the alley after the frantic men and their flock.

It was as much of a distraction as we were like to get. Vaulting over the crate, the two of us made haste to the door.

But our footfalls didn't go unnoticed. The Folquesman spun round in time to see us fly past him.

"Oy! You two!"

But me and Lark had no intention of being caught. With all the speed we'd got, we tumbled through the door, slamming it with all our strength in the face of the enraged man. Thick fists rained down blows on the wood outside, and curses not fit for a royal wedding celebration split the air.

"By the White Lady, he's sore," panted Lark.

I cringed, listening to the fellow's hoarse shouts. "We're lucky he hasn't got a key!"

"But we probably ought to move before he finds someone who does!"

Lark swung round the tiny room we found ourselves in. It could hardly be called a room at all but an entrance to a winding stair, lit only by long, thin slits in the walls of the tower. There wasn't a soul to be seen.

"But . . . there's no way into the Cathedra!"

I peered up the stair to see if there was any sign of an entrance, but it just wound up and around.

"Oh, seven hells," I said, still trying to catch my breath and cursing my idle months in the palace. "Where were all those folk headed?"

Lark scratched her head. "Well, they couldn't go anywhere but up."

We left the echoing shouts of the Folquesman behind and

began to climb—up and up and up until we almost forgot what it was like not to be climbing. Our knees protested, our lungs begged for air, and *still* there was no door.

Just as I was beginning to wonder if there'd ever be an end to the cursed stair, we caught the sound of voices above. I threw out my arm to stop Lark, putting my finger to my lips. Taking the next few steps with silent care, the light in the stair grew brighter until we found ourselves peering round the corner into a round loft.

There, the robed folk stood in a circle with ropes in their hands that vanished up into the ceiling, chattering nervously.

I realized at once where we were.

"Oh, All, we're in one of the steeples!" I whispered. "Those must be the folks who ring the bells."

I peered out again. Just beyond the bell ringers was a short hall ending in another loft, where I could just about make out other robed figures getting ready to ring the bells in the second steeple. But the thing that made my heart leap was smack in the middle—a door.

"I think I see a way in!" I said to Lark excitedly. "Just there!"

Lark poked her head round quickly. "So . . . we're just going to walk by all those folk and hope they don't ask what we're doing up here?"

"It's either that or go back d—"

I broke off as footsteps and angry voices echoed round the stair. There was no going back the way we'd come.

Lark paled. "Oh, Deep—sounds like he found someone with a key!"

And then the wedding peal started.

Hearing the Cathedra bells from the ground in a comfortable carriage was one thing, but being stood directly under them was like the world breaking apart. It was a thunderstorm made of music that crashed down on us without warning. We jammed our fingers in our ears, but it didn't seem to make a difference— the ringing of the great bells shook us down to our toes.

But the soldiers who appeared below us at the bend of the stair, pointing their fingers at us, didn't seem terrible shaken— just furious.

Hands still clapped to the side of our heads, we burst into the loft, dodging between the ringers, who were so surprised to see two ragged dock boys in their steeple, the peal itself fell into a terrible disharmony. The men hot on our trail added to the muddle, knocking several of the ringers into one another, arms flailing and ropes twisting. The bells rang out wildly for the whole city to hear and wonder on, but Lark and I made for the door in the narrow hall, barely caring where it led, as long as it was away from the clamor of the loft.

Throwing my shoulder to it, we barged through, only to nearly plummet over the edge of a high marble railing.

I'd spent every Matins during my time in Bellskeep sitting in the chancel, gazing up at the Cathedra's beautiful rotunda, trying not to listen to the ugly little jabs the curate made at me in his homilies. The magnificent artwork, done by some long-ago painter, showed the hands of the Mother cradling all of creation. Sometimes, the choristers would even sing from the balcony— their voices sliding and bouncing round the high dome in eerie harmonies. Never in a *month* of Matins did I ever expect to be standing up there myself!

Far below, familiar faces were turning to one another, perhaps exclaiming over the unholy discord above. I could even see Mizzen sat at the feet of Lord Dorvan, shaking her ears, as if that might make it stop.

We threw our weight against the door, but with the first blow from one of the soldiers on the other side, it was plain there would be no holding it.

"There's nowhere to go!" squeaked Lark. "And *tides*, that is a long way down!"

Another blow jarred us from behind. Faces in the chancel turned upward as the violent thumping in the rotunda began to overtop even the complaint of the bells. I didn't know if any of those faces would want to hear what I had to say, but as we'd come to the end of our road, it didn't seem it could make things any worse.

"Lord Dorvan! Lady Mollier! Lord Sandkin!"

The royal councilors squinted up, no doubt wondering who the ragged boy hailing them from far above could be. Mizzen set to barking the short, happy barks that had greeted me every time I entered the council chamber. *At least* she *knows me*, I thought. But she was not the only one.

Lamia Folque, resplendent in gold and crimson, stood up from her seat in the chancel, her face nearly matching her gown.

"Queen's guard! The assassins of the king—they're in the rotunda!"

A dark cloud like pestilence spread round her, dappled green at the edges—as if all the lies she'd kept from me with the help of the stone were determined to show themselves at once. Fury roared up inside me, louder than the bells and the hammering of the guards upon the door Lark and I held shut. With the Mother as my witness, I was going to make sure that Lady Folque never sat upon the throne of Orstral.

We braced our legs against the balcony railing, but it was only a matter of time before the men on the other side would overwhelm us. Lark grabbed hold of my hand.

"I'm glad we did this, even if it's gone wrong," she said. "I'm glad we tried."

But my anger didn't want to hear gentle words of surrender. "We're not done yet!"

I took a quick glance over the edge. Hung from the balcony behind the altar were two great banners—one in Renart blue and silver with the winged bull, and the other in red with the Eydisson stag.

Lark was right. It *was* an awful long way down. But we sure hadn't got much to look forward to if the Folquesmen or the queen's guard laid hands on us.

I squeezed her hand and she followed my gaze to the gently waving banners.

"You've got to be pulling my leg!"

The door behind us shuddered again, nearly coming open all the way. It was now or never.

"I'll count to three," I said, "and then we'll go."

Lark took a deep breath. "It's been nice knowing you, Only. Wind to your back."

"Wind to your back, Lark. One . . ."

The Cathedra below erupted in cries of alarm at Lady Folque's declaration.

"Two . . ."

The door behind us finally burst open.

"Three!"

The ceremony was ill-omened from the start. Firstly, my wife's new cape, which I paid a full thirty gold pieces for, was ruined by some vandal before we even entered the Cathedra. I told her that the cut to the fabric would hardly be noticed, but she was inconsolable all the same. I know the city had suffered through lean times, but that was hardly call for such a breakdown in civility!

Secondly, just as we mounted the Cathedra steps, a flock of white wedding doves was released early, resulting in the befouling of many a guest's clothing (including mine and my wife's) by the winged rats. The common rabble waiting in the square were, of course, delighted by the display.

We had hardly been seated when the terrible cacophony from above began. The bells, usually so melodious, clashed and jangled in such a racket, it gave my dear Viella one of her headaches, of which she complained bitterly. At least, until the shriek of the most honorable Lady Folque in the chancel, at which point Viella miraculously recovered in time to gasp and chatter with Eloisa Giraud, who was *seated in front of us. (In* front *of us! I shall have to have words with Lord Chamberlain.)*

The queen's guard standing at attention in the corners of the chancel rushed off through doors to apprehend the suspects, but as they did, we were treated to the sight of two boys leaping from the balcony of the rotunda.

My wife promptly collapsed in a vapor, but I watched as the two rascals grabbed hold of the royal standards and slid nearly all the way to the floor before the material gave way above and tore from its fastenings with a great rip.

Spoiled clothing is one thing, but never let it be said that Ilbert Hodgekin is not a canny man. With the thought of assassins in the Cathedra, I heaved my insensible wife to her feet and out the commoners' exit.

But blast my caution! In leaving, we accidentally missed witnessing the revelations of one of the greatest scandals the kingdom has ever known.

And the Girauds have never let me forget it.

—Testimony of Ilbert Hodgekin, witness to the almost wedding
of Queen Saphritte Renart and Prince Hauk Eydisson,
from *A History of Orstral*, vol. 2

We were lucky we were more than halfway to the ground before the banners gave way. *Between this and my canopy, if we make it out alive, I'm going to owe a lot of seamstresses a lot of apologies,* I thought.

Lark was a little luckier than me—she landed in an enormous

bouquet of white, blousy snow flowers. My backside hit the stone floor of the altar harder than the first time I fell off Mama's horse, Waymer, when he was at a full gallop. And that was before the whole of the blue-and-silver banner collapsed on top of me, trapping me under an ocean of heavy fabric.

Pandemonium broke out in the congregation. From what I could hear over my own struggling, some folk were sore afeared for their lives—they thought the Ordish had picked just that moment to strike and we were simply the first to show ourselves. Others were angry at the interruption, though I would have thought they'd be glad of something to think about other than the terrible sound of the bells.

I had nearly worked myself out from under my cloth prison when a shrill voice rang out.

"Seize them!" shouted Lamia Folque. "And gag them so they can't speak!"

Somewhere to my left, I heard Lark's scream cut off and muffled. Burrowing frantically, I came to the edge of the banner, but it was too late. I was seized from behind, my arms in a tight cinch and a length of the dratted blue-and-silver fabric forced between my teeth.

"All's nightgown!" boomed Dorvan. "Is it really the Mayquin?"

"Only!" exclaimed Constance Mollier, coming forward.

"Stand back, my lady!" blustered Curate Heyman. "I told His Majesty of her foul witchery and of the evils of the people who scourge the river. Do not let them utter a word, or they may corrupt more good souls!"

"Oh, do be quiet, Heyman!" exclaimed Lady Mollier, stepping from the chancel. "There's no more witchery in these children than there are ice bears in Achery."

The curate's face turned scarlet, but Lady Mollier didn't have any more time for him. She turned her attention to Lady Folque.

"You said they had already confessed to the deed, Lamia. And we were barred from seeing them by your own men." Her eyes narrowed, hard and fierce. "I would hear them speak now."

Lamia drew closer to her fellow councilor. "Constance, dear, you don't know what they're capable of. It's really for the best." Tendrils of the foul lie curved toward Lady Mollier, stroking her cheek and winding round her ears.

Even in my struggling, I couldn't ignore the familiar itch between my ears. *She's using her cunning!* I thought desperately as Lady Mollier's face went slack under the thrall of Lamia's words.

I swung my leg back as hard as I could, delivering a mighty kick to the nethers of the Folquesman holding me. The material between my teeth fell away as the man hit the ground like a sack of flour. I filled my lungs and yelled louder than I'd ever yelled before.

"Liar!"

The Cathedra went dead silent—the only sound being the echoes of my shout bouncing off the marble, accusing Lady Folque over and over. *Liar, liar, liar . . .*

The commotion at the back of the sanctuary turned everyone's head toward the confused and bothered wedding party, making their way up the middle aisle, the queen at the head and her almost husband having to take two steps to every one of hers to keep up. Half the congregation fell over trying to bow or curtsy as she passed.

"What's the meaning of this?" Saphritte hollered, mounting the steps to the altar like some vengeful faerie queen. "Why hasn't the ceremony—"

Her glare swung from the sight of Lamia and Lady Mollier to the writhing Folquesman on the ground, and then to me and the still-bound Lark.

"What are you doing here?" she asked coldly.

"Don't listen to her, Majesty!" Lamia burst out in a voice high and desperate, too flustered to use her cunning. "She'll drive you to madness, just as she did the king!"

Bram, Arnora, Hauk, and Orrad shoved a path to the front of the fray. The King and Queen of Thorvald both stepped back with curses and a great fluttering of hands. "Your *vardmadrleita!*" growled Arnora. "King killer!"

I shook the weak hand of the Folquesman off my ankle and ran toward the royal crowd, ignoring the shouts of distress from the congregation. "Me and Lark didn't kill anyone *or* drive anyone mad. It was her!"

Everyone stared at Lady Folque, who blanched.

"You picked a bad day to stop wearing your fancy pearl," I added, pointing to her neck, which was hung with a heavy gold-and-garnet collar.

Arfrid Sandkin stepped forward, one eyebrow raised. "The poison that dispatched His Majesty *was* Ordish," he reminded everyone. "And then there's the matter of the river token that was known to be in the Mayquin's possession."

"It was stolen from my nameday box on the Day of Misrule!" I answered quickly, before someone decided to take Lamia's advice and stop my tongue. "And the poison came from a book of Ordish herb lore that you'll find in Lady Folque's chambers!"

The royals were stunned into silence. Not taking her eyes off me, the queen motioned to the Folquesman holding Lark to turn her loose.

"Are you going to listen to this little sorcerer?" cried the councilwoman. "Would you let her bewitch you further?"

I fell on my knees before the Queen of Orstral. "Majesty, you're in a heap of danger." I reached into my coat and pulled out the leather roll, holding it up for her inspection. "All because of her."

The queen took the roll from me and unwrapped it, her eyes sliding over the parchment and the crest. The expression she wore when she questioned my brother in the Wood descended over her face like a dark cloud. Bram and Arnora peered over her shoulder.

"What is the meaning of this?" barked Bram. "Whose colors are these?"

But Saphritte was already opening the envelope. "Who is Roysa Beale?"

An unexpected cross voice came from the chancel.

"She was an old hunting partner of my father's," said Borin Folque. "Though in the years since, she's been known to receive coin for taking lives."

"Shut your mouth, brother!" hissed Adalise. "You don't know what you're saying!"

"My folk have been hosting a friend of yours for a little while," Lark said, boldly approaching Lamia. "Master Maddock Beir had a few things to say about your ambitions. And about how you tried to frame us for your burning!"

"Lady Folque hired Roysa Beale to put an arrow through your heart after the ceremony, Majesty. All so she could talk her way onto the throne with Hauk!"

The Thorvald prince looked like he'd taken a bunch of knuckles to the face. "Is this . . . true?"

"Not only that, Highness," Lark explained to Hauk, "but she planned to weasel her way onto the throne of Thorvald by wedding her daughter to your brother!"

One of Orrad's eyebrows shot up so far, it nearly launched itself off his forehead. He gave Adalise a lewd smile, earning a slap to the back of the head from his infuriated father.

"*Fifl!*" snarled Bram. "This is not a compliment!"

"There is no proof of any such thing!" Lady Folque shot back shrilly.

A boom shook the Cathedra as the great doors burst open.

"I hope we're not too late, my dears, I hope we're not too late!"

Jaws fell open all over the sanctuary. "Master Dodd? Master Warin?" cried Lark in disbelief.

I could hardly believe my eyes. "You came back!"

The little man swept off his hat. "Well, we had a bit of a change of heart, my girl, a bit of a change. We figured maybe a little politicking might not be such a bad thing."

He and his giant partner strode up the center aisle, Warin carrying a struggling figure over his shoulder. But stranger still, the big man was wearing a rough gray gown and apron that were much too small for him and a prim, starched white bonnet on his head.

Queen's guardsmen moved to block them from coming near, but Saphritte turned to me.

"You know these men?" she asked.

"Aye, Majesty." I grinned. "They're good fellows." A small twinge hit me between the eyes. "For the most part."

The queen waved off her guard, allowing the petty crooks to approach.

"I say, is that fellow wearing . . . housemaid's clothing?" boomed Lord Dorvan, not quite caught up with the turn of events.

"You'd be surprised how little trouble you get being a maid who looks like my friend here, my lord," Dodd said, slapping Warin on the back. "Funny, though, no one seemed to want their rooms made up." He jerked his thumb to the figure over Warin's shoulder. "'Specially not this one in room twenty-five."

Warin turned so we were face-to-face with the silver-haired woman who was dead cross to be hanging from the big man's shoulder like a prize goose. Her hands and feet were bound, and Dodd's belt was lodged firmly between her teeth, but her glare was nearly as deadly at the Ordish bow the little man pulled from his canvas sack.

"This lady was up to some wicked mischief, my good folk, some terrible wicked mischief. And well-paid mischief at that!"

He reached into the sack and brought out a leather purse, which he handed to the queen with a bow.

Saphritte tugged open the strings to reveal the glint of gold coins. She looked back to the letter and then at Lady Folque. "Two hundred gold pieces. This is what my life was worth to you? What my father's life was worth? What the *crown of Orstral* was worth?"

The queen dashed the purse to the floor, the gold scattering with a jingle on the stone. Dodd raised his eyes to the heavens, likely beseeching the Mother for the willpower not to bend down to pick it up. Saphritte, in all her wedding finery, advanced on Lamia, who took a few nervous steps backward.

"Y-Your Majesty," she stammered, her cunning itching my ears once more, "there . . . there's been a grave misunderstanding."

"No, there hasn't!" I shouted, breaking her spell again. "Ma'am, do you remember, back in the herbery, when I told you Lady Folque was cunning? She can make folk do what she wants 'em to—including go mad, like she did to the king."

I didn't want to tell the next part—to share my disgrace in front of the whole city. I'd promised myself I wouldn't cry, that I'd take what was coming to me like a tough green apple, but the sight of all the royals standing there in their wedding best had tears spilling down my cheeks like a waterfall.

"She said . . . she said she wanted to do what was best for Orstral." I sniffed. "And I did, too." I squeezed my eyes shut in shame. "She said she could talk the king off the throne. Replace him with you. And you'd stop bothering the Ordish and let the indentures go and the attacks on grain stores would stop . . . of course, they weren't the ones attacking—"

"Only—" began the queen.

"Because now we know it was her all along, ma'am, and everyone's hungry, and I went and got her a book from the library and tried to talk you into taking the crown, and I understand if, after this is over, you wanna throw me in the dungeon—"

"Mother's milk, *Only*!"

I stood before her, trembling, silent, and snotty, waiting for her to shake me, take up a sword, or unleash all seven hells on my head, since I more than deserved it. Lark rushed forward to comfort me. Members of the queen's guard moved silently behind Lady Folque, cutting off her slow backward retreat and leading her through a side door. Borin clapped a hand round his sister's arm, forcing her back down into her seat, where two more soldiers came to escort her after her mother. Warin gratefully handed over the still-bound Roysa Beale.

To my surprise, Saphritte Renart knelt down on the floor in front of me.

"Even before Lady Folque, my father allowed himself to be led by fear," she said quietly. "Fear of appearing weak, fear of losing control, and fear of things he couldn't understand. A kingdom can't flourish in fear. And she knew those fears inside and out."

I looked up, still not wanting to meet her gaze. "But . . . I was afraid, too, ma'am."

"You're a child! You're supposed to be afraid of things! You've known nothing *but* fear since the moment this all began. And if I hadn't been so willing to allow my father to indulge *his* fears, perhaps you might have looked to *me* as a champion rather than Lady Folque. She gave you a reason to trust her, however misguided that trust was." She gave a disgusted huff. "And I looked the other way when my father had a little girl retching on her knees in front of the throne."

She took my hands and kissed them. "You could have hidden the moment you escaped, but for some reason, even after you were free, you came running back into danger because you felt my life was worth saving."

I could hardly believe it. The queen was *forgiving* me, even after all I'd done.

She turned her attention to Lark. "And you—that you should return after the misery my father caused you, I owe you double thanks."

Lark held her head up high. "I came for Only," she said, keeping her tone respectful. "And for my brother."

Saphritte took no offense. "I will make it the first order of my rule to release the indentures and to treat with your people. There are many wrongs to undo."

Bram clapped his hands together. "So, we can now go ahead with the wedding, yes?"

"Your Majesties," the queen said slowly, "I'm afraid I cannot."

Dodd pointed to the trussed Roysa Beale. "Iffen you're worried about this one, Your Majesty, I don't think she's in the position to do any more harm."

"No, master, my thanks, but it isn't an assassin I fear."

Hauk's face fell. "What does this mean, *isabrot?*"

"Perhaps this new queen would prefer a wolf to an *ulfrlitt,*" suggested Orrad, flexing his arms in a way that showed off the depth of his chest. "I am always happy to—"

He was silenced by a vicious elbow to the gut from his younger brother. "Call me *ulfrlitt* one more time on this soil, and I will remove your tongue!"

"Gentlemen, please," Saphritte interjected. "I wish to honor all of the treaties of land and trade made in my father's name. Despite everything that has happened, Thorvald and Orstral can still be joined—but in the bonds of friendship rather than marriage."

Bram's beard quivered in outrage, but Arnora put a hand to his arm. "Go on."

"My prince," Saphritte said to Hauk, "you are a good soul and a wise one. I have no doubt we would have grown to be fond of each other, but . . . my affections have always lain elsewhere."

She put out her hand to the chancel. Everyone's head swiveled to see who would be the one to take it. Lark grabbed my arm as Borin Folque stood up and walked over to the queen, a look of wonderment on his face.

"We were children together," said the queen, looking into his eyes. "We fought together in the practice yard. We studied together at the lyceum. We read together in the library."

Borin's chin quivered. "I've been there ever since. It was the last place we were . . . happy together."

Saphritte put a calming hand to Borin's shoulder. "To be the ruler I wish to be, I must be allowed to choose my own path rather than the one my father chose for me. And I choose to walk it with Lord Folque. It was a path we chose long ago."

An uncomfortable silence fell upon the throne room, finally broken by Arnora.

"My *moder* chose another *herr*, another husband, for me." She looked lovingly at Bram. "Do you remember, my *svass*?"

"He had more gold, a better name," the king admitted. "But my Nora, she chose me instead."

"And together, we make a strong Thorvald, yes?" The northern queen smiled. "So, this . . . this is something we know."

Hauk stood frowning, his arms crossed over his chest, but he nodded curtly. "I have no wish to be second in my wife's heart." The Thorvald prince gave a stiff bow. "I wish you joy, *isabrot*."

Orrad's voice came from the chamber floor, where he'd been clutching his stomach. "Are you certain in your choice, Majesty? Because I—"

Hauk's boot silenced him a second time.

"Words cannot express my gratitude, Majesties," Saphritte said. "There is much to discuss, but first, we must have a care of this city. It is angry, fearful, and hungry. We must contain their anger, quiet their fears, and put food on their tables."

"We offer what help we can," Arnora declared. "You have but to command it."

"Come, then. We'll return to the palace to hear the rest of the tale from our young friends."

Lark cleared her throat.

Saphritte nodded. "And to see about some better conditions for our guests from the river until they can be safely delivered home."

The queen looked down at us both with hope in her eyes. "Let us go and begin to build this Orstral for everyone."

Epilogue

⇥✳⇤

The rain that spring seemed like it would never end.

It poured buckets straight out of the sky, turning everything to muddy soup. The rain poured through the fields and down the hill into the river, swelling its banks, where the fast-flowing water took everything in its path.

When the rain finally stopped, the earth erupted. Tree blossoms were bigger and more fragrant than they had been for years, bringing swarms of bees. The lavender bushes grew thick and lush, promising a bountiful late-summer bloom. And, not to be left out, Non's vegetable garden produced some of the fattest, ripest beans and carrots we'd ever seen.

The house was even quieter than it'd been when I left, though it wasn't sad. While I'd been gone, Mama and Papa'd relented and given Ether leave to be prenticed at Dorvan Bay. He and Jon may not have been with us, but they were content and free from harm, making their absence easier to bear. Mama, Papa, Non, and I pulled our chairs closer round the table and filled our bellies and hearts with one another's company.

As the light breezes gave way to the warm, sticky summer air, eagerness stirred in me. The wheel was turning. The harvest was coming.

On my nameday, I woke early to the mouthwatering smell of Mama's apple crumble and fat bacon rashers. Non made me two new frocks to better fit my body, which seemed to have a mind of its own since I saw my first moon that winter. New hips and bosoms poked and bunched my old things, making it hard to swing an ax or use a hoe. Mama and Papa surprised me with a trip to Lochery, where I was allowed to pick a book from a traveling merchant they'd got word of. To their surprise, I didn't pick *Mistress Bayard's Fairy Stories* or *Verse of the Countryside*, but rather *A History of Orstral*.

"That's a bit of a dry read, ain't it, Pip?" Non asked. "You sure?"

"Yup. It'll be like visiting with an old friend," I replied, ruffling its pages fondly.

That evening, as the sun dipped behind the trees, we all sat in the garden, dinner sitting heavy on us, when a melody, balanced on the edge of the breeze, teased the air.

"Do you hear that?"

Mama, Papa, and Non stopped sipping their cordial and turned their ears to the wind.

"Do you know, Ellis, I believe I *do* hear something," Mama said, the corners of her mouth turning up with mischief.

The same playful expression lit Papa's face. "Maybe something at the sanctuary?"

Twinkling sparks burst to life around him. *What are they up to?* I wondered as the song grew louder, whispering through the tall grass and the lavender.

Non's eyes twinkled. "You know, it sounds to me as if it's coming from the river."

I pricked my ears harder. Non was right—it *was* coming from the river.

> *The boughs of the trees are heavy,*
> *The fruit weighs down the vine.*
> *We come,*
> *We come with willing hands!*

I leapt to the top of the wall. The shining ribbon of the Hush, stretched far to the north, was dotted with red sails.

"They're near a week early!" I breathed. "Why . . . ?"

Papa looked out over the wall with a smile on his face. "I got word from Master Fairweather a few weeks back. They finished faster'n they expected at a farm just south of Oldmoor. We ain't the only ones keen to celebrate your nameday this year."

Non looked up at me with an apple-cheeked grin. "I reckon we should be neighborly and meet 'em at the shore, don't you?"

With a wild whoop, I bounded over the wall and into the fields. The lavender's heavenly scent arose with every brush of my skirts against the purple blossoms as I tore through the rows, bursting with impatience to make the riverbank. The Ordish greeting song rang clear over the water.

The earth is rich and ripe,
The river, slow and easy.
We come,
We come with happy hearts!

I burst from the blooms, raced past the oak tree, and skidded to a halt on the wide, open bank, my toes poking just over the edge. The first barge was just rounding the river bend, and on its roof were the furiously waving figures of Lark and Rowan. I waved back, barely able stop myself just diving in to meet them. Behind the *Briar*, more familiar prows came in sight—the *Greenling*, *White Lady's Bane*, and the *South Wind*.

Together we are at last,
The wheel has turned again.
We come,
We come with open arms!

The *Briar* cleared the willow grove first. Lark and Rowan launched themselves from the roof to the towpath and thundered toward me, summer dust rising up behind them. We all crashed into one another at the top of the hill and fell to the ground in a heap of giggles, trying to screech months' worth of hellos at the same time.

"Look at you! Your hair's grown back!"

"You got so *tall*! What've you been *eating*?"

"Is that a new frock? It's the shine on the apple!"

Mama, Papa, and Non appeared, all grins at the cleverness of their secret-keeping.

"I can't believe you're here!" I cried. "And for my nameday!"

"Oh, you ain't seen nothin' yet, Only Fallow!" crowed Lark. "We brought all manner of surprises."

"Mama! Papa!"

Ether came streaking over the hill. Mama gave a delighted cry and caught him up in her arms. He didn't even utter a complaint, though he'd long insisted he was too old for the sort of cosseting he'd got when he was wee. Papa joined them, slapping my brother fondly on the back and tousling his hair. When Mama'd let go her grip, he came grinning to me. "Told you in my letter, didn't I, that I'd be back for harvest?"

I hugged him gratefully. "Good met, you sneaky flatfish! Lord Dorvan gave you leave?"

"You were right about him—he's a kindly fellow, no mistake. Oh, he wanted me to make sure you got his *warmest and most affectionate greetings*!"

My brother bellowed the last few words, just like his lordship, which sent us all off into fits. "Mizzen sends her love, too." Ether laughed. "But I ain't sure you want me to deliver it as she would."

Laughing, I shoved him away. "Not on your nelly! Did you come with Jon?"

"I did," he answered. "He's just helping Maura along. She ain't quite as fast as she usually is."

"Good met!"

Jon's shout turned every head as he and Maura appeared over the hill's crest. Mama, Non, and I ran to greet them and make a fuss over Maura's huge, round belly.

Mama hugged her tight. "Oh, you do look well!"

Maura blew some of her sweaty curls out of her eyes. "I feel big as a barge," she groaned.

I gave her a kiss on the cheek. "Wouldn't it be fine if the whelp was birthed while you were here?"

"All I know is, babes don't come till they're good and ready!" declared Non.

"Speaking of good and ready, Mistress Beulah." Maura sighed, putting both hands to her back. "I reckon I've had enough swollen ankles and midnight trips to the privy to last a lifetime." She took my wrist and placed it on the side of the great swell of her belly. "She's been squirming like an eel these past few minutes."

As if in response to her voice, the hard knob of a elbow pressed into my palm. "She?"

"Auntie Maven thinks it's a girl," Lark said. "Least, that's what the egg yolks, tea leaves, and her gold ring say."

"Auntie Maven ain't never wrong," Rowan insisted.

Maura looked sideways at Lark. "She was wrong at least once *I* can remember."

"She said *I* was getting a *sister*," Lark whispered in my ear.

Rowan heard her and stuck out his tongue.

All along the riverbank, the ring of mallets on mooring stakes replaced the music of the Ordish song, but swelled tender in my chest till I could have just about burst. The bank under my feet was still warm from the afternoon sun. Its dying rays shone off the folded red sails and the tents that'd already begun to unfurl along the river. It was my nameday, the orchard was ripe, and all the folk I loved were within arm's reach.

"This might just be the best day I ever had," I said, hugging Lark.

"Oh, it's not finished yet. We've not even given you your present!"

"You mean all *this* isn't my present?"

"Well, it's part of it," Rowan admitted. "But we got you somethin', too. Had to ask the queen for it and all!"

"You saw the queen?" I asked excitedly.

"Papa went up along with the other clan leaders in the spring. Had a big shindig with some of the nobles, just to get acquainted. They were a little chilly, but Her Majesty gave 'em a talking-to and their noses came down out of the air a touch."

"The new curate's not so bad, either. Even invited us to Matins in the Cathedra!" added Rowan. "It was dead boring, but she spoke kindly of us to the folk of Bellskeep."

"Oh, and Master Warin and Master Dodd send their greetings, too." Lark made a disgusted face. "They *wanted* to send fish."

My stomach turned. "I'm glad it was just greetings!"

"But here's the good part." Lark fished a large envelope from the pocket of her overlet. "This is for you."

The paper was thick—finer than any I'd ever seen. My name was written on the front, the dark blue ink looped in fancy dips and swirls. The wax seal on the back had a silver token set in it

and elegant blue ribbons trailing below. With a crack, I broke it
and carefully pulled out the message inside.

His Lordship, the Master of Ceremonies
is commanded by the **Queen** *to invite*

Only Fallow and her good family
to the marriage of

Her Royal Majesty
Saphritte Bethan Fisroy D'Abreu Renart

to

His Lordship
Borin Ansel Yssac Folque,
who shall thereafter take the name of Renart

on First Day, this year of our Mother,
at the second afternoon bell

Non'd come to peer over my shoulder. "Fancy us being invited
to a royal wedding! I'll have to pack my best bonnet."

The old straw hat with faded yellow piping round the brim
hung on a peg by the herbery door. "I didn't see no one wearing
bonnets last time, Non," I said quickly.

"What's the other bit say?"

"Other bit?"

Non poked her finger inside the envelope, where another

piece of thinner paper was tucked. I eased it out, a smile spreading over my face as I recognized the hand.

"It's a message from Her Majesty!"

My dear Only,

Our friends the Fairweathers have kindly agreed to deliver this invitation to your hands. I hope that you and your family will join us as honored guests when Borin and I wed this Yule. You have my personal guarantee that the wedding feast will not involve any livestock.

Thanks to King Bram and Queen Arnora, Lady Folque has lately taken up her new residence at the outpost of Kaladrengr in the north of Thorvald, where she will spend the rest of her days living in simplicity and humility. I've been told the cold there is so fierce, a horse might freeze mid-step. I wish her a comfortable stay. As for Adalise, Borin believes she might have suffered under her mother's thrall, and she has been exiled to one of the Folques' country properties until her head might be clear enough to determine what measure of guilt she must bear.

As part of our new accord with the Ordish people, work has begun to dismantle Kester's Weir. Bellskeep is to have a real river once more, so that all the people of Orstral might feel welcome. I asked the clan council if they would give the river its new name, and without hesitation, they replied, "The Fallow."

Each morning, when I look out upon my city, I thank the Mother for your friendship and your bravery. Though it was my father's fear that brought you to Bellskeep, it's my hope that you will feel ever welcome here, so long as we both shall live.

I wish you joy and a bountiful harvest, and I look forward to seeing your face on our most happy occasion.

Ever yours,
Saphritte

Post Script—Miss Lark and Master Rowan have borrowed something of mine to make your nameday one to remember. I pray you use it gently and send it back in one piece.

I looked up from the letter into the shining eyes and sly smiles of my friends.

"It's not that giant glass vase from the ballroom shaped like a lady, is it?" I asked suspiciously.

Lark laughed. "It's not near as breakable as that."

Rowan leapt onto the bow of the *Briar* and knocked on the front door. "It's even been pretty handy in the fields!"

The small stable doors of the barge swung inward and a freckled face popped out. Weeks in the sun had added a host more to his cheeks, his nose, and his forehead, but the grin below was unchanged.

"Many happy returns of the day, Only Fallow," said Gareth.

AND SO, WITH the sun going down, me and the steward found ourselves sitting together on the top of that same boat, watching the riverbank come to life.

Gareth stretched his arms into the sky. "I swear, after the first few days on the river, I found places I didn't even know could get sore."

"A bit different from napkin folding, then," I joshed him.

"Cheeky." He grinned. "Do you want your nameday present or not?"

"What, there's more?" I exclaimed. "You brought yourself—I can't ask for more'n that, surely!"

"This one isn't from me, mind, although maybe we can use it later this evening. It's from Master Iordan."

I gaped. "Master *Iordan* sent a gift for my nameday?"

"He won't admit it, but I think he's a bit bored without someone needling him all the time," the steward said, leaning over the lip of the roof to reach inside one of the open windows. He came up with a box, which he set heavily in my lap. "Open it."

The ebony casket was long and elegant, with pearl inlays that made it look as if it was covered in the night sky. I'd never seen anything so fine. The two sturdy silver catches flipped open under my thumbs, and the box opened to reveal a series of strange silver tubes with curved glass at their openings, set snug into cradles of black velvet.

"Mother's breath," I murmured, running the tips of my fingers over the thing. "What's it for?"

"Read the note."

I picked up the piece of paper that lay atop the contraption and opened it.

Miss Fallow,

I regret I was never afforded the time to give you a proper astronomy lesson. Please accept this gift so that you might be able to observe the heavens upon your leisure. As you so eloquently observed, the nights in Presston are "dark as a watchman's pocket" and should make for excellent stargazing.

Near the next new moon, you will find the constellation of <u>Helvia Hyalus,</u> the Queen's Mirror, in the northwest sky just after sunset—you'll know it by its six stars, which form an irregularly shaped circle. I have no doubt that as you ponder its mysteries, you will always be able to see your own face reflected in its light.

Yours ever,

I

"A telly-scoop," I said wonderingly, the cup of my heart brimming over. "That old stuck-up's got a soft spot and no mistake."

"Oh!" he exclaimed. "Speaking of Master Iordan, there's one more thing."

"It's too much!" I said, pressing my hands to my overheated cheeks. "I feel like the queen must on *her* nameday!"

"You'll like this, I promise." He reached his hand into his pocket. When he pulled it out, sitting in his palm was the Liar's Pearl, flashing and burning in the twilight. It'd been cut round and put in a simple silver cup hung from a leather cord, but there was no doubt it was the same stone.

I leaned back. "Sweet All, what do you think I want *that* for? After all the mischief it caused?"

"I know it doesn't seem like much of a gift, but the inquisitor had a theory he was hoping you'd test for him. Put it on."

I didn't want to touch the stone, let alone slip it round my neck. But neither Master Iordan nor Gareth would have me do anything ill, so I held out my hand. I flinched as it touched my skin, expecting it to burn, but it didn't—it was just a smooth, flat weight in my palm.

"You sure about this?"

"It won't *hurt* you, if that's why you're worried. Master Iordan thought it might even help."

"Help what?" I asked suspiciously.

"Oh, for the love of All, just put it on!" He laughed. "I swear it won't bite."

I put the cord over my head and the stone fell just beneath the hollow of my throat. "What's supposed to happen now?"

"I'm going to tell you a lie," the steward informed me.

I crossed my arm in a pout. "I don't like the idea of you lyin' to me, Gareth Farway."

"It'll just be a foolish one, I promise. Are you ready?"

"What kind of question is that? I'm *always*—"

"This morning, I ate a bear for breakfast."

Twinkling white flashfire danced around his head. "You could still see that, couldn't you?" he asked.

"Sure I could! Did Master Iordan think the stone would stop my cunning from working?"

Gareth shook his head. "Not exactly. Lady Folque was still able to use hers while wearing the stone. What he hoped it would stop . . . well, now I need you to tell *me* a lie."

My heart quivered. "You know I can't do that. Not without—"

"I know," he said, grasping my hands. "And you can tip me right over the side of this barge if anything ill happens. And I'll carry any message back, no matter how foul, to deliver to Master Iordan with my own lips, but . . . just try it."

I took a deep breath, getting ready for the familiar stab of agony between my eyes. "Well, you should know . . . and don't go gettin' a big head over it or nothing . . . that I wasn't at all pleased to see you today."

I cringed, waiting for the familiar pain to crash over me . . . but it never did. I opened my eyes and blinked at Gareth, who looked terrible uncertain.

"That . . . that *was* a lie, right?"

"Of *course* it was, you egg!" I cried, giving him a joyful shove. "The inquisitor thought since the stone protected Lady

Folque against your cunning, it might protect *you* against it, too. Looks like it worked!"

Rowan's head appeared over the lip of the barge roof. "What worked?"

"Ro, look out, you got a great spider on your shoulder!" I shouted.

The boy let go of his grip on the barge and fell to the towpath, brushing at his tunic. "What? Where?"

I toppled over backward, cackling with glee. "Oh, this is the green on the grass!"

Lark emerged from one of the tents on shore. "What's eating you?" she asked her brother, who was still turning circles and batting at his clothes.

Gareth grinned. "We just proved Master Iordan right."

Rowan stopped flailing and scowled. "Oh, I see. Yeah, a barrel of laughs."

"I'm sorry, Ro. Oh, but that was a merry thing." I slipped the pendant off from round my neck.

Lark rested her chin on the roof. "You don't want to keep it on?"

I paused. How fine would it be to be able to say what I liked? To be able to use words like Papa's sturdy wall round the garden, just like everyone else? But watching the blue-green fire dance in the heart of the stone, I knew my answer. "I think I've got used to the truth. And besides, other folks have got used to me tellin' it."

"Do you want me to take it back?" asked Gareth.

I winked before slipping it into the pocket of my overlet. "It might come in handy when Non asks for my notion on what to wear to the queen's wedding."

The Fairweathers hopped up onto the roof to join us. The sun had quit the horizon, leaving behind the rich purple robe of evening that fell thick over the river. The bonfire rose up, licking at the first bashful stars, and the cry of Master Harven's fiddle winged low and sweet across the water. Dear faces glowed by the fireside—Mama and Non fussing over Maura; Papa, Jon, and Bula jawing over some light matter; and Ether wrestling with Fen Piven in the dancing shadows.

A chorus of voices joined in the fiddle's song—a gentle tune to welcome the night. There was no need for words among us four on the roof of the *Briar*—my fingers stole overtop of Lark's, and Gareth's head drowsed on my shoulder. Rowan lay on his back, his head upon his sister's knees, watching the great, dark welkin above our heads spark to life.

The hours bend to evening,
We gather closer in,
The bright world's shades are deep'ning,
Oh, what a day it's been!

The sweat from all our labor
The shame from all our sin
Are washed away till morrow,
Oh, what a day it's been!

I sighed, contented right down to the soles of my feet. "Ain't that the truth?"

> *Our lives are like the twilight,*
> *Where joy and sadness twin,*
> *Where endings make and dawns awake,*
> *Oh, what a day it's been!*

ACKNOWLEDGMENTS

✠

"'Turn the wheel of the heavens, the seasons, or the tides, the slowest to turn is the wheel of change.'"
"What does that mean?"
"It means," said Non, "it's easier to get a chicken to lay a stone egg than for some folk to admit they were wrong."

THIS DELETED EXCHANGE from the second draft of *Riverbound* has stuck with me since I wrote it. I couldn't have imagined, when I began this duology back in 2014, which way the wheel of change would turn or how many vulnerable people it would grind beneath its progress. First of all, I'd like to thank all of the artists, writers, makers, and creatives who have continued to make good art and tell good stories during this time—especially the work that shows *everyone* they're seen and they have value. It's hard but abundantly necessary work to show that there is still good, still hope, and still things worth fighting for.

Thank you to my wonderful agent, Jen Linnan; ever-patient editor, Arianne Lewin; her assistant, Amalia Frick; and the rest of the Putnam/PRH crew who've been so good to me.

Thanks to Vivienne To, whose beautiful cover art brought Orstral to life.

As ever, huge thanks to Tom and Marlene England and my beloved mess at Curious Iguana in Frederick, Maryland, for their love, support, and dedicated hand-selling. Thanks also to Judy Samuels and the PRH Westminster gang for their great work!

To Nick, who brought endless cups of tea and patted my hair when I was sure I'd never be able to finish my sophomore novel, and to Wren and Ellie for only *occasionally* busting into my office to ask what the Wi-Fi password was or how to make mac and cheese, thank you.

To Mom and Dad, whose love brings them to our door so often when things break, need cleaning, or need looking after: You are vastly appreciated.

To the community of folks online and in real life who've supported me during this journey by reading, reviewing, buoying up, and spreading the word, I cannot thank you enough.

Here's to hoping that when we meet again, the wheel of change is turning in a kinder and gentler direction.